The

YEAR
of the
BARBARIAN

DRAGONFLY TRILOGY, BOOK ONE

Elizabeth Ann Boyles

To Elaine,
I hope you enjoy the
journey to a fascinating
land!
E. A. Boyles

This is a work of fiction. All of the story's names, characters, incidents, places, and dialogues are products of the author's imagination or are used fictitiously. Any resemblance to actual events or persons, living or dead, is coincidental.

Scripture quotations are from the King James Version of the Bible.

Cover design by The Killion Group, Inc.

For supplementary insights, visit the author at
www.elizabethannboyles.com/my-books

To my husband, Dale—
whose unwavering faith and dedication to the Lord
provide a bright light for me and many others.
With all my love.

Dear Reader,

Decades ago in Tokyo, I became acquainted with descendants of my great-great-uncle, the first United States consul in Nagasaki, Japan. My cousins commented on how congenial their grandfather had been. I wish I'd probed to discover more details about this ancestor. If only I'd realized that someday I would imagine stories around a fictional consul's life.

In the story, the Japanese family names are given first, following the country's custom, but I took liberties with the complicated use of Japanese titles and phrases reflecting status. For example, the straight-forward title of *Shōgun* is used for the exalted ruler.

You can find lists of the characters and selected terms in the back material.

So now, the daughter of a samurai and a New York adventurer are waiting to entertain you as their quests begin.

PROLOGUE

July 1848 (Year of the Monkey), Nagasaki, Japan

Seven-year-old Taguchi Sumi stood by her home's vestibule, erect and still, as suited the daughter of a samurai, even though her heart pounded like a drum and her feet wanted to dance. As soon as her father finished his breakfast of *miso* soup, they would bow to her grandfather and make their way toward Nagasaki Harbor for the most fascinating sight imaginable.

Ever since she could remember, she had wanted nothing more than to accompany her father to watch the arrival of the annual Dutch ship. Last New Year's Day, he promised to take her when the tall sailing ship reached the port.

Today was the day at last. If she were lucky, she might even glimpse one of the strange-looking foreigners. The painting she'd seen at a street stall showed a tall man with red hair all around his face and a long nose. Her chances of seeing one would increase if her father, Dutch Scholar of the Second Rank, were asked to interpret at the customs house. If that happened, she'd also get to see the curious cargo the barbarians' ship disgorged.

Her grandfather slid back his room's panel and stepped out. "Kenshin," he called to her father. "I must speak with you about those plans you have." Impatience filled his crackly voice.

A butterfly jumped in Sumi's stomach and lodged in her throat as her father quickly rose. She crept after him, the *tatami* floor's straw mats muffling her footsteps. Early morning shadows helped cloak her as she approached her grandfather's room.

"You cannot take the child." His words stung like angry hornets. "Encouraging her interest in the barbarians will surely anger the spirits of our ancestors."

Tears sprang to her eyes. She rushed toward her grandfather and stamped her foot. "No, I must see the ship! Father promised. I cannot wait another year."

Sumi clasped her hand to her mouth. She had done the unthinkable.

Her father's eyes grew stern. He removed her favorite kimono with its pattern of blue dragonflies, leaving only her long under-robe. Her face grew hot. She wanted to collapse on the mat beneath her, but she couldn't. She was the daughter of a samurai.

A whimper escaped from somewhere deep within as her father half-picked her up, then pushed her out into the garden.

"Your impertinence is intolerable. You will learn respect for your elders before you reenter." He slid the back entrance closed in her face.

"I am sorry," she cried. Leaning her ear against one of the panels, she heard nothing. She put her right eye up to the slim crack between the two panels, but the tight closure blocked even the tiniest view.

She called out her apology again, this time to just her

grandfather. By now her father had left for the harbor. Without her. He might even interpret for a foreigner. Without her. She couldn't hold back a sob despite belonging to a long line of samurai.

Lunchtime came and went. The afternoon dragged on. Kneeling by the door, she cried her apology many more times, but no one came. The sun slipped behind the trees. The blue hydrangea blossoms that charmed her the previous day now looked pale. Ghostly.

All of a sudden, a dark shape among the clouds cast a shadow. Could it be a *tengu,* a goblin? Their maid often told her how *tengu* grabbed bad children with its sharp claws.

She gasped. There it was, half-hidden by clouds, hovering over their neighbor's pine tree. Glancing over her shoulder to see if it came any closer, she hurried back to the door.

"Please, please, let me in! I am sorry. I will obey." She dared rap on the panels' frame.

No voice, no footsteps came from within. A thought struck her. Maybe her grandfather would be happy if the *tengu* took her.

If her family wouldn't save her, she had to save herself. She darted her eyes over the garden's pear and maple trees, the small pool with its fountain, the bushes encircling the jutting rocks, the garden's own pine tree at the back. There was no place to hide. None.

But the miniature bridge in their neighbor's garden—it might shelter her.

She dashed for the narrow gap where the walls of the two properties came together and squeezed through. She slid under the edge of the bridge's arch, thankful now she didn't have on her best kimono. Hunched between the bridge posts, she tried to remember if the maid had talked about anything dangerous that might lurk in the black pond at her feet.

Darkness settled around her. An angry insect buzzed by her head. Her legs ached, but she couldn't leave her perch.

Her mother's voice floated from her family's back garden, then her father's, calling her name. Were their voices real? Or was the goblin trying to trick her?

The calls began again from a distance, probably from the road in front of her house.

How terrible that the neighbors would know of her disgrace. She had to get back into her garden even if a goblin saw her. Trembling, she crept through the gap and waited by the door. "I am sorry, Honorable Grandfather," she murmured one more time.

The door slid open. Her grandfather grabbed her arm and yanked her through the house to the front veranda.

"Stay here." He twisted her to face him as he spoke. "Do not move." He picked up a lantern and strode out their front gate.

She hardly dared breathe, let alone move.

Her elders, with a few neighbors, headed toward her in a pack, lanterns swinging wildly.

"Where have you been? Were you hiding?" Her father's scowl hurt, like a splinter piercing deep into her chest.

She opened her mouth to explain about the *tengu*, but no sound came out. It was as if all the eyes staring at her stole her voice. She couldn't stop shivering.

Her father squatted and pulled her toward him, his tunic's sleeve brushing her bare arm. "You are here now and safe." He didn't sound as angry. "Why didn't you answer when we called? Were you in danger? Did someone try to kidnap you?"

"A *tengu.*"

"A *tengu* does *not* exist." Her father gripped her shoulder. "There is no such thing. Do not add foolishness to today's bad behavior."

Sumi's head jerked up. She'd been fooled. The maid had seemed to truly fear those goblins. She looked at her grandfather standing over her. He was watching her intently, in the same way he studied a tree or flower before painting it with his watercolors.

"Enough questions." Her grandfather's voice had also softened. He nodded to Merchant Omura and his wife and bowed to another man who lived nearby. "We thank our kind friends for their aid and apologize for the inconvenience."

After adding his own bow, her father accompanied the chattering neighbors to the gate. Before the gate closed, Sumi heard Merchant Omura say it was wise to curb a child's unnatural interest in the barbarians. But she didn't think her interest was at all *unnatural.*

"Come." Her grandfather turned on his heel. "We shall offer thanks for the child's safe return." He led her mother and her into their home.

After preparing the sticks of incense in front of the god shelf, he turned with the lit sticks. "You are too like your father," he said as he handed Sumi hers, "not cherishing our ancestors' ways."

Just as she opened her mouth to give the required apology, her mother interrupted, her voice as gentle as the whisper of a summer breeze. "I am sure my husband has never meant to offend you or the revered ancestors. He wants to do that which pleases you."

"I can see what is happening. I am old, but not blind."

"You have been more than patient." Her mother handed her stick over to Sumi, then knelt and touched her forehead to the straw mat.

Sumi sucked in a breath. To bow down and try to make everyone happy must take the patience of silkworms spinning cocoons. Or maybe a hen waiting for her eggs to hatch.

And on top of that, pleasing people required selflessness. No one knew what the poor silkworm felt the minute before it was killed for its cocoon, the precious result of all its tedious work. Maybe it didn't care. But she knew chickens resisted foxes wanting to steal chicks. She was much more like a combative chicken than a silkworm—or her meek mother.

For one thing, she would never give up her wish to see the hairy barbarians.

Never.

CHAPTER 1

Seven years later
July 1855 (Year of the Rabbit), Nagasaki, Japan

A hungry mosquito flew under the hem of Sumi's kimono and attacked her ankle. She dared not swat it while old Suzuki-*sensei,* her tutor, knelt ramrod straight on the cushion opposite her, expounding the virtues found in the *Tale of the Heike.*

"With true samurai spirit, Lady Nii took the seven-year-old Emperor's arm and propelled both of them off the ship and into the foaming sea." A hint of enthusiasm colored his recitation. "Emperor Antoku's mother leapt in after them, intending to save her son's life, not his honor."

The mosquito bite itched, but Sumi held firm. She would not lick her lips. She would not sway. And she would not allow a muscle's quiver. If she concentrated on the fascinating account, she'd forget the urge to scratch. She was sure of it.

Suzuki closed the worn text and bowed. "I shall continue the history next week when the young student is able to concentrate." He clamped his lips together.

"*Sumimasen,*" she apologized, her heart plummeting. She'd kept her eyes cast down and had held perfectly still. How did her tutor know that her mind wandered for a second?

Waiting a week to find out if the three drowned in the sea was disappointing, but worse was this newest failure. Now that she had turned fourteen, the standards for a samurai's daughter rose impossibly high. In the last lesson, she had left out two phrases from her long recitation. In the lesson before that, Suzuki-*sensei* scolded her for asking a foolish question about whether women could be samurai in the Western countries. And in the prior weeks? Countless mistakes, no doubt firmly fixed in her elders' memories.

"Perhaps fresh air will improve your mind." Suzuki's knees creaked as he rose. "I shall observe your progress with your weapon." He gestured toward the open panel and walked down the hall leading to her home's back garden, his slight limp betraying his age of more than sixty years.

Following at a respectful distance, Sumi held her breath as they approached the closed panel leading to her grandfather's room. Would her lapse be reported to the Eldest?

Suzuki hesitated a moment, then walked on, the *tatami* emitting soft puffs as he crossed them.

She practically tiptoed the rest of the way to the garden.

At Suzuki's word, she grasped the lacquered black shaft of the *naginata,* a smooth, long spear ending in a curved steel blade, and then waited for his next order.

"Pick the ripest pear. Not one leaf with it."

Squinting at the bright sky, she studied the nearby tree. The yellowest pear nestled close to the top on an inner bough. She'd never be able to avoid striking the branch. Yet she had to try.

Careful not to entangle a wisp of her long hair, she made a

quick thrust at the pear. Amazingly, she hit it, but a twig full of leaves accompanied it into Suzuki's outstretched hand.

"How many hours did you practice last week?" An icy politeness frosted his words.

"Seven hours. One . . . one each day." She'd practiced early each morning before the summer heat siphoned her energy, and had endured the chore before breakfast, half-starved.

"Two hours a day this week, and three the next if you do no better. The spear must become an extension of your arm."

Sumi bowed her assent. At that rate, no pear or branch would be left on the wretched tree. Maybe she could do imaginary battle with leaves instead of fruit, while melting under the sun. For a moment, she envied the merchants' children. Most of them were privileged to learn to read and write like herself, yet had the leisure to fly kites, roll hoops, and play games like the top-spinning competition, *beigoma.* They didn't have to train for nonexistent battles. Yet she couldn't help being proud of her line of valiant ancestors.

"Taguchi Sumi-*san,* are you listening to me?" Suzuki-*sensei* clapped his hands twice.

"*Sumimasen,*" she apologized again. Her neck grew warm.

"You have an hour left to perform with the *naginata.* Then review the first five precepts of *Higher Learning for Women.* Memorize those precepts. Word for word." His voice rose slightly. "You must train your mind to concentrate and your ears to attend to your elders."

He gave a stern nod and reentered the house.

Sumi bowed to his back. There was no question about the disappointing report he'd give when he came to her grandfather's door this time: Failure to keep still. Failure with her weapon. Failure to listen.

Sighing, she wielded the weapon again, decimating more twigs.

A movement on one of the branches on the other side of the tree caught her eye.

A snake! Headed toward a sparrow's nest.

The mother bird frantically flapped her wings, but the reptile slithered on.

Sumi circled to the far side of the tree until she had a clear view. Only two branches between her and the snake. Heart pounding, she thrust out the *naginata.* It cut through leaves, but missed the snake, now poised to snatch a hatchling from inside the nest.

Gritting her teeth, she hacked at the monster again.

Missed, but the snake turned to the side.

Once more.

Struck in half, the snake plummeted to the ground.

But, horror of horrors, the mother bird fell next to it, one wing sliced off, flapping the other.

Sumi collapsed.

She sensed her grandfather before she heard him.

"I will take care of the bird and the nest. The sun still shines. Despite your failure, the sun goddess has not forsaken the world."

Tensing her body lest the forbidden tears break out, Sumi pulled herself up. She looked away from the flailing sparrow and grasped the *naginata*.

"You are dismissed from practice." His voice conveyed resignation.

She bowed, replaced the weapon, and fled to her room.

Grabbing two cushions, she fell onto them and sobbed as silently as possible. She had slaughtered the hatchlings' only source of life. They would starve. More sobs wracked her chest.

She would never be a worthy samurai's daughter. How could she yank a child into the sea? She couldn't stand to kill a bird. Her sobs ended in a moan.

But perhaps the sparrows would come back to earth in a different form. She mulled over the thought. The Buddhist priest claimed a person's behavior determined the next rebirth. People might become a bird or even sink down to be an insect. So if one became a bird, would he have another life beyond that? And how about the child Emperor if he had drowned?

She might ask a priest at the Suwa Shrine to enlighten her about such mysteries if a priest's acolyte hadn't treated her recent question as though she'd spoken treason. Mustering her courage, she had bowed under the shrine's *torii* lintel, then approached the solemn young man standing to the side of the coin box. "Excuse me," she'd said as he leaned toward her. "Could you tell me how much respect I should give the foreigners if I ever meet one . . . according to the gods and spirits? Might they be equal to our country's artisans or the lowly merchants?" She'd known foreigners couldn't rank among those privileged to be born at the top, like samurai, or next to the top, like farmers, who grew the nation's food.

The acolyte stepped back as if she'd slapped him. "Barbarians are lower than Untouchables—like animals," he'd growled.

Her face burned at the memory of his glare, amazed she'd dared to respond.

"But how can they be lower than Untouchables? Dutch Scholars, like my father, wouldn't spend time reading their books if they didn't have something worthwhile to say."

"Who are you to argue?" he'd sputtered, then waved his

hand for her to leave.

Another tear slid down her cheek. Maybe she wouldn't find out what happened to birds when they died—or people—until she met the same fate. But she knew all too well what had happened to the mother bird and her babies in this life.

Sumi nibbled her breakfast of rice and dried *nori*, keeping her eye on the entrance to the guest room. Curiosity about the discussion going on behind the closed panels supplanted her three days of regret over the sparrows' demise. From the determined looks her parents aimed at her before disappearing through the door, she had to be the focus of the unusual meeting, which included her uncle and an infrequent visitor named Kato, whose home was a day's journey away.

A strange, momentous meeting.

The door slid open. She set down the half-finished bowl, not able to swallow another bite.

Her father gestured for her to enter.

She paused at the door and bowed, grateful her mother had instructed her to wear her attractive, lemon-colored kimono. Raising her head, she flinched. Every eye was trained on her, examining her from head to toe. She followed her mother's nod to kneel on the empty cushion.

As soon as she sat back on her heels, her grandfather turned toward Kato. "Our humble family accepts the outstanding Hino family's proposal for my granddaughter, Taguchi Sumi, to be betrothed to their honorable son, Hino Makoto. As agreed, the consummation will take place in three years during Makoto-*sama*'s twentieth year and our girl's seventeenth year."

Bolts of anxiety crashed through Sumi.

Her grandfather affixed his seal to the scroll without a glance in her direction. “We thank our good friend for serving as *nakōdo,* successfully mediating the match.”

Sumi bowed her thanks also and lowered her eyes while her elders carried out the closing formalities. She ordered her mind to remain placid, her nose not to twitch as the hazy smoke from the men’s pipes tickled her nostrils. This agreement equaled a thousand mosquito bites.

Could her family be so disappointed in her that they would sentence her to marry into an ignoble family? Or into a distant clan in the hinterlands? On the other hand, had they possibly discovered the perfect husband for her despite her many shortcomings?

The men filed out, and her father slid the panel shut, leaving her with her mother.

“I have joyous news for you.” Her mother scooted her cushion next to Sumi’s and patted her arm. “We have managed a splendid match. The Hino family even boasts a noble ancestor.”

A ray of sunshine broke through the fog. “And do they reside near Nagasaki?”

“No. They are of the Ōkubo clan on the main island, close to Edo.”

Sumi gasped. “Then I’ll never see you or Father or Grandfather.”

“That is the way with brides. You know that.”

“Couldn’t our family adopt Makoto-*sama* and my marriage continue our Taguchi name?”

“The betrothed is their only son, so they would refuse, and the sons of your Edo cousins are carrying on the Taguchi name well enough." Her mother shifted on the cushion. "Kato-*sama* told us your future mother-in-law is reasonable and has two personal maids. You will not have to give her massages or run a thousand-and-one errands." She gave a weak smile. "Above all, you will be part of a family with an excellent reputation as well as an annual allotment of rice greater than ours. You will have shelter in a big tree's shade."

Sumi's head swam. Leaving her family, leaving her city—alarming, no matter how splendid the tree. And the most important question hadn't been brought up.

"I understand a good-tempered mother-in-law and a respectable family are treasures, but may I ask about Makoto-*sama* himself?" She dared to rush on before her mother could stop her. "Did anyone speak of his nature? Might he have an interest in art or poems or valiant tales, like Grandfather has? Or an interest in the world lying outside our country, like Father?" She held her breath, as if perched on a wire above a chasm.

"Whatever his interests, you will adjust to them and support him—without fail."

"But in spite of my efforts, isn't it possible I might disgust him? His family could despise me, and I'd have nowhere to turn." The chasm yawned wider.

Her mother looked as if she wanted to shake Sumi. "It is your *duty* to please him in every way, so you will *not* be despised." She puffed out a breath. "But why assume the worst? And remember, all else will pale in importance when you are with child."

Sumi pushed down her queasiness about the mysteries of married intimacy and held her tongue. Apparently the matchmaker hadn't told her elders anything about Makoto-*sama* himself.

Her mother reached for a lacquered box, its cover decorated with inlaid mother-of-pearl. "Look at this. It's your beautiful betrothal gift." She drew out a richly brocaded sash. Smiling again despite the vacant expression in her eyes, she caressed the sash's design. "See the stitching of the bridal flower—the plum blossom. Every bride expects some hard times in marriage. The bold plum flowers poke through snow-covered branches." She folded the sash and replaced it in the box. "Follow nature's example and resolve to . . . persevere."

Sumi's pulse quickened. "I wish very much I could persevere closer to home."

"You have begged to explore outside our city as if it were a matter of life and death."

"Forgive me. I do want to see new things. Have adventure." She gathered her courage to speak boldly. "But not *exile*."

"Enough of that. You must express your genuine appreciation to your grandfather for the good match."

Sumi followed her mother from the room and waited for her grandfather and father to return from bidding their guests farewell at the gate. Her face felt frozen, while her emotions churned. How could her family send her to a distant domain to live with someone they knew nothing about? Surely she hadn't failed so miserably.

Maybe there was an unseen force wreaking havoc like the poet Bonchō's *haiku* hinted.

A sound reverberates
Alone with no one around
The scarecrow tumbles

She shivered. A *tengu,* the goblin she'd feared as a young

child, didn't exist. But what about another ghostly presence? Might the spirit of the bird she had maimed be seeking revenge?

When her grandfather came into the room, she offered a deep bow. "Thank you for the honorable match." She made an effort to sound sincere. "And for overlooking my many faults."

"It *is* a good match. We shall see if you prove worthy of it." He raised her chin with his long painted fan. "The Hino family will not care that you falter in wielding the *naginata.* Instead of skills of self-defense or scholarly attainments, they desire a woman who excels in the feminine arts. Flower arrangement. Tea ceremony. Stitchery. Proficiency in the *koto*'s music. You will pursue mastery of such skills immediately."

She bowed, not revealing her dismay at more hours of practicing pointless techniques.

After her grandfather left the room, her father motioned for her to sit with him by one of the low tables. Her mother poured both of them cups of golden tea, then also left them alone.

"Kato-*dono* confirmed a message your grandfather received last week. I think it will interest you." He slurped his steaming tea, teasing her with the promised revelation.

Sumi waited, doubting any information could soothe her heart.

He set down his cup, then met her eyes. "The Shōgun has agreed to a treaty with a powerful foreign country, the United States of America. Its diplomat will be posted at Shimoda, not so far from Edo and fairly close to your future home in Kamakura."

A tingle shot from head to toe. Unbelievably good news! Her father had shared the one piece of information that could comfort her.

"So what do you think?" A smile threatened to break

through his usual mask.

"Does that mean you might be an interpreter there? In Shimoda?" She couldn't hold back. The questions came tumbling out. "That I could visit you? That you might introduce me to a hairy barbarian? That I . . . you . . . could learn all about their country?"

"I won't be assigned to Shimoda, but this may be the first snowflake of an avalanche."

"Many more foreigners will come, over the seas, onto our land?"

He nodded.

"Do they speak Dutch in the United States of America?"

"They speak English, unfortunately. But Governor Nakamura gave me two books confiscated from an American ship that violated our waters ten years ago. I received help in deciphering the language from an imprisoned American whaler who survived a shipwreck."

"I didn't know you mastered English too." Admiration bubbled up for her father.

"Not mastered. The whaler and I mainly used drawings and gestures to communicate. But now, I have been ordered to study the language in earnest. Our city's governors graciously chose me rather than the proud interpreters who inherited their ranks. I will teach you a few words from time to time." Compassion crept into his eyes.

The scarecrow had tumbled, yet the ground might not be too unyielding.

One more question pricked her mind. "You said Grandfather heard about the treaty last week. Why did he keep such momentous news a secret?"

"The treaty and its concession to the American demands to

open our country may have been an unspeakable calamity for him."

"Not all foreigners can be evil, can they? Or like beasts? Lower than Untouchables?"

"Not lower than Untouchables. But how good? Or how evil? It's hard to tell."

The hairs on Sumi's arms stood up. Should she be happy or terrified at the news? Of course, every country had to have a few civilized people. Otherwise, the nation couldn't function. Her father treasured his foreign books. Spent hours hunched over them. Muttered their phrases like incantations. Sometimes he acted as though he'd been transported to the distant countries, leaving only his body at home. Now perhaps she wouldn't be left completely behind.

Despite her worrisome betrothal, a light glimmered in the shadows.

CHAPTER 2

September 1855, Yonkers, New York

John Cardiff watched Catherine Gray sketch the rolling hills stretching beyond the back boundary of the Gray's property. It still amazed him she'd agreed to his courting her. But how would she respond to the disagreeable information he planned to share? Although he'd gained permission for the courtship three months earlier, their opportunities to speak to each other alone had been rare indeed. The present chance had arisen when her ever-attentive, hawk-eyed lady's maid had been excused from the stroll and picnic due to a twisted ankle.

John scratched under the chin of his dog Sam, short for the fierce Japanese *samurai*. Sam was anything but fierce, but an old hermit, who had persuaded John to take the pup, favored the name over the others John considered. "Might bring you luck if yore dead set on tradin' in that savage country," Uriah had said, chewing on a straw. "Lost a good deal o' money meself, countin' on a blamed ship stayin' afloat. Guess you know tradin' companies that make big are scarcer than a two-headed cow."

Which is like once in an eternity, John had thought when the old man paused to spit.

"But usin' a Japanner word as if'n yore there, that's like prophesyin' yore avoidin' calamities."

John had doubted Uriah's logic, but appreciated the effort to support his aspirations.

Seven years had passed since he'd invested a large part of his inheritance in Bick Trading Company, eager to get in on the ground floor. Pudgy Sam had grown into a sleek, loyal dog, and John had become Bick's leading salesperson, always envisioning his experience as a stepping stone toward establishing a Far East trading company himself. Often, while running his eyes over one of Bick's merchant ships in New York Harbor, he imagined how it would be to sail his own ship to the ends of the earth. Reaching Asia—especially mysterious Japan—he would search out delicate porcelain and rolls of dazzling silks for his new company. The opportunities for profit were tantalizing enough, but even better was the idea of encountering temples, stone castles, arched bridges, tea ceremonies, and other quaint Japanese customs that the German, Engelbert Kaempfer, described in his 17th century history.

But now, a darker side of Bick's threatened to make Uriah's so-called prophecy of success closer to a prediction of failure.

He shifted his gaze away from Catherine, deciding to bring up the thorny subject after she finished her drawing. "I'll let you concentrate," he said, surveying the horizon. "Sam needs a romp, and wildflowers on that hillside look like they're waiting to adorn the hands of a pretty lady."

She wiggled her left hand's fingers in acknowledgment,

apparently too deeply enthralled with her project to comment.

John removed his coat and whistled for Sam to follow. After getting himself and the dog over the property's back stone wall, he jogged along a path wild goats had once taken. At the top of the hill, he paused to catch his breath, letting the pasture's bracing smell and the canopy of blue sky ease his worries.

While Sam chased butterflies, lizards, and possibly mice in the tall Indian grass, John set about gathering handfuls of yellow sunflowers and purple coneflowers, hoping Catherine would appreciate them as a memento of their outing. Adding strands of maiden grass around the bouquet's edges, he decided it was downright attractive.

When his fob watch showed an hour had passed, he called Sam. If he wasn't careful, there wouldn't be any time left to divulge his concerns. And besides, Catherine didn't like to be kept waiting. He headed down the hill, but halted halfway to the bottom. One of the Grays' servants had stepped out from the grove of maple trees separating the picnic spot from the house.

The man peered up at John, no doubt sent by Mr. Gray to check on John's propriety, then after nodding to Catherine, ducked back into the trees.

Reaching the quilt, John held out the bouquet. "For the prettiest lady in New York."

Catherine looked up from her drawing and wrinkled her nose as she took the flowers. "Well, if you two aren't my retrievers." She chuckled, then stopped Sam from licking her hand. "I'll lay them here, and they can serve as our centerpiece . . . although they might have been a little better looking on the hillside."

John moved over to the nearby tree trunk, leaned back, and

petted the dog. Judging from the glance he'd gotten of her drawing, he and Sam would probably be better off on the hillside, too, since she clearly needed more time to finish. However, on the hill, he wouldn't be able to take surreptitious glances, admiring the wispy auburn ringlets framing her delicate face, her porcelain-like skin, her long eyelashes. He didn't always understand Catherine Gray, but without question, she was an exquisite young lady.

Twenty minutes later, she held up her sketch for John's praise.

"It's a beauty, Catherine."

"I plan to hang it in our home's entryway after I add some color."

"A good place for it." He moved back onto the quilt, careful to keep a proper distance lest any eyes among the trees register disapproval. "You have so much talent, I regret . . ." John swallowed. "I regret I haven't demonstrated the same amount of talent in my business venture."

Her head jerked up. "I'm sure your work is more than satisfactory."

He met her eyes, ignoring the wisp of her hair caught by a breeze. "It's not a problem with my work, per se. It's with the company. Bick's officers are hiding something. I'm almost certain."

Her blue eyes became unusually cool, appraising him. "Can't you come right out and ask whoever's in charge? The Board of Directors or whoever? I should think your considerable investment and years and years of sales effort deserve, at the least, a clear accounting."

"No argument there." Her challenging tone caught him off guard. "But the members who know will not be forthcoming if the company's doing something illegal . . . like smuggling."

Her eyes widened. "Smuggling? Good heavens." She set her drawing on top of the picnic hamper, anchoring it with a small mirror from her reticule. "That sounds dangerous. Are the criminals aware you suspect them?" She ran her gaze along the edge of the grove, then back to John.

"No, I'm sure they aren't. And not all smugglers—*if* that what's happening—are killers, as I'm sure you know." He smiled, but at her frown, added, "I'm telling you my suspicions, only preliminary ones at this point, because I don't want secrets between us."

"I see." Her frown deepened.

"Of course, I'll be careful when I investigate. And I won't continue with Bick's if I find it's truly involved in any illegal trading."

"I certainly hope not. Now that we're seeing each other, your career may affect me and my family as well as yours." She pressed her lips tightly together.

"My goal is to bring only honor to your fine family." He decided it was time to change the subject. No need to get into the distressing implications for his income until he knew if he'd actually have to resign from Bick's.

He picked up her drawing and studied it for a moment. "I don't know how my closest friend managed to keep a pretty lady like you hidden from me for so long—and an artist, to top it off. Your sketch captures the scene perfectly."

She twitched her shoulders. "You thought of me as Phillip's grammar-school sister with pigtails even when I was in Miss Brooks' Finishing School."

He carefully replaced the picture. "I was blind as a bat, as they say . . . actually blinder since bats aren't totally blind."

She offered a smile at last and slid the sketch and her drawing pad into a leather case.

John joined her in gathering up their things and picked up the bouquet.

She shook her head. "They're already wilting. Just leave them there. But I do appreciate my retrievers."

"My French poodle here is more of a standout." He grinned and took hold of her hand, feeling its softness.

She snatched her hand away. "How could you, John? You're practically calling me a snippy dog." She shot a glance at Sam, who gave a tentative wag of his tail.

"Retriever, poodle—to my way of thinking, they're both dogs."

"Yes, but . . . but a young lady must be treated more genteelly." She pulled on her gloves, adjusted the hang of her teal-colored gown, and smoothed the lace on the edges of her sleeves.

John checked for a sign she was teasing, but a puckered brow declared she'd been miffed. "Oh, then I beg your pardon," he murmured. It was a half-hearted apology. His effort to confide in Catherine, to become closer, had been far from a success.

John sat in the Grays' parlor, wishing he'd never brought up the subject of Bick Trading Company with Catherine the previous day. After accepting the light for his cheroot from Mr. Gray's Lucifer match, he joined his host in puffing out smoke while waiting for the inevitable questions.

"What's this talk of smuggling at Bick's?" Mr. Gray

flicked his ashes into a tray on the writing desk between them. "You must have some basis for your suspicion."

"I'm concerned, sir, because of a recent incident on the docks. You see, I make it a point to be on the wharf every time Bick's two ships offload cargo. The sailors have gotten used to me. Also, none of them knows I studied Greek, a Hamilton College requirement."

Mr. Gray tilted his head, offering no comment, so John forged ahead. "A week ago, two Greek sailors off Bick's merchantman were talking within earshot, and I caught the gist. Three unmarked crates were leftovers from Shanghai and weren't on the manifest, so those crates were to be loaded onto a barge—a dingy one barely visible by the pilings under the adjacent pier."

"And the purpose?"

"Most likely, I'm afraid, to avoid questions about the crates' contents and why they weren't listed." He adjusted his coat and steeled himself for the next question.

"Is there a reason you didn't demand an accounting right there on the wharf?" Mr. Gray's voice had grown stern.

"I confronted one of the sailors to do just that. But a gang of longshoremen lowered the crates to the barge and rowed away while the sailor pretended not to understand my Greek."

"And what would you guess was in those crates?"

"My guess—purely a guess—would be opium." John swiped his fingers across his damp forehead, hoping his discomfort wasn't obvious.

"Humm." Mr. Gray's brow furrowed. "That drug draws more than a little attention these days."

"Yes, after the incident on the wharf, I read up on the substance. Among the many favorable articles, a few were troublesome. A doctor in one medical journal argued that opium is so addictive it should be illegal except for carefully supervised treatments. I understand it's against Chinese law to import it into China for any use."

Mr. Gray clicked his tongue. "I question the danger of addiction. I've taken doses of laudanum to ease a fever with no adverse effects whatsoever." He raised an eyebrow. "However, I grant that usefulness doesn't justify smuggling. Your concern about this situation speaks well."

"Thank you, sir." John couldn't help smiling at the compliment—the first Mr. Gray ever offered him.

"If I may ask, is the company paying fair dividends for your investment?" He ran his eyes over John's run-of-the-mill, brown frock coat. "A company that is fraudulent in one area, or turning a blind eye to misdeeds, may be less than honest in others."

John drew in a breath, seeing no way to avoid revealing more of the murky situation. "Actually, the comparatively low rate of return on my investment also makes me suspect something underhanded. I'm definitely not losing money, but my income doesn't come close to what the top management earns, judging from their mansions, carriages, and such." John bit back his words in time to avoid commenting on the owners' number of servants. Catherine's family employed at least twelve, compared to the three servants in John's home, not counting the part-time yardman.

Mr. Gray's eyes narrowed. "You're still eager to begin your own company, I assume. I am sure you realize the need for more financial stability before you seek my daughter's hand."

"I understand, sir." John blinked back his dismay.

"That stability could be achieved more quickly by taking a

managerial position in the family's factory. We have one open now since Phillip is trying his hand at corporate law in Pittsburg. And doing well, I might add." Mr. Gray gave a ghost of a smile.

"I applaud Phillip's success—well deserved, and appreciate your kind offer." John shifted in his chair. "However, I still hope to meet your standards through a trading company." Working in the Grays' carpet factory would be even worse than practicing civil law, whose grasp John barely evaded after finding his undergraduate law studies about as engaging as counting grains of sand would be in the Sahara.

Mr. Gray glanced at the ceiling and took a puff on his cheroot before meeting John's eyes again. "I suppose there is a chance you're assuming too much from the three crates. They could have been an anomaly. Or even those Greek sailors' secret scheme. Have you considered taking advantage of your brother Edward's situation and checking out Bick's activities overseas? Didn't you tell me once that Edward had moved to the same Chinese city where Bick has its overseas offices?"

John's stomach clenched. Was Catherine's father trying to get rid of him? Separate him from his daughter so she'd find a better prospect? One more successful? One perhaps more pliable? "Uh . . . I have given thought to such action, but—"

"Young man, you've heard the phrase the Roman poet expressed, 'Absence makes the heart grow fonder.' If two people care for each other, they need not fear a period of separation, a period that could bring them together more quickly in the end."

John searched for words. Traveling to the famous Chinese port of Shanghai, where Edward had become one of the top managers for Rubert and Company Trading House, would be an amazing adventure—in line with his fondest dreams—but could he afford to take a leave of absence from his job? And could he bear to leave Catherine?

"I'll carefully consider this advice, sir."

"I seem to recall that my brother recommended Bick's to you." Mr. Gray flicked off more ashes. "I'm disappointed his endorsement guided you into, at best, a mediocre venture, and at worst, one profiting from illegality."

"I don't believe he could have foreseen this problem, if what I suspect is true. I certainly don't think poorly of him for trying to improve my lot."

"Nevertheless, if you decide to venture into the Far East, I am prepared to make an investment of half the journey's roundtrip expense, whether it be for the passage or for exploration into a more legitimate and profitable trade."

"Oh, no, begging your pardon. I could never accept." John felt his face redden.

"It's not charity. If all goes well, I'm confident you will repay me in full. If you, er, come to a dead end in the trading business, you can repay me by putting your talents to work in the factory. Think about it, keeping in mind that if you make the journey, I want you to have these funds."

Mr. Gray set aside his cheroot and rang for a servant.

John took another puff, struggling to think calmly. Surely, he wasn't expected to decide at that instant. For one thing, he had to discuss such a far-reaching decision with Catherine and his family.

"However"—Mr. Gray broke into John's thoughts—"I would object to a man courting my daughter, but continuing an association with a possible smuggling operation. Mr. Cardiff, it seems your choice is either to venture forth and thoroughly investigate the matter or accept different employment."

Minutes later, the butler was handing John his hat and informing him that Catherine had gone out with her mother.

John walked the five blocks to his family's comfortable, but decidedly more modest home, deep in thought. When his courtship with Catherine began, he never would have envisioned a time he could leave her for a month, let alone for two or more years. Yet he could conceive of it now even though she was the most talented, beautiful girl he'd ever met. Was it because of the small cracks that occasionally showed up in their relationship? The inconsequential, often silly misunderstandings? Perhaps a time apart would help. Actually make their hearts grow fonder. Permit them to see past the minutia.

If he resolved the issue with Bick's or discovered a better investment, there would be one less obstacle to their marriage. Sailing to Shanghai could demonstrate his respect for her family's wishes and his devotion to her. And as a bonus, he would embark on one of the greatest journeys anyone could possibly experience.

The opportunity of a lifetime.

CHAPTER 3

September 1855, Nagasaki, Japan

A shadow fell across the *tatami* floor of Nagasaki's most profitable bronzeware shop. "Merchant, are you Omura?" a gruff voice demanded. A lone samurai stood in the entranceway, his hand next to the longer of the two swords slung at his side.

"I am, Sire." Merchant Omura sprang up from the cushion next to the brazier and offered a deep bow. His gaze traveled down the samurai's once fine, blue silk tunic and *hakama* trousers, and then quickly up again. He guessed the stern, wiry man to be in his late-twenties. His attire spoke of high status in the Chōshū clan, but also of a great setback.

"I am honored by your visit to my humble shop." Omura chose one of his nicest pieces of bronzeware from a nearby shelf and held it up like an offering. "Perhaps I could interest you in this pitcher or another object of its caliber."

His visitor struck the pitcher so that it flew across the room and clanged against the staircase.

Omura jerked back, darting his eyes from the pitcher to the

samurai.

"What do I care for your filthy merchandise!" The samurai surveyed the shelf as though looking for another item to hurl.

"Forgive me." Omura took a shaky breath. "I . . . I meant no offense." After another deep bow, he extended his arm toward the back of the shop. "May I invite you into my garden?" Although a curious person standing in the street could see through the two six-mat rooms into the small, manicured garden, no one could overhear them . . . and nature was known for its calming effect on irrational people.

The samurai strode through the shop ahead of the merchant and stopped on the rear veranda to slip into clogs for the garden. Then stone still, he stared at the rhododendron bush next to the step. "This bush is like a tree. An untidy jumble," he pronounced.

"Please excuse my pitiful garden's lack of attention." Omura struggled to hide his distress. Did the warrior abhor plants as well as material goods? He beckoned to the maid, who had hurried from upstairs to bring cups of tea.

The samurai waved the girl away. "Enough!" He pivoted to face Omura. "Although you became a blood-sucking leech, trampling your samurai calling, perhaps your words at the Ōhira Inn last week reflect a dribble of your previous training."

"I do not recall—"

"What you said about the devilish barbarians." The intruder's tone grew icier. "Now, sober, do you stand by those words?"

Omura forced his mind back to a night befogged by *sake*. A night out when he'd drunk a good deal more than usual. He'd been defending himself from a taunt that his sale of a few Dutch goods could be disloyal to the country. A couple of his tipsy phrases came to him: *The foreigners pollute our coast . . . But relieving the barbarians of their filthy coins helps us bear their stench.* The courtesans clinging to each of his arms had gaped at him. His friends had guffawed at his pretended repulsion, knowing how he craved foreign trade. But his drinking partner hurried him out amid the merriment.

"Watch your tongue," his friend had muttered. "The governor's officials are everywhere and can twist whatever you say."

Beads of sweat pebbled Omura's forehead. The governor's officials were the least of his worries now. How could he avoid getting entangled with this unbalanced reactionary?

"Your answer?" A vein throbbed in the warrior's neck.

"I always try to say what I mean. But I am a simple man, an insignificant grain of sand, and I . . . drank too much."

"Unworthy, certainly. But a simpleton could not monopolize this city's bronzeware trade." The warrior clenched his fists. "The barbarians think they can worm their way into this country, but, by the gods, they will be repelled! And their two-faced accomplices will not escape *my* wrath—the wrath of Ōta Nobumitsu."

Omura flinched. Did the warrior consider him an *accomplice*? And then the name registered. He fell to his knees and flattened his face to the damp ground. The Chōshū warlord's relative—right in his garden!

"Stand up." The warrior kicked Omura's thigh hard, like someone would a stray cur. "You cannot have lost all sense of duty. Does your loyalty lie with the Divine Emperor, who calls the barbarians animals, or with your money?"

In spite of his throbbing thigh, Omura pushed himself up. "With the Divine Emperor, Sire!" Although he rarely thought about the distant emperor and held money in high esteem, his interest above all was in keeping his head attached to his body.

A recent scene flashed before his eyes. A samurai, irritated by the loud, carefree song of a drunk peasant, had sliced off the man's head. The detached head had rolled until it knocked against the post by the entrance to Omura's bronzeware shop—like an omen from *Naraka* hell.

"Then you can serve our country even as a bumbling merchant since you live close to Taguchi Kenshin." The samurai gestured toward the point where Omura's garden touched Dutch Scholar Taguchi's property, located in the section reserved for higher samurai. "I suspect you know the family well."

"Ah yes," Omura spoke barely above a whisper, not sure what to admit. "I have had contact with the translator over the years." The samurai's hand tightened on his sword's scabbard, and Omura quickly added, "You see, my family cannot easily avoid these neighbors. Taguchi Kenshin's wife and my wife are . . . from the same clan." He stopped himself from revealing the two women were distantly related.

The warrior swept out his long sword. The cold, sharp edge hovered against Omura's throat.

"Is Taguchi's wife above the Divine Emperor then?" The warrior's lips held a sneer.

"No, never!" Omura rasped, desperate to step back, but terrified to move more than his mouth. "The Divine Emperor—above all!"

"Remember those words, Merchant. You will begin your service by being an *eye* for me." The sword moved away slightly. "Keep a record of the traitor Taguchi and his family's actions, words, visitors. Let nothing escape your observations."

"Oh, I will keep a record. Such a record. Nothing will escape my eyes."

"You will not speak of this to anyone." The samurai lowered his sword. "I will come back—when least expected."

Omura took a big breath and bowed his acquiescence. When he looked up, the garden was empty, but his rhododendron bush lay sliced to a nub. He stood still, listening, fearful the intruder might reappear like an old tale's phantom. When convinced the horror had ended, at least for the time, he stumbled into his shop and dropped down by a low table.

Almost at once, the young maid brought him a pot of tea and his pipe. Still unsteady, he motioned for her to serve him, then return to the family's residence upstairs.

He slurped the yellowish tea with his eyes closed, allowing its mild fragrance to soothe his churning senses. The smoothness and warmth of his old friend, the *chawan* bowl, felt good in the palm of his hand. After drinking a second bowlful of tea, he blessed the gods who had provided such an elixir for mankind. The exquisite liquid lifted the fog from his thinking.

He only had to spy a little. Why not? The Shōgun, who really governed the country in place of Emperor Kōmei, had his spies. The ever-present informers wrote down all the words and actions of every warlord and high government official. The temple priests recorded each birth, marriage, and death. The neighborhood headmen kept records on every local home. So what would be wrong with his keeping an extra record on his neighbor?

In fact, such sleuthing had appealing features. Taguchi Kenshin's scholarship had given him a new stature in too many people's eyes—a stature that might not be deserved, even apart from the Chōshū nobleman's censure. When one considered how Taguchi surrounded himself with foreign ideas, the so-called scholar's allegiance to the Divine Emperor could well come into question, much more so than his own loyalty due to his indulgence in a little foreign trade.

But what about the eldest Taguchi? Taguchi Yoshikatsu was a true hero of the Chōshū clan. And Taguchi Kenshin's wife? A kindhearted soul. And their daughter Sumi? A cheerful girl. Always interested in his shop and merchandise. Charming—undeniably so.

He shifted his gaze to his tea bowl. *Heroic, kindhearted, charming or not, I have to watch out for my household first, and being "an eye"—that's nothing. After all, as long as Taguchi busies himself in merely translating science books and equally boring government treatises, the scholar and his family have nothing to fear.*

CHAPTER 4

February 1856 (Year of the Dragon)

Sumi ran her eyes over the poem cards spread out on the low teakwood table in the home of her friend Taki. "Ah, there it is." She seized the card, then noticed Taki's pouting lips. "Don't blame me for finding it first. Suzuki-*sensei* had me repeat these poems over and over and over. I could almost say them backwards."

"I knew that poem too, but couldn't find it among all the other cards." Taki withdrew a paper from the sleeve of her bright New Year's kimono and patted her round face. "I don't know how you spot the matches so fast. What's your score? Thirty pairs to my twelve?"

"Thirty-one. So, I guess it's good I had a strict tutor after all. At least, I can win at *uta-garuta*."

Taki nodded, apparently missing the sarcasm.

Sumi forced herself to wait while Taki's eyes searched for the next match. One minute, then another dragged by. Sumi fingered a tassel on her floor cushion until she gave in and picked up the card which had all but shouted its location. She waited for her friend's groan.

Taki burst out with a giggle instead, while holding up the next card from the deck. "I remember this one about entangling love." She snatched up the matching card. It begins with, *I glimpsed you but once, Yet my yearning knows no end.* Doesn't it sound overwrought, like calling a tuna a whale or a puddle a lake?"

Sumi grinned. "Poems of undying passion may appeal more when you're older."

"There's only a year's difference between us. Have you felt passion now that you're fifteen, Great Knowledgeable One?" Taki snickered.

"It's a little soon to credit anything to my turning fifteen, don't you think?" Sumi read the next card aloud and picked up its match while Taki appeared to be still pondering passion. "But if I saw a great warrior," Sumi said, deciding to indulge her friend, "and if he risked his life to protect defenseless people, I might have some kind of *yearning with no end*." She patted her chest, then laughed.

"How about passion for your betrothed? Any there?" Taki teased.

Sumi rolled her eyes. "You know he's a complete enigma."

"Have you already been told about the wedding night?" Taki had lowered her voice. "Just two years from this summer, right?" Her cheeks grew pinker.

Sumi felt her own face blush. "My mother says she'll divulge the secrets the day before I leave for Kamakura. But I know a few things."

"Such as?"

"Such as darkness is the best time for intimacy . . . especially with a man you've just met. What do you know? Has your mother given you details?"

Taki shook her head, read the next card, and slapped her hand over the card's match with a self-satisfied smile.

"It's not fair to distract me."

"Strategy, my friend. Samurai women must become skillful in using the unexpected, according to my—"

"Aeee! Stop!" A woman's scream came from outside the house. Close by.

Sumi's hand recoiled as if she'd touched a cinder in the nearby brazier. The card she'd just taken from the deck dropped from her fingers.

"No! You cannot do this! Nooo!" More screams, the last becoming a high-pitched wail.

Taki jumped up, the swish of her kimono mixing the remaining cards spread out on the table. "It sounds like our neighbor's wife." She dashed over to the nearest *fusuma* panel, and slid it back, revealing a small side garden.

Sumi joined her trembling friend. The opening framed a leafless cherry tree, flowerless azalea bushes, and a high bamboo wall that blocked any view of the neighboring home's first floor or garden. A withered leaf fluttered into the room.

"Let's go see." Sumi whirled toward the vestibule.

"Wait. What if it's an attack to pay back a wrong? Vengeance carried out by some furious warrior? He might attack us too."

"Unarmed girls? I doubt it. Come on." Sumi led the way to the vestibule, slipped into her straw sandals, and hurried down the stone path. The brisk cool wind cut through the cotton wadding of her winter kimono, making her wish she'd paused long enough to wrap up in her cloak. She stopped at the gate and waited for Taki to catch up.

Stepping into the street, Sumi peered in the direction of the continuing wails and commotion. A man entrapped in a policeman's net was being yanked through the neighbor's gate, still decorated with twisted rope for luck in the New Year. The unlucky captive declared his innocence again and again while being trundled toward a large bamboo cage. Sumi drew in a breath. The cage could only mean the man was headed to prison.

"He's our neighbor." Taki had cupped her hand so only Sumi could hear her voice.

"Maa!" Sumi lowered her voice at Taki's warning look. "Your neighbor? Truly? I've never seen anyone arrested."

The captive's wife suddenly rushed in their direction, weaving through the gathering crowd of passersby and curious neighbors.

Taki drew back and turned as though to flee.

Sumi grabbed her arm. "We didn't learn strategy so we could run away. We stand our ground. Remember?"

Coming face to face with Taki, the woman panted to catch her breath, then pointed to the official on horseback overseeing the arrest. "I beg you, tell Chief Inspector Sato we are law-abiding citizens. Loyal to the Shōgun. Your good neighbors. You know that's true."

Taki stood still, saying nothing. Frozen.

"If you know that's so, you must help them." Sumi looked from Taki to the quivering woman. She certainly appeared to be telling the truth.

Taki spun to face Sumi. "Nooo, I can't! They're in trouble. Terrible, terrible trouble! Besides, the official won't listen to me."

"Then I'll speak on their behalf. My family knows Chief

Inspector Sato. In fact, he left his card at our gate and an orange for me this week, like he does every New Year."

Motioning to the sobbing woman to follow, Sumi skirted the ring of three policemen forcing the protesting prisoner into the cage and approached the chief inspector.

"I beg your pardon." Sumi bowed to Sato, seated above her in a large wooden saddle.

He kept facing forward, apparently not aware of her.

Feeling like an unwanted fly that would be swatted aside any minute, Sumi raised her voice just short of a shout.

Frowning, Sato looked down, his shaved pate shining in front of his topknot of hair. Then he bent toward her, his expression slightly softening. "Taguchi Sumi-*san*, this is no place for you. You must leave." He flipped his hand for her to go.

"I beg your pardon. Please let me speak . . . to explain my purpose."

He reared back. "And what could your purpose be? I have no treat to offer. Can't you see I am involved in serious business?"

"Begging your pardon, the arrest is why I wish to speak to you. This lady is the honorable wife of the prisoner." Sumi turned to indicate the lady, only to see no one until she looked down. The woman was kneeling with her forehead on the cobblestones.

Sato was frowning again.

"This lady," she forced herself to speak more forcibly despite her trembling knees, "is a good neighbor to my friend's family. She claims her husband and she are law-abiding people, wholly loyal. If true, might there be a possibility of a misunderstanding?"

"You don't even know this woman, do you? Or their crime. In fact, you are an ignorant child." Sato straightened in his saddle. "Now go."

Sumi lurched to the side and blinked back tears.

The woman, still nearly prostrate, looked up at her, and Sumi hesitated.

"Go now!" Sato's voice struck Sumi as cold as ice. "Obey me! Or else I will report you to your honorable grandfather for impeding police work."

The thought of her grandfather's great displeasure sent a shock of fear. She mumbled an apology, bowed, and scurried after Taki, who had come close enough to hear Sato's last words. Glancing over her shoulder, Sumi saw Sato looking in her direction. He raised his crop, and she didn't pause to see if he was threatening her, the prisoner's wife, or his horse.

At her friend's gate, Sumi dared a last look. The porters were already carrying the prison cage down the street, with Sato seated stiffly on his horse, leading the way. The wife still bowed down on the cobblestones, sobbing. None of the crowd remained to comfort her.

Sumi started to go to the lady herself. But what could she—a stranger—say to lessen the woman's agony? Chief Inspector Sato had indicated he had a valid reason for the arrest. Apparently the lady's husband had committed a heinous crime.

Taki, teeth chattering from either cold or fear, grasped Sumi's hand and pulled her through the gate.

When the gate clicked shut behind them, Sumi's teeth chattered too. She closed her eyes, fighting against the image of the broken wife . . . the protesting husband . . . the New Year's decorations. How could a pleasant day in the midst of festivities bring about such misery? The sobbing lady must have had entirely different expectations when she woke up in the morning. New Year visits with friends. Specially prepared rice cakes, cuttlefish, the *toso* drink. Chatting and celebrating. Not suspecting what disaster lay in store for her and her family.

As for the chief official? He'd always been polite before. Why had he been so insulting this time?

Sumi agreed to Taki's insistence on beginning their game again. Putting their attention on poems seemed better than taking turns at guessing the reasons for the neighbors' downfall.

Taki turned over a card from the deck and read it aloud.

The *waka*'s final two lines about a *folded robe* and *sleep* came from a poem Sumi had known even as a young child, but she couldn't make sense of them.

Taki seized the matching card. "My skills are improving, or yours are worsening."

"I can't think. That poor woman. Maybe I did more harm than good. I should have listened to you."

"You've always been braver than me." Taki gave a wan smile. "I'm proud to be your friend. Chief Inspector Sato could have been more agreeable. Although he is handsome, don't you think?"

"I just noticed his frown and stern voice." Sumi compressed her lips and folded her arms. "Questioning his police work must have made me look foolish. Or impertinent."

"But you acted like a samurai's daughter."

Sumi nodded wearily. "Everything was just horrible. The net. The cage." She cleared her throat, puzzled at her concern for complete strangers. "Do they have children?"

"Three boys. The oldest is, let me think . . . ten." Taki began gathering up the cards. "I guess we should give up our game although it's my chance to gain points while you ponder weightier things."

"The family will be banished, wouldn't you guess?"

"Who can tell at this point?" Taki reached for the bottom drawer under the brazier. "Stop worrying, Sumi-*chan.* You did all you could. You were brave enough to take a risk."

"I entered the tiger's lair and expected to rescue its prey without being bitten. Not too smart."

"But you weren't devoured. Not even really bitten. Just growled at."

Sumi quirked a smile, but then sobered. "The tiger's growl scared me away. Not only that, Sato-*sama* called me ignorant, an ignorant child."

"If you're ignorant, I'm doubly so."

"But how can we help but be ignorant? Look at us, spending hours on these poems." Sumi nodded at the two decks Taki was inserting into the drawer.

"You're the one who asks to play this game every New Years. I've always thought it was because you treasured the poems . . . and liked to win."

"I do love the poems and winning. You're right. But the problem is—we can't study *anything* except ancient traditions. Of course, you also get to practice the *naginata* to fight against twigs and shadows, whereas I'll have to resort to my sharpest hairpin if our house is attacked." She slipped out one of her hairpins and gave a wry smile as she stabbed the air. "How much better if we could also learn about new inventions when they're created, not five or ten years later. Even learn about customs and ideas and other things beyond our borders. Not our city's borders. Our *country's* borders." There. She'd said it.

Taki put a finger to her lips. "Careful. You don't want someone like the chief inspector—handsome as he is—

suspecting you disapprove of the regulations. Besides, you'll be going to a new place soon. You'll join a new clan and learn all about far-away Kamakura."

"Undoubtedly they'll teach me what it means to be a lowly daughter-in-law and an outsider, a rabbit among foxes." Sumi paused, thinking even a friend would grow tired of her grumbling. "But I guess it won't be all bad. Maybe I'll learn a new game of poems or take part in guessing incense fragrances if given time for entertainment." She leaned forward. "And there's also the chance I might meet a foreigner. I heard an American is already living in Shimoda, not too distant from Kamakura. No matter if foreigners turn out to be hairy, ugly, and brutish, meeting one would brighten my life."

A young maid added charcoal to the brazier, then glided out toward the kitchen, her movements barely moving a dust mote in the air.

Sumi rubbed her forehead. When would she learn to guard her words? "Like you said," she almost whispered, "I should be careful. Spies are everywhere."

"Yes, in huts, castles, my home, your home, and Kamakura too." Taki matched Sumi's soft tone and glanced toward the passageway to the kitchen. "But you'll be tucked away as a housewife, whose husband will guard what you say and do. Do you think he'll permit you to *see* a hairy, ugly, brutish barbarian, let alone talk with one?"

"As I said earlier"—she sighed—"I know nothing about Hino Makoto-*sama.*"

"I wish you weren't going far away. If you were still in Nagasaki, I could visit you for advice when my wedding day approached. Get help if I needed courage."

"That's one more reason I try not to think about my

marriage." Sumi attempted a smile. "Even if I meet kind people in Kamakura, they can never take the place of my dearest friend."

A short time later, after exchanging farewells at the gate, Sumi started for home. She slowed her pace in front of the neighbor's house. No sounds of laughter or even wails broke the somber silence. No shadow moved across the thick-paper panels. It seemed as if the officials had already disposed of the prisoner's family and their belongings—leaving a corpse of a house.

A well-built nest, empty of life.

The sounds of boys hard at play came from farther down the road. Sumi hurried on to where six boys were flying their new kites, shouting challenges, fighting to keep their buzzing kites airborne despite the razor-sharp attacks of their competitors. The noisy contest brought a lump to her throat. The neighbor's three young sons had probably received new kites for the holidays too, but they wouldn't be among the happy group. And if the father was found guilty, his boys wouldn't be joining such fun for a long time, if ever.

What if her father were ever accused of a crime, but was innocent? Would their neighbors, such as Merchant Omura, offer help, or would they stand apart and gape while her family suffered? Taki certainly hadn't risked her reputation for her closest neighbor.

Yet who was she to criticize Taki? Her own effort to help had been pathetically weak. Useless.

CHAPTER 5

For three nights after the arrest, Sumi had trouble falling asleep. The morning of the fourth day, she gulped down her breakfast *miso* and set out for Taki's house. She could fit in a brief visit before going to the tea ceremony demonstration she'd been ordered to attend at the nearby park. Maybe the arrest had proven to be a mistake, as she'd suggested to Chief Inspector Sato, and the neighbors rejoiced in their restored home. How wonderful if that were true.

After rounding the corner leading to the main street, she stopped at the sight of Merchant Omura, alone in his bronzeware shop. He had a talent for piecing together bits of gossip, often gleaned in taverns from servants disclosing their masters' conversations. He might know more than Taki.

Omura looked up from the abacus he held and motioned for her to enter.

Inside the dimly lit shop, her gaze flitted over the shelves lining one side of the room, laden with polished bronze mirrors, lanterns, pitchers, figures of mischievous monkeys, sultry cats, and sundry other animals and utensils that usually tantalized her. But not this day.

"Good morning, *Ojō-sama*." The merchant swept his hand toward a cushion on the store's raised two-*tatami* platform, where he usually chatted with long-time customers. "You are out early. And you are just in time to benefit from my newest acquisitions before other customers learn about them."

Omura poured her a cup of tea, then retrieved a bronze figurine of a nine-tailed fox from a back cabinet. It was about one-fourth the size of a real fox. "Can I interest you in this auspicious item?" He squatted, setting the figurine next to the small stand in front of her. "If you position this guardian at the opening to your room, it will keep out those live, shape-changing foxes, known to prowl while the unwary sleep."

A shiver twitched Sumi's shoulders although she didn't believe the tales about spirit foxes, often described as supernatural allies, but also evil tricksters. "I'm not prepared to purchase anything today, thank you. I've been wondering about an incident that occurred recently. When I saw you weren't busy with customers, I thought you might help me understand what happened."

"I always try to help my good neighbors." He poured a little more tea into her cup.

The term *good neighbors* sounded too practiced, too smooth, like a muddy slick waiting to take her feet out from under her. However, she liked the stubby little man, who politely greeted her whenever they met. Many acquaintances looked down on the merchant for giving up his samurai status ten years earlier, but his decision made sense to her. He'd chosen a merchant's comfortable lifestyle in place of the inadequate income of a low- ranking samurai. After all, what good was reputation when your family went to bed hungry?

Yet would a man who sacrificed his honor be completely

reliable?

"I've always appreciated your knowledge of events in the neighborhood," she said, brushing off her odd sense of unease. "My confusion concerns the arrest of a man living next to my friend's home. Not too far from here. His wife was distraught, wailing about the unwarranted action. Is it possible the neighbor broke a law unintentionally? Might there be a new edict that isn't well-known yet?"

"Ah, yes. I know about the arrest." He shook his head. "Bad doings. Not at all unwarranted. A Higo clansman, name of Itō, concealed a prohibited foreign object, one belonging to the Evil Religion, so the scoundrel knew his action was forbidden and had been for hundreds of years. No question. I am sure you've seen the newest placard posted at the ward gate, detailing the generous rewards still offered to informants."

"I have. I read the whole notice." The ongoing attempt to hunt down any vestige of the foreigners' religion had struck her as excessive, but she'd concealed any sign of disapproval from the gate's watchful guards.

"Itō's servant found the item in the stored blankets she pulled out for the household to use on these chilly nights." He raised his eyebrows when Sumi pursed her lips. "We should applaud the maid's careful attention to the decrees. Her loyalty to the Divine Emperor. Isn't that correct?"

Sumi searched her mind for a safe response. "As my grandfather often says, we are nothing without loyalty."

"Yes, indeed." Omura offered a slight smile. "Now the forbidden object, in case you are curious, was a small wooden model of the cross used for crucifying the worst of criminals. Itō-*san*'s fetish had been passed down in his family for generations, from the time the Portuguese and Spanish plotted to invade our country."

"Neither the Portuguese nor Spanish could have such a plot now, could they? Isn't our country too strong?"

"Yes, you make a good point with you excellent insight."

Ever the salesman, pleasing the customer. Sumi gave the required modest shake of the head and drank the last of her tea.

"Our warriors *are* superior," he continued. "Foreigners could never succeed, not long ago and not now. But our officials guard against treachery from within. Good sources say Itō-*san* first claimed the object was a keepsake, to remind him of his grandfather. Naturally, no official believed that was its true significance. When he was beaten at the prison to force out the truth, he sputtered before he collapsed that the cross drew him closer to his god."

"That was his whole crime? Possessing an ancient charm that helped him feel close to a god?" The words were out before she could correct them.

Omura snorted, apparently forgetting to court the customer. "More than enough. If he worships the Evil Religion's god, of course, he's a stealthy *Kirishitan*."

"Oh, that is so, isn't it?" She had to be more careful. "What will happen to him?"

"He will be sent up to the northern wilderness to mine coal for the rest of his short, pitiful life."

"And his family too?" Sumi coughed, surprised the question had come out as a gravelly whisper, as though she had choked on coal dust.

"His wife and sons have already been sent back to her parents. Amazingly, her side of the family was held to be innocent in the affair. The criminal's house was confiscated."

"I see. Thank you." The wife's screams echoed in her

mind. She bent over the figurine and pretended to examine its craftsmanship. After she could trust her expression, she looked up at the merchant. "I knew if anyone could help me understand the incident, you could. I had better be on my way, but I'll keep this fox with its nine tails in mind."

She rose, bowed, and silently commended herself for rectifying the minor slip and not expressing anything else that could be mislabeled subversive.

On the street again, she turned toward Taki's home. A bold, black cricket chirped close to her foot, making her step aside to avoid crushing it. She waited while the insect hopped along on the cobblestones and then into the brown weeds by the side of the road. Fujiwara-*no*-Yoshitsune's poem that had befuddled her at Taki's home popped into her mind.

A single cricket
Chirping in the chilly night
A mat, cold and white

The final two lines that had seemed like gibberish during the card game followed without a break.

Readied with a folded robe
How is it I sleep alone?

She'd never realized the poem's anguish. Had the pleas of Itō's wife been because of passion for her husband? Because she would face a cold, white mat alone after his imprisonment? Or had she wailed because her sons' father was being taken away, covered in shame? Either way, the family's separation was a cruel fate.

Sumi quickened her pace in order to visit Taki and still be on time for the tea ceremony.

Taki greeted her while she was on the path leading from the front gate. "I thought you would visit as soon as you could. Welcome. Welcome. Come inside. You want to hear about my neighbor, right? I can assuage your curiosity." Taki was nearly prancing with excitement.

"I'm not simply curious." Sumi felt her neck grow warm. "I mean, I am curious, but also distressed."

"Still distressed? You are the most sensitive person I know. But at any rate, I've been expecting you."

Once inside, Sumi exchanged greetings with Taki's mother, who then excused herself to tend to her weaving in a back room. Sumi took her seat at the *kotatsu,* a low, quilt-covered table set over a pit in the floor, and waited while Taki bustled about preparing their hot tea and rice cakes. The charcoal's heat emanating through the bottom grate of the pit brought comfortable warmth to Sumi's sock-clad feet. Faint sounds of the shuttle also soothed, as if affirming that life went on steadily. The tightness in her chest loosened.

"I never dreamed our neighbors were so wicked," Taki said, setting the steaming cups on square ceramic saucers.

Sumi jerked up straight, nearly upsetting one of the cups. "What do you mean?"

"The wife—I dare not say *honorable* now—cared for me when my parents went on a month-long pilgrimage. I was only eight, but I hardly missed my family. I guess it was because of the wife's kindness. Her husband, too, was deceptively considerate when he was at home, which wasn't too often." She shook her head. "Perhaps his frequent absences should have told me he was carrying out criminal activities even then."

"Criminal activities? Truly?"

Taki leaned toward Sumi, her elbows on the top of the table. "He had a prohibited object from the Evil Religion."

Sumi's stomach twisted. "Should we assume he was evil and seditious just because he had an old charm?"

"So you already heard about the charges? From Chief Inspector Sato?"

"No, from Merchant Omura right before I came here. I was… troubled by the severe punishment. Banished for life and their marriage dissolved. Doesn't it seem cruel to you?"

"Really, Sumi-*chan*, someone as smart as you should know that no one would keep an Evil Religion's charm if he wasn't involved in treason."

"Maybe I'm ignorant like the chief inspector said, or maybe I'm skeptical because I *am* smart, like you just said." She took a big breath. "Smart enough not to believe everything the officials say, like a sheep following its blind leader off a cliff."

Taki's eyes grew wide.

"I'm sorry." Sumi's mouth went dry. "I didn't mean that. I don't understand why I'm so bothered by your neighbors' fate. I can't even sleep well."

"A bird's death affected you the same way a couple of years ago, didn't it? I guess you can't help being moved by a creature's trouble. But you didn't cause the trouble this time. Our neighbor brought it on himself."

Sumi held her tongue. Her best friend was unlikely to gossip about her, but servants didn't have such compunctions, as the servant's betrayal of Itō confirmed.

Maybe when enough foreigners came, the unbending restrictions on their ideas and beliefs would be removed. In the meantime, she'd best remember that government officials were wiser than she. Laws weren't made to be questioned. Laws were meant to be honored, especially by one belonging to a line of samurai unflaggingly loyal to the rule of the Shōgun.

With a start, she realized she'd stayed longer than she'd intended. Now she had to rush to the tea ceremony, where she would then need to slow down . . . down . . . down, to the pace of a plodding ancient tortoise. While she watched the tea master carry out centuries-old tradition, her disruptive thoughts would surrender to numbing monotony.

And this time, that might be a good thing.

CHAPTER 6

June, 1857 (Year of the Snake), Shanghai, China

Feeling awkward, John gazed out Edward's broad office window at the stunning view of the KwangPoo River while his brother finalized requisitions with an assistant. Western countries' gunships, merchantmen, Chinese junks, sampans, and barges packed the river, a Yangtze tributary. The smaller vessels obviously had to maneuver for space while avoiding crushing collisions. Sort of like himself, John thought. He was a sampan, trying to find the best way forward without scuttling his life.

When the no-nonsense, male assistant left with a stiff nod to John, he crossed the room to the velvet settee facing Edward's imposing desk. His brother's office suite, replete with mahogany furniture and Persian rugs on teak flooring, bore strong witness to its occupant's importance—a powerful merchant, like an unsinkable steamer, at Rubert and Company Trading House.

John folded his arms as Edward strolled toward him. The troublesome subject couldn't be avoided any longer. Even though their close relationship had been suspended when Edward sailed for China more than eight years earlier, they were still responsible to each other as brothers.

"When people back home heard I was traveling here," John said, his eyes following his brother as he sat in the armchair at an angle to the settee, "some congratulated me as though I'd become Lewis or Clark of the Pacific. Others commiserated as if I were going to my grave."

Edward nodded. "Same responses people gave me."

"But the knowledgeable ones talked about this city's infamous vices—prostitutes and opium smuggling."

"Both pervasive problems here." Edward brushed a speck off the sleeve of his white pongee suit.

"I know your stance on the first, but what about the smuggling?" John found it hard to believe he even had to ask his brother about flouting the law.

Edward frowned. "You've hit on a sore point, John. Rubert's not engaged in anything illegal here . . . strictly speaking . . . although reports surface about opium coming in on ships from Batavia."

"Can't you investigate? Stop the practice if it's happening?" It wasn't like Edward to sidestep a straightforward answer.

Edward furrowed his brow. At twenty-nine, he was only one year older than John, but deep lines in Edward's forehead as well as a receding hairline and his dark beard—in contrast to John's full head of wavy brown hair—added to his appearance of age. "It's in the hands of the owners. When I asked about the reports soon after my transfer here, I was told I wasn't paid to be the company's conscience, and I'd better not stick my nose where it wasn't needed."

"Hard to get anywhere when you smack into a stone wall, I'm sure." John took a second to reorient his thinking. "So, if Rubert's isn't engaged in smuggling, what do you suspect happens to opium coming through Batavia?"

"I wish I had a better answer." Edward ran a finger over his mustache, then rubbed the back of his neck. "The truth is that opium from our ships finds its way to independent British traders upriver, protected by the cooperative British consul. Those traders have no problem moving it into China's interior, and our company has no problem recording the profit as miscellaneous cash income. So there you have it."

"How'd the British get involved?"

"Filled in the gap. Our previous consul was ousted due to outrage back home over his part in smuggling operations." Edward gave a thin smile. "Our current consul is a paragon of virtue. Threatens arrest of scoundrels and lectures on morality wherever he gets a hearing—which rarely happens. Afraid his is a futile voice crying in the Shanghai wilderness."

"It's a foul-smelling situation, seems to me."

"Yes, through and through. But hold on a minute." Edward turned toward the lacquered stand next to him and picked up the bottle of claret. "Afraid I've been remiss as a host. A little wine to celebrate your arrival and for your stomach." He poured two glasses and handed one to John. "The water here is teeming with disease, a different kind of foulness. We boil it, but you're bound to get some unboiled residue on food, fingers, and the like."

Edward waited while John took a drink.

"Very good, like the rest of your generous hospitality." John warmed at his brother's pleased look, but then put down his glass, fighting his reluctance to continue the unpleasantness.

"So, American smuggling has gone into the shadows here in Shanghai."

"There's more to tell . . . going back to when I was a peon in the company." Edward sipped his wine, then poured more into both their glasses. "There's no question Rubert and Company was at the forefront of smuggling in Canton although we used bribes instead of force. In fact, there was a saying that the British gunships held the horns, and the Americans milked the cow."

"But bribery, Edward? Didn't that bother you?"

"Yes, but I excused it, knowing a junior assistant like me couldn't change the company's policies. Everyone—no exaggeration—*everyone* said you had to import opium to balance trade. To pay for the silks and tea and porcelain with something other than silver."

"I suspect Bick's could also be unloading opium here. If so, it must be aping Rubert's and the other big companies, bypassing the American consul's prohibition. Right?"

"I don't know of any company that isn't bringing in the drug."

"And how about opium itself? Is it the evil some claim?"

"Let me be the inquisitor and turn the question back on you."

"Sorry. I'm not trying to make a case against you."

"Glad to hear it. For a minute, I thought my lawyer brother had turned prosecutor."

"I'm trying to figure things out." John drew in air through his teeth. "I've a sizeable investment in Bick's. More than you know." He shook his head when Edward started to pour him more wine.

Edward set down the bottle and lurched to his feet. "Keep

talking in a natural tone," he said in a loud whisper. "Could be an eavesdropper afoot." He headed toward the door, the thick carpet muffling his steps.

"You see . . ." John cleared his throat, uncomfortable speaking at a distance. "A visiting clergyman in chapel, back when I was a student, raged against opium. I thought it strange he was so riled up."

Edward motioned for John to continue speaking.

"Before making this trip, however, I did discover the drug was addictive and debilitating to some users, but so is alcohol."

Edward put a finger to his lips, then yanked open the door.

A Chinese servant in a long blue gown stepped back. He gaped for a second before thrusting out a tray of pastries and fruit.

Edward folded his arms with a stern look. "The tray belongs on the table. But first, do you remember what I told you about standing at the door?"

"I knockee. No standee close. Today, before knockee, door open."

"All right. All right. Knock more quickly in the future."

After the servant deposited the tray and left, Edward took his seat and sighed. "Fan's the head chef's assistant, and a good one. Takes over when the chef goes on his all-too-frequent holidays. I'd hate to let him go. If he was eavesdropping and knows more English than he lets on, he didn't learn anything that's not common knowledge. But we may need to be more cautious in some future discussions."

"Guess walls have ears everywhere."

"No question about it." Edward motioned to the tray. "The pastries are generally excellent here—copied from the French Concession. Help yourself." He slid the tray toward John. "At any rate, that preacher didn't pound the pulpit hard enough. My chief comprador, Henry Li, took me to see an opium den a few months ago. Until then, I had the same questions as you. I'd heard the drug praised as a balm for pain, an elixir for the hard blows of life, even as an aphrodisiac for the lovelorn."

"Many doctors swear by its morphine."

"No doubt that's legitimate. But to get back to my visit at the *Huayanguan,* literally the flower smoke establishment, I saw a man in the backroom who was Henry's lifelong friend. He was a living corpse. Henry said he'd been a strapping man with a pretty wife and four children a few years earlier."

"Your comprador let him stay like that? His lifelong friend?"

"No, a couple of years before I saw the man, Henry had taken him into his own home. Henry's family—four generations and two concubines—didn't like that a bit. But Henry stood by him during the weeks of withdrawal. Then the friend went right back to the opium den. Henry tried again. When the same thing happened, he didn't try a third time. 'Black tiger,' Henry said, 'not let go. Ever.' He may be right. By some estimates, one out of every seven Chinese men is an addict, and the number's growing. The drug could bankrupt this ancient country in time."

"That's terrible. Awful." John ran his finger around the rim of his glass, thinking. "Would it be possible to see one of those dens for myself? Observe smuggling's effect firsthand? Bolster my decision to leave Bick and face an undesirable job in New York . . . since there doesn't appear to be any legitimate option for me here. And truthfully, I'm curious about the dens."

"Henry can take you. Without me. Better to have just one foreigner with him in the Old City, the original Chinese Shanghai. That's where his friend is. And when you go, take your pistol, hidden of course. Pickpockets abound although they might be more reluctant to accost someone as tall as you."

John nodded. If he couldn't endure such a small test of his caliber, he needed to turn tail and go home right then.

Edward pulled coins from his pocket. "It'd be wise not to carry anything valuable, not even your pocket watch, but take these copper cash and this silver *tael.* You don't want to infuriate a thief if one slips his hand in your pocket. The best thing is to try to look like an official with authority, not a rich sightseer."

"Have you been accosted?"

"Twice. Drew my gun, but didn't fire a shot and lived to tell it." Edward winked and bit into a madeleine. "Welcome to the wilds of the Far East."

The sweltering heat began early, unusually hot for Shanghai in June, but John refused to cancel the venture into the Old City. The two porters carrying his sedan chair moved at a steady trot as they followed Henry Li's chair down Szechwan Road, across the Yangjingbang Creek's bridge, and through the French Concession.

Between the road and high, white walls of private residences, refugees squatted forlornly in the dirt. John pushed back against the sedan's headrest, his heart hurting. Many of the men had bandaged or even missing limbs resulting, he guessed, from the battles in the surrounding towns between Qing imperial troops and Taiping rebels. Edward's letters had mentioned the ongoing revolt and the contrast between the well-off upper classes and the struggling poor. Now John had to count himself as one of the well-off, having no idea how to address the dire suffering surrounding him.

The porters halted at the gate to the Old City. After Henry dropped several *cash* into the hands of the foremost Chinese guard, they passed through the ancient portal into ranker odors of still more crowded humanity. Hawkers, mules, ragged beggars, water carriers, shoppers, tradesmen, barefoot packs of boys, and a range of simple to ornate sedan chairs filled every inch of space on the road.

He slumped down in the chair to keep his six-foot height from being noticeable. Dust coated the inside of the chair and his sweating face. His porters repeatedly halted and then jerked forward as though fighting through surging tidal waves. Eventually the two sedan chairs turned west onto an equally crowded road, and after a short distance stopped before a narrow alley.

Seeing the dark pathway ahead, John felt for the pistol under the long, pale blue coat Edward had loaned him. Actually, the coat and loose trousers reminded John of what a pirate might wear when wanting to imitate a somewhat civilized person. Maybe a piratical look was good if he didn't have the authoritative-official look quite right.

The porters squatted next to two old men engrossed in a game of mahjong.

Henry gestured for John to follow him.

None of the alley's inhabitants seemed to pay John any mind as he walked along, ducking under the drying laundry, strung from narrow openings in the walls to openings on the other side. He soon let go of the pistol and concentrated on subtle landmarks as one twisting alley led to another and to another and to yet another. His family had often remarked that he had a built-in compass, but he reckoned the best Indian tracker would be befuddled in the maze. At least his height helped him keep Henry in sight. From the back, his guide's gray gown and long pigtail looked the same as that of every Chinese merchant, but he wasn't hard to follow in the alleys because there were hardly any other merchants. Instead, housewives, children, and old men were milling in the more open areas, while individuals who appeared coarser populated the shadows.

At last they turned into a doorway, identical to the hundred or so they had passed except for a red lantern hanging over the entrance. A sickly, sugary smell was already enveloping John as they pushed through a beaded curtain on the inside.

Henry handed a coin to a withered, old woman who met them.

She shook her head and rasped out some words, obviously complaining.

Henry gave a sharp-sounding reply, but offered another coin.

The disagreeable woman tottered to the far side of the room and pushed aside a heavy velvet curtain.

John's stomach turned at the overpowering burnt-sugar smell infusing the darker backroom. After his eyes adjusted to the light provided by two flickering, pine-resin candles, six male figures, lying on wooden beds, materialized in the haze.

Henry walked over to one of the men and spoke to him in Chinese.

The man continued to draw on his long, bamboo pipe, making no acknowledgment that he'd been addressed.

Henry shrugged and turned toward John. "Friend, Hu Lin."

John took a few steps closer to Hu Lin. The man seemed a mere skeleton coated by loose, translucent skin. The only sign the addict still breathed was the thin trail of blue smoke issuing from his nostrils.

John ran his eyes over the other men. One man, whose body appeared unaffected, was watching him, but the other wasted men appeared to gaze at nothing.

Three scantily-clad female attendants were tending the opium being heated at the central charcoal fire. One of them placed a glowing globule into the clay bowl at the end of Lin's pipe, providing more vapors for the man to smoke without interruption.

Another female, perhaps fourteen-or fifteen-years-old, entered the room and began disrobing next to the more alert man.

John signaled to Henry and strode out of the room. He'd seen more than enough. The devastation was seared into his mind.

Fifteen minutes later in the third alley, John suddenly stopped and looked around. Henry was nowhere in sight. Instead of paying attention to his guide, John had been mentally rehearsing his letter of resignation from Bick, pending final proof of smuggling. How could he have been so supremely stupid?

Three unkempt men on the side of the alley eyed him.

Looking lost by standing still invited trouble, so he walked forward. The landmark at the next corner should be a knotted rope dangling from an opening on his right. At least he'd been smart enough to take precautions. He'd find his way back to the main street.

A dog growled. The angry sound of two men arguing came through the wall next to him. A small urchin tried to shove him out of his way, then cut around him. The everyday chattering sounds on the alley had diminished although people still milled about.

No rope was at the corner.

His heart beat harder. Sweat trickled down his back. He struggled to stay calm. After all, hadn't God promised to support those *who took the wings of the morning, and dwelt in the uttermost parts of the sea*? The family's minister, visiting their home before John's departure, had shown him the verse in the Psalms. At the time, John considered it a comforting thought for his mother. Now he hoped it was the truth.

So, he wasn't really alone, was he? He shouldn't worry. He must have simply missed the rope at the last corner. All he had to do was backtrack until he reached the rope or another landmark.

Aware of the watching eyes, he snapped his fingers and whirled on his heel. He reached under his coat and grasped for the pistol.

It was missing!

He flinched. He'd felt nothing. Where could he have been pickpocketed? He looked to the side and saw three men leering at him. One held his gun.

The thief raised the gun, pointed the nozzle straight at John, and beckoned for him to come.

John darted his eyes around him. The alley's immediate inhabitants had melted away.

He took one step toward the thieves.

The man with the gun jiggled it and jerked his head at John for him to obey.

Ducking low, John leapt sideways around the corner in the opposite direction. Heart hammering, he grabbed the coins in his pocket and pitched them back into the alley he'd left, praying the thieves would be distracted.

All at once, a hand grasped his arm and pulled him through an open door.

John clenched his fist, but stopped in mid-swing. The man facing him looked exactly like Rubert and Company's assistant cook.

Was he imagining things? He dropped his fist and took another look at the face before him. It couldn't be, but the features were identical to the man called Fan. Had the shock of being lost and robbed affected his mind? He felt under his coat again. The gun was still missing.

The servant held up his palm. "You safee. Stay." As he slipped into the alley, he pushed the door closed in front of John.

John squatted and leaned back against the wall, trying to calm himself enough to think, to make sense of what happened. Why was the eavesdropper apparently tailing him? And why did he help him? Or was he helping him? What if Fan was a crimp, and John was about to be shanghaied—drugged and impressed on a ship? Chinese were the usual victims, but it had happened to white men too.

And if God were with people who journeyed to the uttermost parts of the sea, where was the Almighty when ships, like the one responsible for Uriah's loss, met their doom rounding the southern capes or scraping razor-sharp reefs or sinking in typhoons? For that matter, where was God when John's father died in a freak mill accident close to their New York home?

A soft female voice and an answering male voice came from one of the adjoining rooms, but the dark room where John waited seemed empty. He listened for any sound—an intake of breath or a swish of movement—but heard nothing. If anyone lurked in the thick darkness, the person didn't want John to know.

How could he escape if Fan were an enemy? He had no idea of the way out of the maze and couldn't communicate. He might walk for hours in the alleyways and even be accosted again. On top of that, he didn't have any coins left to hire a sedan chair if he somehow made it to the main road.

He gritted his teeth and repeated the Bible verse to himself.

The next minute, Henry burst into the room. When he saw John, he threw himself down in a kowtow.

Relief coursing through him, John rose while the comprador poured forth his apologies.

"It's all right. Not your fault, Henry." John tried for a firm voice despite his shaky legs. "I didn't pay close enough attention. It's my fault. Not yours."

Henry raised himself from the dirt entranceway. "Your gun? Gone?" He peered at John's coat as though trying to see under it.

"Yes, but I can get another."

Henry pointed at the assistant cook. "Fan know many people. He get gun back."

"I don't want to endanger him. I'm thankful he was here. Maybe saved my life."

Henry scowled.

"Thank God for you, too, Henry. You came back for me."

"Manager Cardiff skin me alive, like Indian do, if I lose you."

John smiled in spite of himself. "Surely not."

Henry didn't return the smile. "I give coins. We go through rooms. Come out on different alley. We go now. Quick. Quick."

Henry led the way, and Fan took up the rear until they reached the waiting sedan chairs. John settled onto the chair's silk cushion as the porters began the return trip to Rubert's compound. Despite another layer of dust already forming on his sweaty body, he'd never in his life appreciated a ride so much as the swaying, jerky one carrying him at that moment.

CHAPTER 7

Two hours after John's return, Edward shook his head as he listened to John's account. "I doubt those ruffians would have shot you. They probably wanted to rob you of more items, but you never know. Anyway, it seems you've had a baptism by fire. Still attracted to the Far East?"

"Yes, very much, but got a lesson in watching my surroundings I won't soon forget." John took a bite of rice curry, already feeling stuffed from the fish soup and mutton in the five-course meal provided in Rubert's first-class dining room. "I'll have to resign. Turn in my company shares. Of course, I'll check into what's actually happening first, but not much doubt in my mind." He heaved a breath. "As I explained earlier, I invested a good amount in Bick's. Actually, over half my inheritance."

Edward's eyebrows shot up. "Didn't figure it was that much."

"I received enough disbursements over the last eight years to live on. Put some surplus into savings, but, depending on the Shanghai market, I may come out short of the initial amount."

"Sounds like it could be worse."

"Yes, I could be wandering in circles or dead." John couldn't force a chuckle from himself or Edward.

Edward narrowed his eyes. "In addition to whatever you recover from Bick and have saved, do you have more funds available?"

"The remaining part of my inheritance—for a sure thing—and a small amount of Mother's nest egg, a forty-dollar *investment* from a hermit called Uriah, and, uh . . . a loan from Catherine's father. I tried to refuse money from all three to no avail."

"Ah hah. Do I detect the love for the pretty Catherine behind this journey? I think your letter mentioned courting her . . . when? Over a year ago?" Edward's eyes twinkled like they had in his and John's boyhood days.

John rolled his eyes. "I expected that. And yes, we're to all purposes engaged. We made a commitment to each other before my departure, but her father withheld final approval. Wants my finances to improve and a resolution of the trouble at Bick's."

"It seems congratulations are in order."

"Well, hopefully. At least, I'm working on the smuggling issue. And I'm here. Mr. Gray left me little choice about making this trip."

"From what I gleaned, he's a hard man to buck. And you say the hermit Uriah invested too?"

"I got to know Uriah better after he left our paper mill. He was bitter about the hand providence had dealt him. Said the Almighty relented when Jonah prophesied to the sinners in Nineveh, but didn't relent in sending him calamities. However, when he brought me his forty dollars, he claimed he and God were on better terms and that he was doing right well selling turkeys."

Edward nodded. "Glad to hear it. And now, how about the

most surprising of the investments—Mother's? What did *she* say about your excursion over the seas? She acted like I'd sold my soul to the devil when I announced I'd be setting sail."

"She gave her grudging approval in the end. I think the threat of war on our doorstep played a bigger part than any concern over smuggling."

"I have a proposal if your interest in this part of the world is large enough—great enough to stomach a good deal of risk."

John's pulse rose at the intensity in Edward's eyes. "I'm interested in whatever you propose. You're the expert here."

"I still have most of my inheritance along with the savings deposited in the Agra and United Services Bank down the street." Edward leaned forward. "If you're not afraid of starting a new venture too soon—jumping from the pot into the fire, as Mother says—maybe you and I could manage something extraordinary—truly extraordinary." He stared at John.

"What are you suggesting?" John's mouth had become dry.

"Taking majority ownership of a hundred-fifty-foot, three-mast, screw steamer a Russian tycoon wants to sell quickly."

John jerked back. "You can't be serious!"

"Oh, but I am. The tycoon's grandson, half Russian and half Chinese, has been arrested, accused of aiding the Taiping rebels. The Russian is desperate to raise money for the young man's defense in the Chinese imperial courts."

"Buy our own ship? Outright?" John nearly choked on the words even though he'd longed for that exact thing all his life.

"A majority share, at least. Maybe the whole ship, depending on the value the Russian assigns it and our bargaining powers. We could start our own company. Take cargo on consignment." Edward's eyes glittered. "What do you think?"

Although the two British couples at the next table appeared

deep in conversation, John lowered his voice anyway. "If we actually got the ship, reckon we could carry on trade under the noses of Rubert and Bick?"

"Rubert's the one that could hurt us—resort to cutthroat competition." Edward had lowered his voice too. "We can put the company in your name to smooth the waters. I'll have to stay in my present position until our new company can hold its own. But you can take on whatever cargo we manage to get from the Russian. Most likely seal skins and a ton of whale oil."

"You've already thought this out. In so much detail."

"Seemed an impossible dream. Then you appeared."

Still seemed impossible to John, but his mind was clearing. "So, you're proposing we'd trade up and down China's coast?"

"Well, after trading down the coast, you could cross the South China Sea and sell the remainder of the cargo at the LooChoo islands. Wouldn't meet any Rubert ship over there."

"The LooChoos? Doesn't Japan hold sway over them? Guard them jealously?" John conjured up a map of the islands.

"Japan has complete control over the northern portion of the chain—islands to be avoided at all costs. But the chain's southern islands are shared with the Qing emperor." Edward nodded to the waiter to take their plates. "Are you still obsessed with Japan like you used to be?"

"More than ever. I met an impressive Japanese chap named Manjiro when he visited New York a couple of years ago."

"Never heard of him."

"An American ship's captain rescued the young fisherman after his boat sank. If he returned to Japan, he could be sentenced to death—as I'm sure you know—but he was willing to risk everything to provide for his elderly mother."

"He was staying true to his Confucian morality—duty to

parents is paramount here."

"And besides Manjiro, there was the hoopla when Commodore Perry sailed from New York to bring Japan into the *civilized* world—possibly a misnomer, considering how the North and South are at each other's throats."

"Well, I asked about your interest because the LooChoos could be a bridge to Japan proper. The Chinese comprador we'll have to hire could handle the LooChoo trade negotiations too. The Chinese get special charters for trading not only at the southern LooChoo port, but also for Nagasaki."

Nagasaki! A shiver traveled up John's spine. "What I wouldn't give for a charter like that. But it sounds awful tricky, Edward. Finding a good enough comprador. Hoping to somehow be granted a spectacular charter." John could hardly believe he was carrying on with the idea even theoretically, as though he'd plunged into waters with an irresistible undercurrent.

"Martin Li, Henry's younger brother, is trained to be a comprador and would leap at the chance to work for us. And here's the best part: the American Consul General is in Japan right now, negotiating with *Nippon*'s high muck-a-muck to open a few of its ports for trade, most likely including Nagasaki. Imagine when that happens—an escape from the most vice-riddled, densely packed city in the world into territory virtually untouched by outsiders. And we can be on the ground floor."

The familiar words grated. The ground floor hadn't worked well for John, and much worse for Uriah. Still, here was an unparalleled chance to draw close to mysterious Japan, as if a genie had appeared and offered to fulfill his biggest wish.

"And you think we have a decent chance of succeeding?" John stopped speaking at a waiter's approach. He shrugged off the sensation of being watched. Of course, the waiters were watching, ready to serve the next dish. He nodded to the offer of raisin pudding.

"Yes, as much as I know in this unpredictable world."

John ate a little of the pudding, using the chance to think. What if he lost the rest of his inheritance? Lost everything? He would lose Catherine. And his loss would be Edward's also, a two-fold devastation in his mother's mind. But at the same time, what if he and Edward were on the threshold of a great enterprise? Could he live with himself if he didn't try?

"You know," John said after a minute, "I'd hate to regret for the rest of my years that I'd thrown away a one-in-a-million opportunity. Let me check out Bick, with your help. If the company's selling opium to independent dealers, then I say, let's try to get that ship. Fan the flame."

Edward thrust his hand toward John. "Partners then?"

"Partners." John shook hands while working to quiet his racing thoughts. "I hate to ask my next question."

"Spit it out."

"All right. How would we split the company?" John blew on the coffee the waiter had just served.

"Fifty-five, forty-five. Sound fair?"

"More than fair."

"Just to be clear, your share is fifty-five."

"What?"

"Fifty-five, or it's no deal. Because you're going to be investing all your funds. Not only that, you could be in danger at the LooChoos. I mean, Commodore Perry cleared the way when he showed up at the southernmost island with his warships and got coaling rights, but situations change without warning. Could turn ugly. In fact, nothing 's for sure when you're talking about a trading company in Asia."

John sucked in a breath. "I understand."

Edward watched the waiter walk away after topping his coffee cup, then pulled out two cheroots and handed one to John. "Fan no doubt contributed much to the meal. Too bad I'll have to dismiss him for trailing you. On principle. Or, maybe we can transfer him over to you since you say he may have saved your life." He struck a match for their cheroots.

John took a couple of puffs and watched the smoke dissipate. "I find it hard to believe he saved me out of the goodness of his heart. But we will need a good cook . . . if we get a ship."

"The firm of a Hong Kong merchant, Sandwith Drinker, lost a ship when the vessel's own Chinese passengers captured it. I don't see mild-mannered Fan leading a mutiny, but you'd want to keep a vigilant watch if you're even comfortable taking him." Edward flicked ashes onto a saucer.

John nodded, still struggling to get his mind around the huge turn in events.

"Well," Edward said, pushing his chair farther back from the table, "starting a company is like rolling dice when only one number will let you win, but it's worth the gamble, especially if it gives me a future away from Rubert's and the opium trade. In the meantime, you can take the ship and use it well."

"It sounds like you're pretty confident of getting the winning number."

"You, John, came at the perfect time, like a gift from the Almighty. And he holds the dice, doesn't he?"

"In some sense, I suppose. But don't we usually credit a fortuitous happening to his *providence*? Providence sounds better. Although I'm not one to talk. Got too many questions on the subject."

"Call it whatever you want. If we get the ship, I imagine we'll be begging for more of those fortuitous happenings." Edward grinned, then sobered. "Especially you."

"When you want something as much as I want this, it's hard to know what's underneath it all. Presumption? Providence? Opportunism?"

"Or lunacy." Edward laughed.

John managed a snicker despite thinking lunacy might be closest to the truth.

CHAPTER 8

October1857, East China Sea

The crane swung a skiff loaded with chests of oolong tea from a Fuchow barge onto the merchantman. For a minute, John expected to wake up and be back on a New York wharf, overseeing Bick's cargo. But the shouts in Chinese flying back and forth left no doubt he was in a Chinese port, standing on his and Edward's ship, aptly named the *SS Retriever*. Cardiff & Associates had become a pulsing reality. A reality, John thought with a slight shiver, dependent on the ocean's moods, market vagaries, and the competitors' strength or weakness. Clearly, he'd taken one of those dare-devil leaps off a cliff, like in his boyhood, only this time he didn't know what the water held. Or to use Edward's questionable analogy, the roll of the dice might omit the one desired number.

However, so far, so good.

A group of Chinese hands began moving the tea chests toward the ladderways leading into the ship's belly. Boxes of well-wrapped, blue-and-white porcelain already lined the bottom of the forward hold to protect the tea from the seawater that seeped into the bilge even in tight ships like his. His comprador, Martin Li, watched the tea's progress, no doubt bursting with well-deserved pride.

Braving thieves and pirates, Martin had traveled from Fuchow up the Min River to bargain with the oolong tea processors. Often called black-dragon tea, its plants thrived on the upper slopes of the Wuyi Mountains, far into the Chinese interior. Martin returned with five large boatloads, as well as a contingent of ragged escorts acting as guards for the prized tea. The payment for the guards and transport had been unbudgeted, but would be worth every silver *tael* so long as Martin and he managed to trade the tea in the LooChoos. And if they failed, a nightmare lay in store.

Martin shuffled a handful of papers—receipts for the goods, John guessed—then walked around winches, coiled cable, and the massive spider webs of rigging to where John stood.

"An excellent cargo." John raised his voice to be heard above the din of thuds, shouts, whistles, and clanking machinery. "Our competitors must be green with envy over your triumph with the tea. Jealous too of our success with the skins and whale oil." He smiled at Martin. "An auspicious start. I couldn't be more pleased."

"My duty." The glint in his comprador's eyes conveyed his pride. "Porcelain and tea accounted for, sir. I check Indian spices coming now." He motioned to where the tackle's crane was lifting another skid of boxes onto the deck and hurried in that direction.

John glanced up at the quarterdeck where the *Retriever's* sailing master, an American by the name of Jim Whitson, was issuing orders that translated into the dizzying beehive of activity reaching up to riggers at the crow's nest—a staggering eighty feet above the main deck—and down to Fan, cooking in the galley on the orlop deck, as well as to all the seamen on the three decks between the extremes.

Captain Whitson noticed John and motioned for him to stay where he was. He scooted down the ladderway with remarkable agility despite his squat stature and middle-age paunch. After buttoning his tight-fitting jacket at his waist, Whitson strode over to John. "We're on schedule. We'll steam out first crack of dawn tomorrow, then use faster sail and save coal." He raised his felt hat and ran his hand through his bushy dark hair. "Spending the night on board?"

John's pulse rose. "Yes, on board, and eager for the open sea."

The captain gazed up at the cloudless blue sky. "We've a promise o' two, mebbe three fine days. After that, only Mother Nature knows what mis'ry she's stored. S'long as the weather holds, should be a quick crossing, an' I hope as uneventful as one o' them ladies' quilting bees."

John chuckled. "I'm all for uneventful. Help counter the stress where we're going."

"Worryin' o'er trade with those ornery natives, I reckon. You can rest easy 'bout the handling o' the ship. This here's a good ship, thank the saints above, and manned by able seamen."

"Manned as well by a sailing master who has my full confidence. I heard a proverb the other day you might like: *Too many captains run the ship up the mountain.* I'm partial to ships on water, so I'm here to trade. You're in charge of the ship."

"Suits me fine."

John rubbed the back of his neck. "It *is* the LooChoo trading, as you say, that's worrisome. We've had an example of

Martin's remarkable shrewdness, so I'll have Martin negotiate with the merchants first. Maybe he can convince them we're not a threat to their lives or their country's survival, and they won't claim empty shelves while their back rooms are stuffed to the rafters."

Whitson's brow furrowed. "Shrewd trader or not, I wouldn't want my fortune dependin' on success in a country closed tighter than a clam, or its outpost islands either. And pleased I am enough funds to pay the crew's sittin' in the bank."

The captain excused himself with a lift of his hat, and after bawling out a sailor who had stopped work to stare, headed back to the quarterdeck.

John watched him go, thankful to have him on board. The captain's long-time experience on the Pacific more than compensated for his brusqueness. When Whitson agreed to stay with his old ship, he'd retained five American crew members, one Englishman, and four Russians, claiming they were the best of the lot. Then he'd overseen the recruitment of eight more American seamen, including a ship's surgeon, from a storm-battered whaling ship sitting in dry dock. Henry and Martin Li had helped Whitson recruit the eleven Chinese hands straight off the Shanghai wharves. John's only concern with the crew was Fan, the one man the captain hadn't chosen.

The rough-and-ready captain's reference to a quilting bee brought to mind the hours of ladies quilting John suffered through growing up. Now, he wouldn't mind any amount of tedium if it meant a safe trip and a toehold of trade at the LooChoo port of Naha. Failure at Naha would slice the profit of the company's maiden voyage in half. He'd probably end up back in Fuchow and Shanghai, selling the precious tea at bargain prices to beaming rivals, like Bick's, able to carry it to

Britain or America. The sharp rocks of a dive into unknown water could cut deep. But the leap was underway, and one couldn't change his mind in midair.

The mention of ladies quilting and thoughts of home prodded John to retire to his room, situated in front of the captain's Great Cabin. He'd have to finish writing his mother, younger brother, and Catherine so the letters could go on a fast clipper ship leaving that week, sailing around Cape Horn, and arriving in New York at the end of three or four months.

He scooted his straight-back chair up to his narrow writing desk and dipped his steel-nib pen in the inkwell, ready to share the recent exciting events. He paused. What would Catherine find interesting? The attainment of oolong tea? The ship's progress? The members of the crew? All would bore her. He supposed she would like an account of the Shanghai bund, so he set himself to describing Edward's splendid suite, the magnificent gardens at the entrance of the Rubert and Company's compound, the Shanghai settlements' race course, and of course, in conclusion, how he wished she were with him.

Then with something akin to relief, he turned to finishing his mother's letter, assuring her of his continuing good health and success—a much easier task.

Three days out from Fuchow, John spotted the first of the short mountains of the Diaoyu tai jutting from the sea, barely visible on the ship's port side. These uninhabited cones of rock marked the half-way point on the age-old route from China across the East China Sea to Naha.

Two dolphins zigzagged away from the ship as the

Retriever's sails hummed and snapped while glittering waves slapped the hull. The ship's bow had been smoothly cutting through the moderate ocean swells on the entire course—uneventful, as hoped. And lucky, since realistically much could go wrong. John shook his head, picturing how planks of wood less than a foot thick and a thin copper sheath kept the dark depths of the ocean at bay.

Now if the second half of the route would only continue so well.

A minute later, a noise like a sheep's persistent bleats caught John's attention. He stood still and listened. Had he heard right? Why on earth would a sheep be on deck? He made his way toward the sound coming from the ship's stern and stepped around the screened-off area the American hands used when not on duty. There stood Fan next to the taffrail, talking with a group of five Chinese sailors, one of whom, sure enough, had hold of a sheep. The sailor—an especially burly man—removed a rope from around the animal's neck and hoisted it in his arms.

"Stop! What do you think you're doing?" John strode toward them.

The man holding the sheep looked at Fan, who said something, resulting in the animal being roped again and plunked onto the deck.

"Givee sheep to sea." Fan grabbed onto the rope and pulled the sheep closer to himself. "Makee ship safe. Here come Blackee Water. Sea god angly."

"We need all our sheep," John said, his voice authoritative. "We need them more than any sea god."

"Sea god wanchee sheep."

"Fan, I want you to talk to Captain Whitson. He knows

about oceans. He can explain the water's darkness."

"He know north ocean. Not ocean here."

"No, that's not right. Henry Li got the captain a good rutter for this sea. It tells the best routes and compass points." John waved his arm indicating the points, hoping Fan would at least get the gist even if his English was truly rudimentary. "So the captain knows the currents, shorelines, reefs, harbors, channels, even the tides. He can keep us safe."

"No givee god sheep?"

"No. We need every sheep. We'll be fine. You'll see."

Fan bowed, not managing to hide a flash of indignation. He muttered in Chinese to his five companions, using words, John imagined, that would make polite Chinese blush. As Fan and the men shuffled off with the sheep in tow, John caught the Cantonese words *fan kuei*, foreign devil.

The men juggled the sheep between them and disappeared down the ladderway hatch toward the hold containing the other two sheep, chickens, ducks, and turtles.

Too bad, John reflected, that he and Edward had taken a chance with Fan. But maybe, if the smooth sailing continued, the men would see they had nothing to fear and the incident would be forgotten. In the meantime, he'd ask the captain to post a guard so a sheep wouldn't vanish during the night.

The next day, standing at the ship's bow, John studied the dark clouds lowering over the ocean in the far south, replacing the previous day's cotton ones. Surely the Chinese hands with the sheep wouldn't blame the wrath of the sea god for less favorable weather.

He turned to see Whitson hurrying toward him, grim-faced.

"What is it, Captain? Bad weather ahead?"

"The least o' worries. The main mast lookout's sighted a

ship's top gallants. Following our path, adjusting its course each time we tack, gaining on us. Haven't seen its colors yet. Dread the sight."

"Cantonese pirates?" John shuddered at the thought.

"If pirates, prob'ly out o' Fuchow. Hid behind the Diaoyu tai to intercept us. Don't matter where the devils are from. Pirates are pirates."

"Can we outrun them?" John peered through the maze of ropes toward the stern but saw only slate-colored ocean beyond the wake, stretching to the horizon.

"Our canvas is at full stretch, and, I repeat, she's gaining. The fresh wind favors a light schooner, without heavy coal and cargo like ours. But with that squall line on the starboard, mebbe the south'ly wind will pick up. Not 'commodate sails like hers."

"And if it does pick up?"

"We'll tack to the southeast and then switch to steam and go straight south. Put us off course a little. If she's a pirate ship, she won't have steam. Their crew'd hafta reef and furl sails, so they'd quit the chase. Problem is, the ship might reach us 'fore the wind strengthens."

"What kind of chance would we have in a fight . . . if overtaken?" John worked to keep a brave face despite fearing he knew the answer.

"We're priming the four cannon, but eighteen pounders ain' no match for a well-armed pirate schooner. We'll resist surrender till one cannonball short o' going under, but hide any valuables you got."

The captain turned on his heel and headed up to the quarterdeck, shouting for First Mate Brewer to call all hands ahoy.

John hurried to the stern and pulled out his spyglass. The

topgallants of the suspect ship's sails now showed above the horizon. Nightfall's cover was a good three hours away. His heart in his throat, he headed up to his cabin, not to hide valuables, but to get his second revolver. Fortunately, he had replaced the stolen pistol with two newer ones before leaving Shanghai.

Reaching between the blankets lying at the bottom of his wardrobe, where he'd hidden the revolver, he found the gun had shifted from the center to the left. He picked it up, his stomach twisting. Had the ship's constant rocking caused the movement? Or a person?

Taking a breath, he inspected the barrel, cylinder, and trigger with unsteady fingers. Each mechanism worked. How could anyone have tampered with the gun anyway? His door had been locked, and the sentry had been on guard by the captain's cabin. He needed to get hold of himself, not let fear make him irrational. He loaded the gun, then holstered it under his coat on the side opposite of his other pistol.

He climbed down to the main deck while assessing the ship's defenses. Buying four additional cannon, each a twenty-four pounder, would have been a wise investment, but no use thinking about that now. Could well-aimed bullets deter an attack before either ship fired their cannonballs? According to Robert Fortune's account in *Three Years' Wanderings*, he had held off two pirate ships—one after the other—single-handedly, with only his rifle and pistol. Unbelievable, but verified by witnesses.

But if the pirates weren't deterred? He rubbed his forehead. Falling into pirate hands—unthinkable. Horrible accounts of slaughter were told in the foreign settlements. If their attackers behaved as usual, most of the Chinese sailors would be killed quickly. But he and the others would be held for ransom and slowly, savagely tortured to death to force out ever more desperate pleas to friends and family.

If worse came to worst, it would be better to cause mutual destruction of the ships and drown.

Drown!

Catherine's beautiful face came to mind. How heartbroken would she be if he died? At least, she'd know he and Edward had owned a trading company and a ship. He'd risen beyond marketing the imports of a shady firm.

So, would owning a trading company be his life's one accomplishment? If he died that afternoon, his proud achievement would be worth . . . what? He closed his eyes and grimaced. Worth nothing financially. There would barely be enough funds from insurance claims to let Edward make the reimbursements and break even. And worth nothing otherwise because who cared about a dead person's status?

However, if he lived, he could tell Catherine he'd battled pirates while pursuing his fortune to advance their wedding. She'd question whether his desire to explore wasn't the bigger reason for his dangerous venture, but she'd be impressed, nevertheless.

And he would fight! He wasn't ready to die. Especially not in the ocean, where blood-thirsty sharks would feast on him. He would fight. Not end up as a bloated, half-eaten body.

CHAPTER 9

John took up his vigil at the main deck's stern, staring through his spyglass. The stalking ship's billowing upper sails formed in his view.

The bosun rushed up. "Pirates for sure. No ensign at her masthead. No reply to signals. Captain requests your presence."

"God help us!" John darted a glance at the distant ship's skulking beauty. "I'm on my way." He climbed to the quarterdeck two rungs at a time. A strong gust, carrying the smell of rain, whipped through the canvas as though demanding attention. The clouds to the south were a good deal closer and blacker. He joined the bosun, chief engineer, First Mate Brewer, and Second Mate Crowder leaning in around Captain Whitson.

"We'll steam straight into the big blow as soon as the wind strengthens," Whitson said, his voice gruff. "This is typhoon season. But anything nature dishes out beats the curse o' pirates."

"One hour to full power if all goes well," the engineer said, obviously for John's benefit. "With permission, going below, sir."

The captain gave his curt permission and turned to John. "If the enemy maintains their speed, we'll hold off the attack with our hand weapons first. Four o' my men have rifles. The pirates' firearms will be short-range, old muskets if they've any at all. But we can't withstand their heavy cannon if they get too close."

"I'll join with my two revolvers if the distance shortens enough," John said. "The rifles are a godsend. We'll win! We have no choice."

Even before John finished speaking, the captain turned away. He issued orders and headed to the helm where the helmsman was holding a steady course.

John climbed back down the ladderway while First Mate Brewer bellowed through his trumpeting horn for the riggers to take to the yards. As John stepped onto the main deck, Brewer's order came for the Russian gun master on the berth deck below to open the hatches and prime the two starboard cannon.

Only two starboard cannon, four rifles, and two revolvers to face the enemy! Woeful!

Back at the stern, John could see the full schooner without his spyglass. With the glass, the deadly black cannon protruding from its eight gun ports were clearly visible, like a monstrous spider raising its legs. He estimated another hundred yards was needed for the American riflemen to target the crew before the schooner turned broadside to fire.

An angle began to form between the two ships. John watched, puzzled, then realized the *Retriever* was turning in order to make for the squall's wind.

Sensing movement, he edged over to make room for the riflemen and turned to acknowledge them.

Fan stepped next to him.

"What—"

The cook hung a huge black flag with white Chinese characters painted on it from a shroud at the stern's starboard side. "Wanchee give up. No die. No meetee sea god."

"No! Never!" John yanked the flag off the shroud and hurled it overboard.

"Chinese wanchee sullenda." Fan slipped a long knife down from his sleeve.

"You dare mutiny? Alone?" John stared at him, sliding his left hand under his coat.

"Not know *mutinee. Sullenda.*"

Five Chinese sailors, the previous ones with the sheep, loped down the deck toward John like a pack of wolves. Knives glinted in their hands.

John lunged, connecting his right fist to Fan's chin.

The cook toppled backwards.

John whipped out both revolvers and pointed them at the five men, now running toward him, while keeping an eye on Fan, motionless on the deck's planks.

The five skidded to a stop, dropped their knives, and raised their hands.

"No wanchee sullenda," one called out.

Three Chinese sailors jumped down from rigging. They stopped, stared at John, and broke into confused shouts.

John, palms wet with sweat, raised one of the pistols, not quite in their direction, praying the men weren't part of the mutiny.

One of the three stretched his neck forward and yelled something in Chinese at the mutineers. It sounded like a taunt to John.

The five stayed sullenly quiet.

The three men turned away and began dragging the fire

equipment's engine, pumps, and hoses across the deck, muttering to each other.

In a sudden flash, before John could grasp what was happening, the mutineer closest to the hull leapt into the air with a guttural shout and dove overboard, like a flying fish in reverse. A dull splash sounded a second later.

The remaining men darted a look toward the railing as though considering a similar move.

John glared at the four men and shook his head. "If you try that, I'll shoot." He kept his revolvers trained on them. He'd seen tricks as a kid when facing bullies, but no one had tried to distract him by committing suicide. His stomach revolted at the idea of having to shoot one or more of the men point blank, but he'd do it.

Registering movement beyond the mutineers, John caught a glimpse of the riflemen coming around the black funnel. "Help!" he shouted, while continuing to stare down the four men in front of him.

The men raced forward, guns pointed.

The mutineers fell on their knees and bowed toward the riflemen.

A weight lifted off John's chest in spite of the pirate ship. "Hold these men so we can get them in irons," he ordered as the riflemen slid to a stop and drew into a semicircle out of the rebels' reach. "Our cook's the ringleader." He jerked his head toward the prostrate Fan. "Demanded we surrender. These others joined in. Drew knives."

"No! The blazes they did!" The lead rifleman cocked his gun, and the other three followed.

The kneeling men bowed their foreheads to the deck again and again.

John shouted at a rigger coming down the ratline to relay

the trouble to First Mate Brewer and the captain. After a series of whistles, three sailors—one Chinese and two American hands—rushed up.

The sailors tied up the four protesting men and Fan—conscious but groggy—and yanked the gang across the deck to be hauled below.

After holstering one of his pistols, John took hold of a shroud's rope and leaned out from the bulwark to look for the man who'd jumped.

He was swimming toward the pirate ship with a long way to go.

The riflemen joined John at the starboard side. "Shall I shoot the swimmer?" the lead one asked, eyes narrowed, gun pointed.

"Don't waste your ammunition," John said, sure the man would drown anyway. "Save it for the pirates." Another twenty yards, and the men would be able to hit their marks.

Eighty yards more and the pirates would be in John's range too, while the *Retriever* would be a broad target, well into the pirates' cannonball range. The stalking ship had already made up the distance it lost in its own tack to the southeast. A battle looked inevitable.

First Mate Brewer relayed the order for the riflemen to fire.

John held his breath.

The small figures of the pirate crew scurried around, but the ship drew closer at what seemed an even greater rate of speed. John's blood ran cold like it had when the Shanghai thieves stole his gun.

A rifleman took aim at the pirate's fore topsail mast.

One man toppled, but another could be seen swinging up the rigging to take his place.

The *Retriever*'s cannon fired a second later, the boom deafening.

The smoke cleared enough for John's watery eyes to track the cannonball flying toward the pirate ship's prow.

He groaned as the ball fell short.

The men next to him fired their rifles and shouted vile curses at the pirates.

The pirates hooted and shouted in return, their beast-like yells carrying across the expanse as though they were a few feet away.

A series of whistles came from the *Retriever*'s helm. The funnel belched black smoke. The deck vibrated with the thrumming huge engine. Riggers high in the ropes furled sails as the ship came fully around.

The pirate ship tacked closer into the wind, striving for a parallel track in order to fire its cannon in deadly broadsides before the *Retriever* could escape.

John shifted a few yards toward amidships, held his aim as steady as possible, and got off a round of shots as the ship's prow rose to the top of a swell. Two pirates fell from the rigging, and others disappeared, falling or taking cover on the deck.

John studied the expanse between the two ships. Was it widening? He clenched his jaw, his whole body straining to push the *Retriever* forward. He fired another round of shots, then leaned back and looked up at the sky. "Oh, God, faster," he begged. "Give us speed!"

"God," the rifleman muttered next to him, "hear the man's prayer!"

Black smoke from the pirate ship's side and a shrieking whistle warned of the cannon ball blasting toward John.

He shouted, "Watch out!" and angled away, willing the ball to fall short.

The ball missed the *Retriever* by a couple of yards. Another splashed short of the stern to his right seconds later. Then another angled straight toward the bulwark in front of him.

John leapt backwards and threw himself down on the planks, covering his head with his arms.

Fragments of wood exploded a few yards away. Debris sliced the air and rained down.

After a minute, wondering at the lack of pain, he ran his hands over his body. Although his arms dripped blood from scratches, his limbs were basically uninjured. Then he heard a moan over the ringing in his ears, followed by more.

Turning on his side, he saw large splinters of wood sticking out of the arm and hip of one of the riflemen stretched out next to him.

The injured man waved John away and also the mate who bent over to help him. "Shoot the pirates! Or we'll all die!"

At that moment, a cheer erupted from the men in the rigging behind them.

Not only was the *Retriever* steaming forward, but one look showed the pirate ship had stalled. A skeletal crew could be seen working to reef their canvas as a southerly wind blew in earnest from the nearing storm.

"Sails ho!" came from the crow's nest.

The captain called for his officers and John.

John left the injured rifleman to the care of the ship's surgeon, Dr. Billy Morse. On the quarterdeck, he steeled himself for the next round of terrible news.

"Where there's one pirate ship, there'll be two or three more devils," the captain said. "They work in packs. We're going to steam farther south, then east."

"Into the storm?" John asked when the two mates and bosun were grimly silent.

"A short ways 'til the fresh sails the lookout spotted disappear. And, by all things holy, they will."

During the fight with the pirates, John hadn't paid attention to the ocean except for the increasing swells. Now looking down from the quarterdeck, he was struck by how unearthly dark the water appeared. Sullen, roiling, reflecting the swirling black clouds in front of the ship. Not the sea god's work, of course, but the storm emitted malevolence with a will of its own.

He thought of the shipwreck off Cape Horn that sank Uriah's investment. Had the eight survivors watched their mates disappear into a swirling blizzard or actually seen the men swept overboard? Had their lifeboat, said to have been the ship's cutter, held together only long enough for the eight to reach a higher latitude before it too disappeared below the waves?

A lightning bolt streaked in the distance as if warning the *Retriever* not to draw closer.

John retired to his cabin to rest the best he could. It would be a long night, with the looming struggle out of his control. Instead of joining the fight against the wind and waves, he'd be forced to stay out of everyone's way.

The *Retriever*'s timbers shrieked as the ship steamed due east, no longer a pirate target, making for land as fast as possible in case the heavy squall turned out to be a full-blown typhoon. The top sails had been furled, the topgallant masts were already down on deck, and storm sails were double reefed. The highest waves struck the windward side of John's own cabin—towering monsters cascading over the ship. His room shook with each mighty blast.

The storm seemed to suck John, his cabin, the ocean, even time itself into its vortex. The ship tilted from side to side as though about to capsize, each roll making John's stomach clench.

The vibrations from the struggling steam engine abruptly stopped. Every muscle tense, John gripped the edge of his cot, waiting for the thrumming to jerk back to life. The engine stayed still, silent as though it had given up, deserted its keepers, and accepted the inevitability of a watery grave.

A sickening bucking motion took over. The ship climbed giant swells and plunged into deep troughs. With no steam and only the double reefed storm sails, the tempest had to be carrying the ship toward disaster.

John dropped to his knees, grasping his cot's frame. "God, have mercy. Get us to Naha! Please!" He clung to the cot as the room shook, searching his mind. Was he a hypocrite? A believer only when desperate? "If we make it, Lord, I'll take Thee more into account. I swear."

To keep from being pitched across the floor, he wedged himself between the cot and wardrobe. The howling wind and battering waves blocked all other noises. If a sailor struck the bells of the middle watch, John didn't hear the clangs although he tried to pick them out, longing for their reassurance.

Bone weary, but with no chance of sleeping, he thought back to a small toy boat he and his younger brother Matthew had launched into an eddy of the Saw Mill River. How naïve they'd been, feeling outrageously proud of their boat's prowess. They'd had no idea of the difference between an eddy and the sea's green-eyed fury. Other thoughts came: Matthew's grin when John shared his penny candy, sleigh rides in the winter, wrestling with Edward until one of them hollered for mercy—usually John.

He grimaced as the memory that never ceased to haunt him replaced the others. It was an old one, but fresh as ever. In the summer of his sophomore year in college, he'd tried hard to carry out the responsibility his father had placed in his hands at their family's new paper mill. But his father's praise for John's grand effort had dissolved into exasperation as mud oozed from under the massive retaining wall John's crew had finished in record time—record time because they hadn't dug down to bedrock. Another crew under a different supervisor had been hired to reconstruct the wall. And then a few weeks later, his father had died in an accident completely unrelated to John's fiasco, yet always connected in his mind by the time's proximity.

The deep ache at falling short and then losing the man he loved and most admired remained undiminished by the passage of a decade. Would his father have approved of John's Far East venture? Not if the ship ended up at the bottom of the sea.

The *Retriever*, like a racehorse gone wild, galloped on through the storm. But finally, toward what had to be the second day, the ship's bucking eased with only a sixth or seventh rogue wave lifting the boat's prow skyward. Hope rising, John stood, testing his legs.

The engine's vibration started. John stopped mid-step. Waiting. Praying. Then the next rogue wave came, and he grabbed hold of his cot. The engine kept thrumming, however, as though its spirit had returned to stay.

John moved over to the porthole, hoping to see out beyond the gangway rail. A sharp tilting turn scraped his hand off the porthole's edge and slammed him down on his side. He struggled to his knees and darted his eyes around the slanting floor. Were they capsizing? Doomed after all?

The ship righted. Regaining a sitting position on the floor, John drew in long breaths. Side-to-side rolls replaced the waves' battering. Could the ship be entering a harbor? A place of refuge?

First Mate Brewer's voice rose above the other noises in a shout to lower the stern anchor. Then the ship's forward motion stopped.

The tension went out of John's shoulders. He found himself sliding onto the floor as if he were pudding sliding out of a bowl. Lying flat, he treasured the milder rocking of the ship.

The *Retriever* was intact from what he could gather. With all his heart, he hoped no lives had been lost other than the deserter's. As for the cargo, much of the porcelain had doubtless cracked in spite of being extremely well-wrapped. However, the tea should be fine.

Then he slid his palm down the side of his face as a premonition struck.

God help us if we've blown into the Japan mainland.

CHAPTER 10

October 1857 (Year of the Snake), Nagasaki, Japan

"There! I knew I heard a kitten." Sumi pointed to a spot halfway up their pine tree. "See it? Poor little thing."

Taki joined Sumi next to the tree and looked up into the branches, already thrashing in the strong wind. "The animal climbed up. It can get down."

"But there's a bad storm coming. Maybe a typhoon."

"It can get down. You can't climb up there."

"I've done it before." She smiled at Taki's shocked look. "When I was ten. To see the tall Dutch ship in the bay. Of course, instead of sparkling waters, all I saw was an endless sea of roof tiles. Wave after wave of roofs."

"You're older. Your honorable mother would say—"

"A samurai's daughter must be composed, self-possessed." She looked up at the small yellow, bobbed-tail cat. "It'd take just a minute to reach it."

A swirl of dust blinded Sumi. Wiping her eyes, she saw the mewing kitten had moved inward, its white paws clinging to the center trunk.

Taki brushed off her red-flowered kimono. "Those clouds are moving in fast. Look how dark they are. I have to go." She glanced up at the kitten. "Please take my advice: Go inside and let the cat fend for itself."

After their quick farewells, Taki hurried out the side gate.

While latching the gate, Sumi made up her mind. No one was watching. Her father had left hours earlier to check on the status of storm preparations by the Dutch on Dejima. Her mother was shopping for emergency supplies, and her grandfather's paints and brushes were arranged in a semi-circle around him when she'd peeked into his room. She wouldn't even risk hurting a good kimono. She hadn't taken time to change out of her plain, everyday one when Taki arrived.

She'd get the kitten.

She slipped out of her sandals and ducked under the tree's bottom branches. Ignoring the brown prickly needles, she slid under the limbs to the trunk. Twisting and scraping through the narrow spaces, she pulled herself up branch by branch. The strengthening wind whipped stinging needles into her kimono, arms, face, and hair. She used the crook of her elbow to cover her eyes as much as possible.

The kitten stopped mewing and climbed a little higher.

Sumi stretched her hand toward the kitten. "*Tomatte!* Stay put. I won't hurt you."

It went up several more branches.

Sumi looked toward her house. She'd gotten even with the second floor. Using one hand to cling to the trunk and the other to push branches aside, she climbed slowly, narrowing her eyes against the wind and needles.

The kitten scrambled up higher, nearly to the tip.

The tree bent under a powerful gust.

When Sumi peered up again, the kitten had disappeared.

Her heart skipped a beat. Had it been blown off? She eased her body around, then tilted her head to see better. A small limb broke beneath her, but the thicker branch right under it held. She grasped the thin trunk with both hands. Another gust, stronger than before, bent the tree again.

A shout came from below.

Sumi froze, then looked down. Way down at the maid, Kin. Her heart pounded. How would she ever get to the bottom?

A crack sounded.

She slipped and scraped down six or seven branches. At the same time, the tip of the tree crashed and caught in the lower limbs to one side.

Kin shrieked.

Sumi descended as fast as she could. One sleeve caught and ripped. The rough bark tore through her socks and into her feet.

"Get down immediately!" It was her grandfather shouting the command.

She was hurrying as fast as she could.

At last on the ground, she crawled out and bowed low, seeing for the first time that Chief Inspector Sato stood next to her elder.

"A member of a samurai's family does not act immodestly," her grandfather growled, "or foolishly risk her neck. What possessed you to think of climbing the tree, and then to climb beyond a safe limit for even a strapping boy?"

She swallowed and pushed a strand of hair behind her ear. What could she say?

He glowered at her. "Tell me. Surely not to study the churning clouds or look for the barbarians' ships."

"A stray kitten was trapped in the tree. It was frightened." She fought against the threatening tears. "And I am afraid it has been swept away."

"I'd expect even you to have better sense than that." He turned to Sato. "What would you say to such a foolish girl?"

"I would say such a girl should be careful in how she employs her courage. To look for barbarian ships would not be wise. Not at all. Worse, at the time of the New Year, she accosted me while my men were arresting a secret *Kirishitan.* She argued I was making a mistake."

The back of Sumi's neck heated. She yearned to speak in her defense, to say his version amounted to a lie. Her legs threatened to buckle, but she stood erect with her eyes lowered.

"Thank you for bringing this affront to my attention." Her grandfather bowed low to Sato, who returned an equally low bow. "I will address the problem here and now."

He paused and squinted at Sumi, then turned to Kin, who was standing a respectful distance away. "Draw water for my granddaughter's bath. Cold water will do. Do not dispose of her kimono. It will be used tomorrow." He waved his hand to dismiss her.

When the maid had left, he set his jaw. "First, I want to hear your apology to Chief Inspector Sato."

Sumi bowed, a new strength infusing her body. She could handle this. In fact, it was an opportunity.

Keeping her head bowed, she took a big breath. "Chief Inspector, I apologize for listening to the neighbor's wails of innocence. I should not have asked if there had possibly been a mistake . . . even before I knew the charge."

Neither man spoke for a long minute. Was her grandfather absorbing the difference in her version, the true version? Had her *affront* become less odious?

A loose shutter on their storage shed began banging in the wind. The gatekeeper, who doubled as their groundskeeper's assistant, rushed past.

"Add that you have learned not to question our august guest's wisdom or authority." Her grandfather did sound a little less irritated.

She spoke as instructed, glad propriety kept her from having to look up at Sato.

"After the bath, you shall spend the evening in your room with no distractions. No light. No food. It is hoped that fasting in the dark will sharpen your mind and hasten your maturity. Imagine the chagrin of Hino-*sama* if he were aware of your conduct, behavior like that of a wild monkey, not of a young lady soon to be wed. He could have second thoughts about the betrothal. With good reason."

Sumi kept her head down, wishing her betrothed would have second thoughts, especially if he disapproved of rescuing creatures in distress.

"Tomorrow morning, you shall pick up every last needle thrown to the ground by your assault on our pine. The tree's missing tip will memorialize your thoughtless actions."

She bowed again, thinking she didn't need the tree's reminder. Whenever she saw Sato, she would remember his misrepresentation and her shame at being rebuked in front of him, once more treated like an ignorant child. Even worse—compared to a monkey.

When she raised her head, the two men were walking toward the back entrance, gesturing at the roiling sky.

Because of the dark clouds, a gray twilight set in quickly. After Kin prepared the bath water and closed the wooden shutter between the bathhouse and the back of the kitchen, Sumi dismissed her. She hurriedly rubbed her skin with rice bran and rinsed off with the buckets of cold water. Pulling out the needles in her long hair by herself took the most time, but she was finally ready to climb into the chilly water of the tub itself. She climbed out a minute later and slipped into the fresh *yukata* robe Kin had left for her.

Dark wavering shadows, like the storm's fingers, cloaked the stone path leading from the bathhouse to the back veranda. Kin met Sumi at the stairs, holding a vegetable-wax candle, and led the way up to Sumi's room. The maid put the candle on its stand, pulled out Sumi's futon, and readied the mosquito net. As soon as she left, Sumi obediently blew out the candle.

She lay down, doubting an empty stomach and darkness would improve her mind. Perhaps the denial of comfort enabled monks to draw closer to enlightenment if they maintained the right attitude. But she was far from having the necessary detachment from earthly concerns, especially in the face of the oncoming violent storm. The strengthening wind was already moaning around the corners of the second story and rattling the shutters like angry warriors demanding entrance.

While the rain pounded the roof, she thought about the little kitten, imagining its drenched body. If the kitten lived after being blown from the top of the tree, it couldn't endure the beastly maelstrom.

The house shook. The building's screeching protests grew louder and louder, as if struggling to stop the storm from snatching its roof. If the roof were torn apart, some of its heavy tiles would crush her. She pushed her futon close to her cupboard and then squeezed part of her upper torso into the stuffy area. Her bedroom had become a prison, maybe even her coffin.

Could her family not care at all whether she lived or died?

The door to the stairway slid open. A flickering lantern met her eyes, with her mother's shadowy figure behind it. "Come quickly. You will be safer downstairs. This house has stood for more than forty years, but this storm is fierce."

A sob escaped from Sumi's throat.

"Shhh," her mother said, but for once accompanied it with no admonishment other than to hurry.

At the bottom of the stairs, Sumi peered into the room adjoining the main room. Her grandfather was there, wearing his dark robe and holding a stick of incense. His back stiffened as she followed her mother past the open panel, but he said nothing. His silence, she realized, meant he'd given permission for her to come below. But only after he'd left her in danger, she silently accused, fearing for her life.

She swiped at the fresh tear.

The noise of the storm stopped as the typhoon's center moved overhead. In the guest room, Sumi lay awake on the hastily-prepared futon. She pictured the pine standing serenely despite the loss of its tip, lit by the moon shining high, high above. If any spirit cared enough to inform the moon god, *Tsukuyomi*, about a girl climbing too high in the tree, the god, unaffected by even the wildest of storms on earth, would laugh at the tale's insignificance.

Why then did she have to be treated as a scoundrel who'd committed a crime? Like someone being called a murderer for stepping on a bug? Or a thief for plucking a fallen persimmon out of an abandoned grove? Muttering a vow to endure the injustice, she turned over and determined to sleep despite the storm's returning wrath.

She woke to a quiet dawn. The faint tinkling of the wind chimes hanging from the closest eave was the only sound. She stretched, luxuriating in the silence until she recalled the kitten and her grandfather's rebuke. The bright sense of peace transformed into murky annoyance. Picking up all the pine needles would require an hour or more on her hands and knees even if allowed to use the groundskeeper's rake for the bulk of the needles.

Midmorning came, and Sumi was still in the midst of picking up the stubborn individual needles that had resisted the rake when she heard someone clear her throat. She turned, expecting to see her mother with hands on hips, making sure she did a thorough job. Instead, the maid stood there holding a basket.

"You are not allowed to help." Sumi's tone was sharper than she'd intended, but Kin should know better than view her in the ripped kimono, kneeling on the wet ground.

Kin bowed low. "Please excuse my inconsiderate interruption. The Master said to give this to you."

After pushing herself up, Sumi took the basket and slipped open the cover. Inside was the yellow kitten with white paws, either dead or asleep.

"Are you alive?" she asked, short of breath.

The kitten opened one sleepy eye, stretched out a paw on the spotless white towel, and went back to sleep.

Sumi slid the cover into place and looked at the maid. "Which master?"

"The honorable Eldest." Kin's mouth twitched, almost as though fighting a smile. "He found it next to a wall when he went out to inspect the neighborhood's damage. He showed it to me to confirm its identity."

"Has it been fed?"

"Cook gave it fish soup. It drank like a cat twice its size."

"Then set the basket in my room and also a shallow box with straw. I'm almost finished here." She gave a quick smile to the maid and went back to scooping needles.

Even though her robe had become saturated and her hands, lower back, and knees throbbed, she found herself humming. It was a children's song about a frog, reminding her of when she'd shown a small frog she'd captured to her grandfather. He hadn't seemed as distant when she'd been nine or ten, not nearly as demanding. He'd actually seemed to care about her happiness, but that was before she'd failed so often in her training.

However, his kindness with the kitten was amazing. Maybe her grandfather didn't hold her in utter contempt. His concern might be the size of a sesame seed, but that was better than none at all.

She began picking up needles and twigs faster. In her room, a rescued creature was waiting. She would make sure the kitten knew it was wanted and loved.

The eldest Taguchi stood in the shadows of his room, watching his granddaughter through the partially opened *fusuma* panel. He hadn't been able to see Sumi's face when she found the kitten still breathed, but her shoulders no longer slumped. Maybe the time had come to release her from picking up the rest of the needles. After all, she hadn't been at any great fault, obvious from Sato's silence following her own explanation.

But no. Sumi tended to be far too impulsive. Not only had climbing a tree been highly improper for a girl her age, it had also hinted of deception, based on an assumption no one would catch her in the act. She needed reminding that she was to comport herself as a female and not act like the head of the household. Her elders, himself included, had doted on her, their only child and grandchild. As a result, they had a strong-willed young woman on their hands—a potential strength, he supposed, but definitely a problem at the present.

The exercise was also good for her. Now that she no longer practiced with the *naginata*, rode horseback, or shot the bow and arrow, she spent much of her time inside. A few months after her betrothal, he'd had no choice but halt her archery and riding lessons. Whoever heard of a girl wanting to ride with neighbors to visit distant Fuji-*san*?

"But you are a girl," he'd told her. "Females are not allowed on the sacred mountain even if the long journey were not too great an undertaking."

"Couldn't I disguise myself as a boy?" she'd answered, her eyes pleading.

"And infuriate the mountain's powerful spirit?" He'd hardly been able to believe his ears. "That is the talk of a lunatic."

Until that moment, he'd secretly been proud of his granddaughter's horsemanship and archery skills, surpassing a few young male samurai who trained more rigorously. Apparently, she had realized the level of her skill too, and it addled her thinking. Climbing to the tip of a pine tree in the face of a typhoon wasn't the same as wanting to climb Fuji-*san* in disguise, but it sprouted from the same root.

He watched his granddaughter for a few more minutes, then slid the panel shut and took out his pipe.

CHAPTER 11

The ship, according to Captain Whitson's charts, had found refuge from the slashing wind and rain in Tatsugo Bay of Amami Ōshima, an island in the LooChoos. However, *refuge* applied only to the weather. The island lay halfway between the Satsuma warlord's capital city of Kagoshima and the LooChoos' southernmost port of Naha. The Satsuma domain claimed Amami Ōshima. Entrance to the harbor was forbidden to all outsiders.

During the first two days after the storm, no islander or Japanese official had attempted to board the *Retriever* or had even shown his face. But the line of small fishing boats and junks linked together at the narrow mouth of the blue-green bay obviously intended to block the ship's departure. The blockade proved effective because Captain Whitson not only needed time for urgent repairs, but also feared the fishing boats could serve as launches for archers. John, breaking his intention not to interfere in ship matters, had voiced his own objection to plowing through the blockade, assuming the fishermen to be innocent pawns of their masters.

On the third morning, John stood on the starboard side of

the main deck, wishing his spyglass could penetrate the thickly forested hills extending down to the edge of the pebbly beach. Wildlife wasn't a problem. Animals—whatever they were—lurking among the huge pineapple-looking palms, banana plants, and thick ferns couldn't attack the ship, two cable-lengths off the beach. Two-legged enemies could. Were Satsuma samurai massing with razor-sharp swords, invisible in the shadows? Had he been wrong in urging the captain to submit to the blockade for the time being?

He made his way to the prow and stared down the dirt path winding toward sugarcane fields, watching for the return of the little expedition sent three hours earlier to check out a village a mile or so inland. Because of the centuries of trade between the more southern LooChoo islands and China, John sent Martin Li to represent the ship. Martin had taken three of the remaining Chinese hands with him, two of whom were adept in martial arts.

Three hours wasn't overly long, John reminded himself a second time. If the village contained only the native islanders, there shouldn't be any trouble. The LooChoo people were reputed to be gentle, not at all warlike, the opposite of their Satsuma masters. The group should have been hospitably received, not incarcerated or, heaven forbid, slain in a fight . . . unless Satsuma warriors were posted in barracks hidden from the bay.

He pulled out his spyglass again and examined the dense forest more closely, uneasy at simply waiting for the unknown, unable to concentrate enough to write letters or read. And he wasn't alone in his apprehension. The crew hadn't called out "Haul Away and Up She Rises" and other similar chants while working. No banter or lively ditties had swelled from the forecastle in the evening dog watches. Of course, the captain had certainly warned them enough about their location to make them wary.

John thought back to the first morning when Captain Whitson mustered the exhausted men onto the aft of the quarterdeck in misting rain, left over from the storm.

"Men," he'd croaked, his voice rougher than usual from the three days of life-and-death commands, "you've done right good work. I wish this was a safe spot an' you could recover for a day. But it's not. Far from it. Four lookouts 'll stay at attention day and night. You'll be ready for a call on deck at all times. Stay alert, men. Your lives depend on it. We're at an island claimed by the Japanese. In their eyes, we're barbarians. Despised enemies.

"Mr. Cardiff and I've read reports by the few Europeans who came to Japan and lived to tell about it. The military government not only hates Christians, it suspects outsiders o' trying to take o'er their land. Samurai militias defend the borders—men who hold dying for their warlord the greatest honor."

The men's eyes were riveted on the captain despite their fatigue.

"Understand this." Whitson had swept his gaze over the faces of his men. "So far, the blockade's the only visible hostility, and after we repair the worst damage, it 'pears our ship could breach it like a shark goin' through minnows—"

"Aye, aye, sir," a rigger had blurted out.

"But the fishermen ain' the danger, sailor," Whitson had barked. "Samurai archers can shoot at a target from a hundred yards and not miss. Some claim the archers never miss. They can tip their arrows with burnin' tar. If samurai had been on the pirate ship, the *Retriever* would be a black cinder spot dancin' on the waves o' the East China Sea."

Whitson had pointed toward the hill beside the ship, its forest dark and brooding in the mist. "We don't know what's behind those trees or what the fishing boats and junks might hold."

Several men had glanced out the corner of their eyes toward the hills.

John couldn't help checking for movement in the nearest foliage himself. A flash of orange and blue had startled him, but it was only a kingfisher darting over a rivulet emptying into the bay.

After waiting for the men to return their full attention, Whitson had continued with a scowl. "We're facin' a huge unknown. But we know good 'n well what to expect if our hosts choose the more peaceful approach—first off, an inspection on board. So, every Christian item on this ship must be stowed."

"You'll not see me give up St. Patrick," a man close to John had muttered.

Others had frowned or given a covert snort or cough.

Then Whitson described how the Japanese imprisoned and even killed secret Christians. The crew, doing an about face, adopted a thorough-going zeal in surrendering their Christian objects, egged on by their Chinese Buddhist crewmates, who feared guilt by association.

John looked over at three grim-faced sailors, squatting on the deck, pulling apart worn rope fibers to add to tar for caulking the remaining leaky planks. Thanks to the fair weather following the storm, the discontented crew had the repairs nearly completed. The captain was close to ordering a run through the blockade unless Martin brought back good news or

John gave a viable alternative.

Would mowing down fishermen ever be justified?

The eighth bell of the forenoon watch sounded. Taking a last look down the pathway to the village, John reluctantly headed toward the officers' dining area in the Great Cabin.

The replacement cook's stew of mutton, leeks, Chinese cabbage, and rice, even with its heavy dose of salt and a sauce, would have tasted good to John if he hadn't been on edge. Captain Whitson and the officers, apparently absorbed in their own thoughts and worries, offered little conversation at the table.

Before the captain returned to his post, John asked to have a private word.

Once they were seated at the long table by the cabin's aft window, Whitson served John coffee made from his private stash, then leaned forward, balancing his elbows on the table. "I'm not blaming you," he said before John could speak his own mind. "I signed up with my eyes open—but the devil hisself has dogged this voyage's second half. I was on a whaler where a harpooned humpback tried to take us down to Davy Jones' locker, but that was a cruise 'round Nantucket Sound compared to what's plagued this trip." He shook his head, adding to the pale shadows cast by the lantern swinging on a chain overhead. "Our mutineers do blame you, by the way, for not satisfying the Black Water sea god. Course, I don't believe that rot for a minute."

"Doesn't matter who or what they blame now, does it?" John blew on his steaming coffee. "Won't get them out of irons. Now I—"

"Seems the villains' real motive was for the pirates to capture the *Retriever* and sail it to the California gold fields."

"What?" John half rose. "You're telling me that pure poppycock led to all our troubles, or at least, to the attack?"

"One of our Chinese guards heard Fan cursing the pirates for giving up the chase. The cook then spilled his guts, knowing he was doomed anyway. Fan let drop that the pirates lusted after our tea cargo and that he'd guaranteed them an easy capture in return for the ride across the Pacific."

John seethed, thinking how close they'd come to losing the ship and all on board in addition to whatever trouble lay ahead. "A pox on the man and his gang."

"The Chinese officials will deal out more than a pox. Those five'll be nailed to crosses and given the 'twenty-four cuts' while they writhe. You heard o' those cuts?"

John drew back, his anger changing to revulsion. "No, can't say I have."

"The cuts start by taking off the eyebrows and work slowly down the body parts to finally amputatin' both legs. And if the sixth man's alive and is ever caught, he'll earn the same."

John grimaced. "So Fan and his men tried to offer us as sacrificial lambs to their greed." He ran his fingers over his whiskers that were forming a beard. "Nevertheless, I don't wish crucifixion and torture on anyone."

"Well, it's not up to you, so their fate won't be on your conscience."

John ignored the jibe. "The reason I asked for a word with you, I have a plan for our present conundrum. Employing diplomacy over belligerence, subject to your approval."

Captain Whitson heaved a sigh. "I'm listenin'. Just keep in mind, if forced to choose, I'll save our crew's lives, not protect the lives o' unknown fishermen or support your vain hope for future trade with Japanner warriors."

John plunked down his coffee cup. “I’d never sacrifice our crew for trade. I should think you’d know me better than that.”

“A man never knows a person through and through.” The captain tasted the coffee and frowned. “So what’s your plan?”

John let out a breath. “I assume Satsuma cargo ships arrive at this island regularly. Wouldn’t you guess?”

“No doubt the reason for no boarding party yet, or attack. Waitin’ for superiors.”

“I’d like us to agree to an initial inspection of our ship with high dignity—if that’s the course the officials take. Commodore Perry was respected as the *High and Mighty Mysteriousness* when he steamed in close to Japan’s capital, and I want to emulate that. Realizing, of course, we don’t command a squadron of warships.”

“A significant difference.” The captain stirred a heaping spoonful of sugar into his coffee.

“I’d like them to meet you in your full captain’s splendor. You could provide something sweet with wine—plenty of wine—and give them a brief tour of the ship, emphasizing that we have come in peace.”

“Most men would watch for a trick, but curiosity might override their suspicions.” The captain added another spoonful of sugar.

John pursed his lips. “And that brings up the trick. Could you pull off an imaginary emergency? Machinery malfunctioning. Danger of an explosion. The need to lower the pressure by steaming around the harbor—then out of it?”

“Boilers explode sometimes. Not all that farfetched. But if they don’t voluntarily order the blockade broken for our imperiled ship, then do you agree to breakin’ it forc’bly?”

“I have something else in mind if the ruse doesn’t work. I’ll make my appearance and have our old chronometer brought out with much pomp, explain its purpose in giving a ship's location at sea, and then demand they take me to the warlord so I can give it to him personally."

"You mean at Kagoshima?"

"Right. At his stronghold—castle or fort."

"The devil! You thought that out? You'd be a ravin' hostage. Could be months or years until your release. Or never."

"Yes, sure, that's a possibility." *And I'd most likely lose Catherine.* "At any rate, if the cargo ship leaves for Kagoshima with me on board, the *Retriever* can exit the harbor in the cargo ship's wake."

"Have you considered the Japanner ship could have 'nough warriors to try 'n take our ship as a prize? I want you to know: diplomacy is out in that case. We will fight, and we will fire our cannon, and any innocent commoners can get themselves out of the way or meet their maker, Buddha, or whatever."

"Pray God it doesn't come to that."

A knock sounded on the cabin door.

"Come." The captain stood.

"The expedition group is on the path, sir," Second Mate Crowder reported, stepping inside the door. "One man injured. No hostiles in view."

The captain hurried to the bow with John at his heels. John's heart fell, seeing one of the four men limping, his sagging body held up by a man on each side.

First Mate Brewer oversaw the lowering of ropes and a plank to the barge to bring the injured man on board.

"*Habu* got him," Martin reported, once on deck. "Village chief told us about snake danger. We watch feet, but Xi step off path to release his water. Snake struck from tall grass. Two times."

Dr. Billy Morse hurried forward, carrying his black bag. He cut open Xi's loose trousers while the man still lay roped to the plank. After applying a tourniquet, he had Xi's companions take him below to the sick bay.

"Snake's a pit viper would be my guess," the surgeon said, wiping his forehead with an embroidered handkerchief, the source of the hands' nicknaming him, Frilly Billy. "I'll do what I can, but I'm not hopeful. The venom's working fast."

The surgeon, held by all to be an expert in tooth extraction, had come to the ship at Shanghai with a reputation for success in amputations too. But men subjected to the doctor's effort in bloodletting described that experience as horrendous, second only to keelhauling. Rumor had it that Frilly Billy was unsteady not only in lancing but also in the use of the knife. However, from the look of the swollen leg and dark crimson lines extending to Xi's thigh, the leg would be sacrificed to the saw. At least—John shuddered—it would be done in calm waters.

Captain Whitson called his chief officers and John back to his Great Cabin to meet with Martin. John took the same seat he'd had before at the long table. The others carefully sat according to rank.

"Unlucky about Xi's leg," the captain said, addressing Martin at the far end. "The doctor knows his work. However, Xi has three counts again' him. Not only the venom. There's shock and danger o' infection."

John winced.

A shadow crossed Martin's face.

A sad expression dimmed even Whitson's eyes for a minute. "But we'll hope for the best." Whitson gestured to John. "Maybe Mr. Cardiff can send up extra prayers for Xi."

"Yes. Yes, I'll do that," John said, surprised to be singled out. He'd made sure a service had been held both Sundays after leaving Shanghai, but had taken a back seat. Second Mate Crowder had been an altar boy in the Episcopal Church and had read from the *Book of Common Prayer*. A sailor before the mast had offered to read a chapter from one of the Gospels and had taken obvious pleasure in the praise from the eight officers and hands who joined John at the service.

"You met the chief?" the captain, now all business, asked Martin after a nod to John.

"Met headman of village. He island native. Satsuma official in big house not here. Maybe soon come. Only Satsuma cargo ship come to harbor. Other ship forbidden. Headman say word *forbidden* many times. Islander Chinese interpreter make very clear. Cargo ship come each week for sugarcane. Maybe tomorrow come. Interpreter tell us islanders all time work in sugarcane fields. Islanders poor, weak, always hungry."

The captain rubbed his temples. "What about the boats in the mouth? Might they move in response to . . . er, gifts? Food? Whale oil?"

"Satsuma lord order blockade if ship not Japan *tokara* ship. No power to change orders. Headman also say *no power* much times."

"Understood." The captain glanced at John, then turned back toward Martin. "You did all right, Mr. Li. You asked good questions."

"Do my duty, sir." Martin's eyes showed a flicker of pride.

After the captain ended the meeting, John retired to his cabin. He started to pull his Bible from among the Christian objects collected the first morning, but stopped. It didn't seem right to take a privilege the others didn't have. He'd volunteered to keep all the items safe in his cabin: the handful of crosses, three thick Bibles, Crowder's prayer book, six rosaries, and a number of charms. He'd hidden them under rolls of silk in a small wooden chest, already nailed to the floor. If an official discovered the cache, he'd claim ownership and bear the consequence alone.

Leaving the chest locked, he quoted as much as he could remember of the psalm about being in God's hands on the far side of the sea. Then he offered up prayers for Xi, for everyone on board, for his family, Catherine, Uriah, and even the aging dog when Sam came to mind. Finally, he prayed from the bottom of his heart that there would be no bloodshed and he wouldn't become a hostage.

CHAPTER 12

Early the next day, a round-bellied Japanese cargo ship, given a wide berth by the blockade, sailed into the bay and anchored at the port side of the *Retriever*.

John met Captain Whitson as he descended from the upper quarterdeck.

"The officers know about the plan," Whitson said, his voice tense. "They'll pass the word to the hands to be prepared in case of malfunction. If a Chinese-Japanner speaker comes aboard, only Martin will talk to him."

From the shadow of his door, John watched the captain welcome six stern-looking samurai onto the lower deck. Before they could catch sight of him, John reentered his cabin. While pacing the small room, he tried to imagine the six officials' impressions as they were given refreshments and a tour of the ship, a ship more than twice the size of theirs. They had to be a little awed.

All at once, shouts rang out to pump the fire engine and ready the boats. John's pulse rose as the engine's vibrations increased. Chains clanked, pulling up anchors. The steamer jerked forward.

So far, the ruse was working.

Stepping from his doorway, John gasped, horrified. Samurai swarmed over his ship's bulkhead, like Indians breeching a fort out West. Twenty assailants at least.

The engine stopped thrumming. The captain shouted to the crew to desist, no shots. And then, "Bow! Bow, but not too low!" First Mate Brewer ordered the anchors lowered.

The cause of the captain's quick capitulation became obvious. Bowmen on the cargo ship faced the *Retriever,* their arrows aimed. Despite the hairs that rose on the back of his neck, John strode forward, decked out in his white coat with the most brass buttons, white knee-length pants, tall Hessian boots, and his black top hat.

The six officials, standing a little behind the captain, stared at John.

Whitson, no telltale tremor in his voice, ordered the crew to turn and bow to Lord Cardiff. After bowing himself, the captain told John a Chinese-Japanese speaker had boarded with the original group and that the officials had been polite, but restrained.

One of the six walked toward John and bowed.

Not sure what protocol demanded, John removed his hat and returned the bow simply out of politeness. Then he raised his arm and flicked his wrist for Martin to come.

The official snapped an order at a man behind him, who after kowtowing to both the official and John, spoke to Martin in Chinese.

"This official's name is Kawata," Martin translated. "He Satsuma inspector. He in charge of island. He wants you board cargo ship. He also wants know if now no danger from explosion."

"Tell him our efficient crew averted an explosion, and

thank him for his concern. Also say that I have a very important gift for his master, the Satsuma warlord. Tell Inspector Kawata I will be pleased to visit his ship and demonstrate it."

Martin nodded, then cleared his throat. "I go with you. You need Chinese-English speaker."

"You could be a hostage like me for a very long time."

"I do my duty." He bowed low to John.

John turned to Whitson. "Any last words of wisdom?"

The captain grimaced. "You want us to fight if they don't let you return?"

"That's the last thing I want. Follow their ship's wake out and inform our consul at Shanghai."

"Taking your pistol?"

"No. I want Kawata to know we're sincere about coming in peace."

"Then it's your neck," he muttered, changing the start of a shrug into a bow.

The samurai used ropes deployed underwater to swarm back onto the cargo ship. John and Martin crossed the gangplank onto its deck, and First Mate Brewer followed with the chronometer. As soon as Brewer finished his demonstration, he bowed and left, not waiting for questions or even permission. John and Martin were led to Kawata's cabin.

The inspector indicated for John and Martin to kneel opposite him on the silk floor cushions and gestured to a servant to pour them cups of tea. Two of Kawata's assistants and three scribes squatted off to one side.

Taking a sip of the green tea, John nodded his approval despite its bitter taste, then glanced around, amazed at the amount of artistry in the room. A decorative scroll, a flower arrangement, a lacquered box of drawers, and the intricately carved, low table in front of him. Even the bowls for the tea were handsome. If a man cared that much for beauty, he couldn't be entirely malicious, could he?

Kawata spoke in staccato Japanese, the translator used singsong Chinese, and finally Martin translated the inspector's response to the chronometer: "I take your gift to my master. But instrument useful only if lost in ocean. Our good ships never lose sight of land."

"Maybe the chronometer will be beneficial in the future." John smiled in spite of Kawata's hard expression.

Kawata shrugged. "Who know future? Now is problem. This is America ship, not Chinese?"

"Yes, American." John could hardly say otherwise after the officials' tour.

"Why no flag?"

"The violent storm made flying a flag impossible. It forced us into this harbor. We planned to trade in Naha, but we are pleased to meet you."

The lengthy translations afforded John a chance to think. He was in the dark concerning the inspector's intentions . . . as well as the man's range of knowledge. Any accusation of trickery against John or his ship would be disastrous, so honesty, he concluded, had to be the best policy. In fact, considering his pledge to serve the Almighty, truthfulness would fit right in.

"You could not trade in Naha without a charter even if have all Chinese crew. Merchants want to be left alone. Not troubled." Kawata had crossed his arms and was glaring at John.

"We hoped to gain a charter. Mr. Li is our comprador." John gestured toward Martin. "He is in charge of trading and overseeing cargo."

"What cargo you have?"

"Tea, silks, porcelain, whale oil, spices."

"You from China coast, so have opium."

"No opium. I hate opium. I quit a former trading company because it smuggled opium."

Inspector Kawata studied John's face, then nodded. "Your ship part of America group—came up coast three years ago?"

John hesitated. Identifying with Commodore Perry's squadron might help his situation. But then he wouldn't be honest, which seemed almost like disobeying a directive from above.

"No, not part of that group."

"Steamship belonging that group huge monster. Like smoking dragon." Kawata rocked on his heels. "I like honest man. We checked ship already. True about cargo. Why not go through boats in harbor?"

"Our ship needed repairs, and our captain suspected hidden arrows. I didn't worry about the arrows. I didn't want to kill innocent people."

"You felt pity? Men in boats are commoners. No problem if killed."

"Yes, much pity. I—"

The inspector held up his palm and turned to his assistants and scribes. All but the interpreter left the room at his order. He turned back to John.

"Why pity?" Kawata's jaw and shoulders stiffened, like a predator preparing his attack.

Martin's eyes tightened with a trace of fear. His mouth formed a tight line as though warning John to guard his words.

John considered backing off, but acting like a coward also

didn't seem right. "I was once a commoner." He looked Kawata in the eye. "Commoners have desires. Parents who love them. Wives who depend on them. *Precious children* they want to take care of and protect."

The inspector's brows wrinkled in a flicker of confusion before his face became a mask again.

"These poor people," John continued, "work very hard in the sugarcane fields, like animals. They look half starved. Maybe some do starve. I feel sorry for them, for their oppression. Pity."

Kawata gave an abrupt order to his interpreter, who nearly ran from the room. Then he slurped a little of his tea and seemed to study a painting in an alcove behind John.

John sipped his tea, too, his senses on high alert, aware of the distant shouts of sailors, the slow rocking of the ship, the smell of fresh tar. His plan had sounded feasible in the shelter of the *Retriever*. But had he been exceedingly foolish? Downright daft to speak his mind? Was Kawata toying with him? Fattening him up for a more satisfying kill? For an off-with-his-head execution? Or a gleeful humiliation—having him clamped in irons. Maybe restrained in a cage like shipwrecked sailors he'd heard about. If he became a hostage, his poor family and Catherine wouldn't know if he were dead or alive.

And what about loyal Martin? Or even Whitson and the crew if the samurai chose to attack after all? The *Retriever* could sink the cargo ship in a fight to the finish, but many would die on both sides.

John quoted the Bible's verses in his mind, but started, nevertheless, when Kawata leaned over and smoothly poured more tea for him.

After what seemed like half a lifetime, but perhaps just

fifteen minutes, one of the scribes preceded the interpreter back into the room, carrying a scroll.

"You will not come to Kagoshima." Kawata's voice carried a new gruffness. "No need. Here is *Nippon* charter with *my* seal. Your ship can trade through customs house in Naha and Satsuma warehouse in Nagasaki, not here, not Kagoshima. Very small cost—one third your cargo of tea. In return, you take sugarcane in empty space."

John tried for a poker face, struggling to believe his good fortune. He asked Martin to repeat the translation, using the time to compose himself.

"The cost is reasonable," John managed to say without a quiver. Then his gut knotted. What if it was a trick?

The inspector gave John a knowing look, as though comprehending his dueling emotions. "You honest," Martin translated without betraying his own emotion. "I not always honest, but return honesty for honesty."

After sounding out and adding the name *Retriever* in Japanese script to the scroll, Kawata handed it to John with a slight bow.

John received the scroll with both hands and returned the slight bow, feeling as if he were treading on a cliff's ledge that might possibly sustain his weight . . . or crumble into a million pieces under him.

"I ask—command—one more favor," Kawata said, continuing through the interpreters, "in addition to your gift of sailing instrument for Lord Shimazu."

"Please name it." *God have mercy. Here comes the bitter pill inside the sugar coating.*

"Five Chinese men from your hold now on my ship."

John stared at Kawata, who gave a flicker of a smile.

"My warrior good at locks. He open door and free legs of prisoners. Men like pigeons fly from cage. By your rules, these five are bad. For you, they have no value. They have value to me. Work for me in sugarcane fields—work hard, like you say—or I sell to Hollander ship in Nagasaki. Maybe you have not so much pity for the five men."

"They would be killed in Shanghai," John said. "However, the lead mutineer plucked me out of danger once in a maze of alleys. Perhaps it is right he has been plucked out of a terrible death."

"Karma," Kawata said.

"We will record the escape as coming from the crisis on board." Certainly not as a gift, John decided, since he had no power to hand over mutineers. But as the samurai's stern countenance signaled, a refusal would start a battle of wills, if not one with weaponry. The five weren't worth it, especially since the sugarcane fields or the steamy jungles of the Dutch Indies were a far cry from California's hills of gold.

John drank one more cup of tea, thinking back to the hermit Uriah's so-called prophecy. Because of the special charter, John could trade with Japan without waiting for the Consul General's agreement to go into effect. Truly, his company would be on the ground floor. Naming Sam for *samurai* might have served as an apt prediction after all. An unbelievably good prophecy.

He returned to the *Retriever* still in something of a daze.

Captain Whitson, lips puckered, listened in the Great Cabin to John's account of the negotiations without comment. Then he cleared his throat of a wad of phlegm and slid the charter closer to himself. "Bunch o' hieroglyphics, like Chinese," he said tapping the scroll, then pushed it back toward John. "Like they say, if somethin' sounds too good to be true, it ain true. But you're back. No arrows flyin' yet. We'll double our lookouts and see how tonight and tomorrow go."

Yes, John thought while he carefully rolled up the scroll, that's all they could do. Perhaps he should still be worried, but he wasn't. His mind was at peace for the first time since the pirate ship had loomed on the horizon.

On the way back to his stateroom, the enormity of the risk he'd taken with the company and ship struck again. He'd be a fool to think he'd come this far through superior wisdom of his own. For one thing, he hadn't even had control over the results from the oolong tea. First, he'd thought the tea a triumph, then it attracted the pirates, but just now, it helped get the precious charter. So, it seemed reasonable to credit the good hand of providence.

Early the next day, under John and Martin's scrutiny, the Japanese sailors transferred a precise third of the boxes of tea to their ship. Then the *Retriever*'s crane loaded sugarcane bales onto the deck, and the ship's hands and islanders carried them down to the hold.

The gaunt farmers, trudging across the deck, reminded John of weighed-down ants—ants that would receive no benefit other than avoiding death. He went in search of the captain.

John found Whitson studying his rutter. "I want to pay the islanders for their work."

Whitson straightened and frowned. "How do you propose to do that?"

"Supply them with foodstuff. I doubt salt beef or pork would be suitable since they're influenced by Buddhism, if not actually devotees. So, I'd like four barrels of sea biscuit rolled into the village and eight hens and a rooster brought up for the farmers to carry back. We can spare that much, can't we?"

"Aye. You and your brother laid in plenty. Overstocked the ship, if you ask me. But that inspector won't like it."

"Let's get it done before he catches on."

Whitson shook his head. "I wouldn't like to see the upshot if he does."

John narrowed his eyes, and Whitson said, "I'll order it now."

The *Retriever* weighed anchor four hours later. John stood on the quarterdeck and returned each of the inspector's three bows as the ship steamed past. Then the Japanese crew bowed. Before John could react, First Mate Brewer was bellowing for the crew to bow with due respect or swab decks all the way to Shanghai. The *Retriever* followed the Japanese pilot boat past a shoal—a danger they had been ignorant of—and out into the sparkling waves of the deep blue ocean.

John turned as Captain Whitson joined him at the prow.

"Mr. Cardiff," the captain said, "I'm starting to have more confidence in your power o' prayer. Xi lost his leg. Other than that, he's holding his own so far. But by the powers that be, what happened on that cargo ship was like 'n angel dropped down. Paid a vis'tation. Why do you think Kawata didn't attack? Or demand every last pound o' cargo? Or, at the least, take you to Kagoshima?"

"Not sure," John said, pleased at the captain's increased affability, "but I'd guess Commodore Perry's visit at Naha made a difference. Kawata had seen American warships pass by. He probably understood the risk of later retaliation." John drew in a breath. "Yet like you said, there was more. I think he actually feared I'd talk to the warlord about the commoners' despicable life. And for a second, it seemed he understood those miserable islanders were actual people, as if the Almighty—or an angel—touched the warrior so his blinders came off and he could really see."

Whitson furrowed his brow. "Well, that beats all."

"Like they say, 'The proof of the pudding is in the eating.' We'll find out how good our charter is in Naha. A laughable piece of paper? Or the key to trade. My gut tells me it's worth every chest of tea we paid."

"We'll see." The captain slapped the rail, then headed toward the wheelhouse.

John walked to the stern and looked northward. Sailing with the wind for two days would have taken him to Japan proper. What would it have been like to be a hostage in Kagoshima? Terrible. He shouldn't think otherwise . . . but he would have finally stepped foot onto the mysterious country itself.

Yet, he just needed more patience. In the near future, he'd take the *Retriever* on a run to Nagasaki, try out trading through the Satsuma warehouse. In the meantime, he'd better offer what solace he could to Xi. With a peg leg, the man couldn't be a regular sailor anymore. A hard burden to bear. But he could get training as a cook's assistant or even in navigation.

John climbed down three levels to the sick bay on the orlop deck, trying not to breathe too deeply of the bilge's stink of rotting fish. He found a mixed group of sailors around Xi's cot. The injured rifleman stood among them, looking healthy except for his bandaged arm and a slight bulge in the hip area.

While a Russian fiddled a tune close to "Yankee Doodle," the men were singing lustily.

One of the group noticed John, and the men moved aside, their song sputtering to an end.

"No, men. Don't stop. Your singing will do Xi more good than my incomprehensible words ever could. Please carry on." John grasped Xi's hand and squeezed it, then left the bay, deciding to send Martin with a message later.

Back in his cabin, John settled at his desk. At last he could concentrate on a letter to Catherine. He picked up his pen, but paused, imagining his family and beautiful Catherine sitting in their parlors, reading his letter months later. For a moment he wished he could be there, telling them all that had happened in person and how he'd sensed God's hand more than any other time in his life. After they drank oolong tea, he'd give his mother and fiancée each a roll of exquisite silk and see their pleasure.

But then, the adventure would be over. That time in the parlor would be a joyous occasion, a future event to be treasured, but not too soon. Dear God, not too soon. Not before he stepped foot on Japan proper.

CHAPTER 13

July 1858 (Year of the Horse)

Sumi glanced at the empty cushion and untouched food on the low stand next to her. The vacant spot no longer expressed the honor intended for her betrothed in view of the imminent wedding. An official missive had arrived one week earlier with the news that changed everything.

She had watched her grandfather draw out the contents of the packet bearing the Hino family seal. He read the two enclosed scrolls and scowled.

"You will not wed Hino-*sama*," he said.

She had grasped the door frame to steady herself. Had Makoto-*sama* heard some horrible rumor about her? Maybe someone said she actually resembled a monkey.

"The cholera plague has claimed your betrothed's life," her grandfather had gone on to explain. "His body was cremated a month ago. His parents were also ill, but recovered. Here is the betrothal contract—canceled." He held out the contract, then rolled it up, and inserted it into his tunic sleeve.

Sumi had bowed and stumbled up to her room. An

unexpected sympathy for her betrothed's parents had brought tears to her eyes until the disquieting thought struck that seventeen was old not to be married or at least betrothed. But then, relief that she wasn't being sent far away supplanted her other concerns with one exception—her unease about the offerings to the dead man's spirit, placed right next to her at each meal.

"Father, may I ask a question that troubles me?"

He put down his rice bowl and nodded for her to continue.

"Might Makoto-*sama*'s spirit actually be here watching us?" She glanced up at the ceiling's polished beams, imagining his ghostly presence.

Her father glanced at the ceiling too, then at the eaves, visible in the twilight through the open side panels. "Most likely his spirit hovers in his Kamakura home. But even if his spirit should pay a visit here, you need not fear angering him. We will be careful to pay the necessary respect. A samurai's daughter must face the spirit world with the same courage she faces the visible world."

Sumi bowed an acknowledgment while thinking she'd certainly take a look at her betrothed if she had been the one to enter the spirit world. She forced her eyes to stay away from the ceiling and tried to swallow a little of the fish soup. The liquid caught in her throat, and she took a quick sip of hot tea to wash it down. Once the stone tablet bearing Makoto's name was delivered and placed on their family's god shelf, the food to please his spirit would be offered there. That couldn't happen soon enough. If her courage in facing invisible spirits were a measure of her overall bravery, she fell far short of everyone's expectations. As usual.

In case the spirit did check to see how she and her family

behaved, the Buddhist priest had urged her family to offer the dishes for the usual fifty days. As for Sumi's mourning, the priest pronounced that wearing a somber kimono for the period would do. Since her betrothed had never laid eyes on her while alive and the funeral had already occurred in far off Kamakura, she need not cut her long hair off at the neck. Thankfully, she could continue to arrange it in the piled-up, bouffant style of a grown woman.

In that respect, she was more fortunate than her eighteen-year-old cousin, who still dressed in mourning clothes. Kiyo had moved into their house four months earlier after losing both parents in the same terrible plague. Sumi had looked forward to sharing her bedroom with her cousin, excited to have someone who could be like a sister . . . until Kiyo's first day in their house. Her cousin's bitter sourness had turned Sumi's stomach, and Kiyo's bossiness day after day had destroyed all the sympathy Sumi originally felt.

Her grandfather rolled up an ancient scroll that had seemed to claim his full attention. He cleared his throat and squinted at Sumi. "Your mother once implied that you chafed against the betrothal, not because of Hino-*sama"*—he too glanced at the ceiling—"but because Kamakura did not suit you."

Sumi sat up straighter and lowered her eyes. "My betrothed's passing is most regrettable. I am sorry for his parents. But I am grateful to remain in our home."

"You cannot remain here indefinitely. Your marriage is expected." Irritation tinged his words.

"I pray I may contribute to our honorable line." She bowed her forehead to the mat, then gathered her courage. "Perhaps if I truly master the feminine arts, a Nagasaki family will not mind that I am somewhat old and unspoken for."

Sumi glanced at her father to see if she'd been too bold. To her relief, he nodded and picked up his bowl of rice.

Her grandfather rose. Although dressed informally in his dark blue robe, his erect figure and alert eyes commanded genuine respect.

Sumi and the rest of the family stood and bowed as required.

"We shall see how well you progress." Her grandfather pointed to her flower arrangement in the alcove. "You must apply yourself more diligently in the next months than you have in the last two years. As a minimum, learn to incorporate a gracefulness into your artistic effort."

After he left, Kiyo gave her a prideful look. "Here, let me show you how this should be done." She pattered over to the arrangement and straightened the sunflower, fluffed its leaves and adjusted the lower stem of pampas grass so that it curved into a half arc.

Sumi could see the difference. The lines of the plants were balanced—gracefully.

Kiyo turned toward Sumi. "Better, don't you think?"

"Umm . . ."

Sumi's mother frowned.

Before her mother could speak, Sumi mumbled, "Yes, better." She resisted the unbecoming urge to ask why men hadn't materialized to marry such an artistic, accomplished person as Kiyo. Her cousin was also not betrothed, having lost her promised one, not to the plague but to a competitor.

When everyone resumed their meal, Sumi made sure Kiyo wasn't watching, then scrutinized the flower arrangement. She had to admit she'd plunked the plants into the vase, eager to get the tedious task finished. Next time she'd take more time. She would make the tallest branch seem to reach for the heavens and the other two stems embrace it in some kind of beautiful swirls, forming a lovely triangle. She tried to picture the effect, but couldn't work it out even in her imagination. She hastily drank some tea to clear the new lump in her throat.

At the end of the meal, her father took a few puffs on his pipe, then moved with Sumi's mother onto the cooler veranda to view the moon. Kiyo, morose as usual, trudged up the stairs.

Sumi strolled over to her father's desk. A new item, tied up in a brown *furoshiki* scarf, lay there. The large bundle clearly contained a thick, rectangular book. Her father always allowed her to handle his books. Occasionally, when they were alone, he kept his promise to teach her some vocabulary from the two volumes written in English, reminding her she might meet an American in her future home. That wouldn't happen now, but the predicted avalanche of foreigners would include Nagasaki someday. After all, until Shimoda, her city had been the only port where any foreign ships had been officially allowed for the last two-hundred-and-fifty years. She closed her eyes for a minute, picturing tall Westerners with round eyes, red or yellow hair, and long noses parading down Nagasaki's main thoroughfares.

The scarf's knot came loose when she tested it. She paused, holding the bundle in her hands. Would it be a problem to go ahead and slip the knot open without asking first? As long as she put everything back exactly as she found it, her father shouldn't mind. Depending on who her grandfather chose to replace the deceased Makoto, she might not have as much opportunity to sample her father's books in the future . . . or any foreign books for that matter.

Sure enough, when she opened up the scarf, a book lay

inside, only it was partially burned on the edges. Her hands shook. Could it be a confiscated book that her father rescued from destruction? Her finger traced the title, *HOLY BIBLE.* She had never seen either word before, but guessed they were English.

If the book were really a prohibited one, the consequences of being caught with it in her hands would be terrible. Itō's banishment showed what happened to people who disregarded prohibitions. But more likely than not, the book had simply been saved from a house fire in its mysterious past.

She glanced around, then held the book under her kimono sleeve and moved into the empty guest room. After sliding a cushion close to a lit lantern, she listened for any sounds in the adjoining room. The house was quiet.

Making herself comfortable, she thumbed through the pages until she reached what appeared to be the first page—at the wrong end of the book. Her father had told her English words were written from left to right, but he hadn't told her the pages were positioned from back to front.

She ran her finger along the mysterious letters. She understood the first three words: *In the beginning.* So perhaps this was a history book. The next words, *God, created,* and *heavens,* were unknown ones. The last word in the sentence, *earth,* might mean "land." So perhaps it was a science book.

"What are you doing?" Her cousin stood over her.

Heart hammering, Sumi slid the book's burned edge under the fold of her kimono.

"What does it look like? I'm . . . trying to read."

Kiyo's eyes gleamed like a cat's watching its prey. "You can't read it under your kimono. If it is a good book, a permissible book, why are you hiding in here?"

"I'm not hiding. I hoped to read where I wouldn't be disturbed."

"Then let me see the book for a moment, and I'll disturb you no longer." Kiyo held out her hands.

"It's one of Father's foreign books. You'll have to ask his permission." Sweat trickled down Sumi's sides. If the book were prohibited and Kiyo reported it to her grandfather, he would be furious with both her father and her.

"Did *you* ask permission?"

"Maybe I did, and maybe I didn't." Sumi shrugged, as though the whole thing were a game. Why couldn't her cousin be her friend? Why couldn't they help each other keep out of trouble with the elders? Instead, Kiyo tried to shove her into trouble, the deeper, the better.

Sumi offered a false smile. "I don't know why you're interested since it's in English."

"Let me see it anyway." Kiyo held out her hands again.

"What do you want to see, Kiyo-*san*?" Her father stood in the doorway, the scarf in his hand.

Sumi didn't know whether to relax in relief or curl into a ball of shame.

Kiyo's face flushed and she moved back. "I . . . I wanted to know more about the big book Sumi-*chan* is studying so intently. However, she refuses to show me even its cover."

Her father stepped over to Sumi, leaned over between Kiyo and her, and tied the book into the scarf. "This book is not suitable for either of you," he said as he stepped away. "The concepts are much too difficult even if you could understand the language. Come with me, and I will find good reading material for both of you."

He led them to the bookshelf over his low built-in desk and

handed Sumi a volume of ancient *haiku* she had read a hundred times. To Kiyo, he gave a packet of papers demonstrating embroidery. "In the future, Sumi, ask permission before taking a new book. But no harm done."

Sumi bowed, then quirked a smile of victory at Kiyo. Despite being forced to totter on the edge of a pit, she'd survived.

Her father said goodnight to Kiyo and turned toward Sumi. "Come. I wish to discuss a question with you. It will be cooler on the back veranda with a breeze."

Once they settled by the back step, he removed the book from the scarf. "How much did you understand?"

"I read only the first sentence before Kiyo interrupted. I understood *in the beginning* and maybe *earth.*"

"It is a very dangerous English book." His voice had fallen to a low, intense tone. "It contains information about the Evil Religion that the Portuguese and Spanish invaders tried to use to conquer our country. The *Kirishitans* fought and died for books like this." He cleared his throat twice. "I wanted to keep it so I could compare the vocabulary with the same Dutch book that occasionally falls into my hands. Now I see such a plan is too dangerous. Far too dangerous. I will destroy this tomorrow."

Sumi winced. The pit had been much deeper than she'd imagined. "I'm sorry I took it without asking."

"You must not speak of this book again. Ever. Do you understand?"

"Yes, I understand." Her voice trembled. "It is a dreadful book."

"As I said, dangerous without a doubt. But dreadful? Who knows for sure?" Her father sighed.

Sumi's heart went out to him. Like her, he wanted to know what lay outside their country's confines. She must have ruined an opportunity he deeply desired.

"Don't fret," he said as though reading her mind. "Foreign books are multiplying. Fewer will be forbidden. Other opportunities will arise."

"Father, you are kind to me." His unusual candor gave her courage to risk impertinence. "I hope I can be betrothed to someone like you." She offered a tentative smile at his surprised look. "Please forgive me for speaking boldly, but I long to marry a man who opens his mind to exploring new ideas. Like you."

Not returning her smile, he stood abruptly to reenter their house. "My father will choose a suitable husband for you."

She wanted to repeat *someone like you, Father.* But he'd answered the best he could. She had to accept her fate whether it turned out to be good or awful or something in-between. She followed him and bowed before heading upstairs to her bedroom.

Kiyo was already asleep, softly snoring, but Sumi's nerves still jangled after the close call. She picked up the book of *haiku* and sat close to the dim light issuing from under the lantern's half-closed night shade. The page before her contained beloved poems by Bashō, but she couldn't concentrate. The Evil Religion's book had captured her mind although she'd held it only a few minutes.

Why would people die for a book? Of course, people died for their liege, but why for a book? If it were truly a god's book, couldn't the god take care of it himself? When necessary, gods could do their own fighting. Look at how the divine wind had sunk the ships of the Mongol hordes.

This was precisely the type of question that made her feel like a thousand prickly thorns encircled her. Could she never break out? Never investigate such mysteries? The foreign books might hold answers impossible to imagine.

If only the avalanche of foreigners would hurry up and come.

CHAPTER 14

October 1858 (Year of the Horse)

Wanting to please the moon god, *Tsukuyomi,* Sumi checked to make sure the rice dumplings, sweet potatoes, brown chestnuts, and orange persimmons were perfectly arranged on the temporary, altar-like table in their back garden. These items, suitable because of their round shapes, represented an offering to the deity, whose festival her family would celebrate as soon as the twilight yielded to nighttime.

More than two months had passed since her betrothed's death, so she was free to take part in the festivities as well as to wear a pretty kimono. To fit the occasion, she'd chosen a blue one embossed with silver shooting stars. She glanced up at the moon, perfectly round, shining in splendor. Of course, the god, so distant from life on earth, wouldn't notice a kimono, but perhaps their guests, old acquaintances of her grandfather, would appreciate the effect.

Voices of porters at the front gate, negotiating for the return trip later that night, jolted her from her reverie. She quickly added more oil to the base of a flickering lantern, one of the eight glowing along the stone pathway. Then she took her place near the back veranda, ready to welcome the visitors into the garden.

A few minutes later, her grandfather and the Kurohashi family emerged from the house. Sumi bowed, then swallowed her surprise at seeing a pallid-faced, young man eyeing her. She'd heard the family had a married daughter and an unmarried son named Keiji, but hadn't heard the son was close to her age.

The way the young man wrinkled his forehead a second later indicated disdain, yet the lantern's light caught a glint of interest in his eyes. Was it possible he was not yet betrothed?

Kiyo came from the house last. She walked past Sumi with a slight jerk of her head, which could be an imperious nod or a nervous twitch. Most likely an imitation of nobility, Sumi judged.

Sumi trailed the visitors and her family to the wooden pallet, placed in a spot offering a good view of the moon. The men had knelt on the cushions placed on top of the pallet's right side, leaving the other side's cushions to the women. She knelt down in the one remaining place, unfortunately at the end, next to Kiyo. Her vision of an enjoyable time dimmed.

Little of the conversation between the two women was audible where Sumi sat, but she heard every word of the men's louder conversation. Their talk soon centered on one of their clan's scholars.

"After the black ships invaded our waters, it was nothing short of treason for Yoshida Shōin to beg the barbarians to take him to the United States of America," her grandfather asserted. "An ambush of our clan's good name."

"He clearly flouted the shogunate's decree against leaving the country." The Kurohashi grandfather's voice trembled with indignation. Then he looked at his son expectantly.

"The man deserved his imprisonment. His appalling ignorance made him spurn the law," the second of the Kurohashi men obediently added. He looked at the next in line.

Keiji puffed out his chest. "I heard he compared our country's seclusion policy to 'holding one's breath in a dark room.' If he continues in his delusions, he will regret not having more breaths to hold when the sword descends."

Sumi drew out her fan and whisked away a mosquito, while thinking that seeking information about another powerful country had to be prudent, not in the least unwise. Even if foreigners turned out to be horrible barbarians, her country's fighters would be better off knowing their enemies' strengths and weaknesses.

Her father kept quiet. Like herself, he no doubt empathized with the scholar's illegal desire.

"If Shōin-*sensei* had been a better student of Confucius," the eldest Kurohashi said after a moment, "he would have taken the right path." He turned to the grandson. "You studied a relevant passage yesterday. You can quote it for us."

Keiji recited a long passage from one of the Confucian tomes about man's duty to obey those over him. He glanced at Sumi and finished by emphasizing the woman's duty to obey her father, husband, and when widowed, her eldest son.

"Well done." Sumi's grandfather nodded his head in approval. "It is the duty of elders to be certain the next generation is trained properly and not misled by false ideas." He gave a pointed look at her father.

"I heard more secret *kirishitans* have been discovered." The eldest Kurohashi spoke in a confidential tone. "A man who lived not too far from here, named Itō, has been banished, so perhaps *his* three sons will think better of emulating their father's criminal activity."

"He'll learn to serve our country by digging in the northern coalmines. A well-deserved punishment," the second Kurohashi said.

Sumi began to fan her burning face.

"Yes." Keiji gave a humble bow for speaking up. "Itō should be glad he was not crucified or dangled by his heels inside one of the dung pits—the smell to match that of the rotten religion."

Sumi drew in a sharp, protesting breath. If Keiji-*sama* really had much knowledge about the Evil Religion, he would be guilty of delving into forbidden information. So, he was parroting an opinion with no regard for the facts . . . or compassion for the Itō family's tragedy.

The eldest Kurohashi turned to Sumi. "You appear to be listening to our words."

"*Mōshiwake gozaimasen,*" she apologized in the humblest manner, then bowed, hoping he hadn't detected her gritted teeth.

He dismissed her apology with a wave of his hand. "Our political talk must seem irrelevant to you with your feminine training. Have your elders read *Higher Learning for Women* to you—a very instructive book for young ladies?"

"My tutor assigned me to read it, so I did." The less she said, the better, although speaking about the tedious book was far safer than the previous topic would have been.

"You must speak up, pronounce your words clearly." The eldest Kurohashi frowned. "Did you say you read it yourself?"

Sumi's grandfather also frowned.

"Yes." She lowered her eyes with all the meekness she could muster. "My tutor, Suzuki-*sensei,* assigned lessons from the book to improve my female character."

"If I may ask"—Keiji glanced at his elders, who nodded—"do you think those lessons succeeded?" His eyebrow arched.

A trick question, Sumi realized right before she spoke. Answering *yes* would sound inexcusably proud. An answer of *no* would imply her tutor and the book's author, the venerable scholar Ekken, had fallen short of their goals.

"Perhaps a woman should not be expected to be a good judge of her own character," she replied with yet another bow.

The grandson squinted at her, his face a yellow hue in the lanterns' glow. "And so, do you plan to be fully obedient to your elders, to your future husband, and then to your eldest son in your old age, as you have been taught?"

"To the best of my meager ability." She raised her fan level with her eyes, making sure no one glimpsed her grimace. The young man's questions sounded like he might be baiting her, most likely so he could demonstrate vast superiority.

"My mother already considers my opinion above her own. Would your *meager* ability rise to such a level?"

"If my son were as wise as your honorable mother judges you to be, I would rejoice in his exceptional insight." Surely no one could object to that answer.

Everyone chuckled except Keiji and Kiyo.

"Well put," the eldest Kurohashi said.

"Not that a female's opinion ever matters, but what would you do if your son were foolish?" Keiji persisted.

"Then I would also have to bow to him since he inherited my foolishness." She could hardly believe the words that spurted out of her mouth. Would anyone realize they offered an alternate explanation for his mother's submission? Possibly a more realistic one.

"I have one more question." Keiji looked at his elders, who nodded again. "Would you apologize to the eldest son if he said a kimono's design looked contrived, even ridiculous in the moonlight?" He wore the expression of a grand master making a *go* game's winning move.

Sumi held back any reaction and waited for the eldest Kurohashi to correct such uncalled-for rudeness. Surely he realized his grandson referred to *her* kimono with the shooting stars.

All she heard were the chirrups of a locust undeterred by nightfall. None of the elders spoke, apparently baffled by the question.

Sumi raised her own eyebrow. "Yes, I would apologize and provide *him* a better one." She came close to laughing at his puckered lips.

"I believe we have dwelled on the topic long enough," the eldest Kurohashi pronounced. "Our hosts have a fine tradition of upholding duty to their superiors."

"Your stiff spine and witty remarks," Kiyo whispered, "just showed up an educated man from a good family line, who might have become your betrothed. You outwitted yourself."

"I couldn't be happier." Sumi glanced at the moon and hoped the deity, if he listened to mere mortals, wouldn't judge her forwardness too harshly.

The conversation turned to the ancient story of how the moon god had angered his sister, the sun goddess, by killing the original provider of the earth's food. From then on, *Amaterasu-Ōmikami* refused to be in the same part of the heavens with her brother.

Sumi ached to point out that the story was a perfect example of how a female didn't bow to a foolish male. But then a wayward thought struck. Her father had explained how the Western science books claimed the earth circled the sun. Not only that, but apparently the moon circled the earth and always had. Although the sun goddess ruled the world, the orbits of the moon and earth didn't seem to depend on her decision to live in a separate part of the sky.

If the foreigners came, she could find answers to such questions. After all, they had managed to invent the *teresukopu* to study the stars, so they could doubtless explain the relationship of the two orbits to the god and goddess.

Her grandfather picked up his empty cup. "We require *sake* for our toasts."

Sumi's mother gestured to the cook, standing by the back entrance. A servant brought warmed *sake* with small individual trays of steamed *awabi* sea snails, dumplings, and round rice cakes filled with sweet beans.

"We honor the moon god tonight in his perfection," the eldest Kurohashi said, standing and raising his cup.

"*Kampai*!" everyone chimed in, then took a drink. More toasts followed to the health and prosperity of both families.

Sumi's throat burned, and tears came to her eyes from the strong liquor, but being treated as an adult was worth the discomfort.

The eldest Kurohashi clapped his hands. "Now we hope for the privilege of hearing the two young ladies' excellent pleas to *Tsukuyomi*."

"Kiyo-*san,* you shall be first since you are older," Sumi's grandfather instructed.

Kiyo pulled out a piece of paper and carried it over to the little table. “I am honored to read my petition.”

Great Moon God, make my heart as pure as your moonbeams and as perfect as the brightness shining above.

She bowed and inserted the paper into the round *sake* cup in the middle of the table.

The elders drank a toast to her words.

It would take more than a hypocritical prayer, Sumi reflected, to make her cousin pure and perfect. She pulled out her own slip of paper and walked to the table.

“Instead of repeating the same requests from all the previous years, I have chosen two *haiku.* One of Sodō’s and one of the woman poet Chiyo’s.” She had decided to add the second poem a minute earlier even though she risked a later rebuke from her elders.

“Let’s hear the first,” her father said.

She bowed and read,

My shadow leads me
From the moon’s awesome splendor
To my waiting home

The eldest Kurohashi cleared his throat. “A nice expression of domesticity. Females should value their home and hearth more than the expanse above.”

Sumi bowed, hiding her amazement that their guest had completely missed Sodō’s point, that awe compelled him to return to a familiar place.

"One is enough," her father said.

With a bow, she inserted the paper into the *sake* cup, fairly certain her father had figured out which poem she'd intended to add.

"I would like to hear the second poem," Keiji said. "If you would indulge me."

Her father's mouth formed a stern line, but he nodded for her to recite it.

She stepped back to the table, picked up her paper, and smiled her sweetest. "Chiyo's words encourage me tonight." She pretended to look over the words. "Her ancient poem says,"

Whatever our clothes
We transform into beauty
When viewing the moon

"Yes, I understand your need for encouragement." The eldest Kurohashi wiped his thin lips with the tray's damp napkin and accepted more *sake* from the bowing servant. "Poetess Chiyo expressed a woman's viewpoint well. There is no harm in tolerating a lady's fascination with clothes."

The grandson balanced a dumpling in his chopsticks and solemnly nodded.

Sumi wanted to ask how anyone older than a three-year-old could think that was the meaning, but bowed instead while imagining the bedlam that would have erupted if she'd followed her inclination. Raising her head, she noted her mother's contented expression. At least her mother, the peacemaker, was pleased.

After she took her place, Keiji turned and stared at her, his smug expression making him downright ugly.

Instead of modestly ducking her face behind her fan, she stared back, her chin high. Such indiscretion should guarantee he would never consider her as a possible wife.

Her next thought sobered her. The two grandfathers were perfectly able to agree on a betrothal without consulting either Keiji-*sama* or her. In fact, laying the groundwork for such a proposal could very well have been the evening's chief purpose.

A chill gripped her heart despite the pleasant breeze and the round, perfect moon.

CHAPTER 15

October, 1858, Shimoda, Japan

John took another bite of roasted pheasant, appreciating the fine dinner hosted by Townsend Harris, the American Consul General for Japan. In addition to himself, Harris had invited Captain Whitson and another American merchant, George Jennings, to dine at the temple, which doubled as Harris' residence and the location of the U.S. legation. The Consul General's young secretary-interpreter, Henry Heusken, joined the dinner as well.

Mr. Jennings, who called himself an art critic, antique collector, and financier, struck John as a person to watch. The red-haired merchant had somehow finagled a passage on the U.S. frigate making port at the town of Shimoda three weeks earlier and had missed being on that frigate when it left for China two days later.

"So, do I understand that the frigate simply steamed away, stranding you here?" John looked across the table at the merchant, sensing a fairytale in the making.

"Took a hike in the hills the second afternoon," Jennings

said with a sly grin, "but got lost. Wanted to ask for help, but the ignorant peasants I met took off like I was an ogre. Maybe my red hair. Spent the night in a damp cave, holding off a nosy fox and a bigger animal, probably a bear."

The Consul General frowned. "Haven't heard of any bears close around here."

"Whatever it was, it was gone by first light of day when I struck out." Jennings appeared unfazed. "Didn't want to delay the ship, but I seemed to go in circles. Finally climbed up the hill high enough to *see* the harbor. And what treachery met my eyes?"

John could guess.

"Smoke from the frigate making for the open sea like a bat out of hell. Then the local posse acted like *I'd* robbed the stagecoach or something. Told me I'd have to take the next foreign ship out."

"The *Retriever* leaves tomorrow for Shanghai, third bell of the first watch, weather permittin'," Captain Whitson said. "Be on the longboat at the first bell if you go with us. There's one cabin available for a payin' passenger." He paused and looked at John, who nodded. "And the fo'c'sle for ordinary sailors who earn their way."

"Aye, aye, sir." Jennings gave a sloppy salute. "I'll be taking the cabin."

John swallowed the last bite of pheasant and leaned back. "Mr. Jennings would have missed a pleasant time tonight if he'd made it onto the frigate. The good food and fine company, with no translation needed, make me feel like I'm back home in Yonkers. I'm sure Mr. Heusken here is also relieved to enjoy the evening without parsing each word that's uttered." He smiled at the interpreter.

"It's a welcome change . . ." Heusken wiped his mouth. "I have to say, though, I like languages, even the little Japanese I've struggled to learn."

"In that case, how about acting as my comprador in your spare time?" Jennings leaned forward to see Heusken better. "I'd pay well for those services."

"My interpreter," Harris huffed, "has more than enough work—crucial work—for the consulate, and will be even busier in Edo when the terms of our hard-won treaty go into effect."

"My apologies." Jennings raised chin looked anything but apologetic. "I was trying to find a way to get around the mind-twistin' language the heathen yammer here."

Harris grimaced. "The order for you to leave should end your disagreeable language problem."

"Of course. Of course." Jennings gave a crooked smile.

The Consul General raised an eyebrow at John. "If your purpose is trade at Shimoda in the near future, Mr. Cardiff, you're also wasting your time, along with Mr. Jennings. The natives here are over-taxed and barely able to scrape out a living."

"That's become clear, sir," John said, covering his surprise at the chiding tone. "As soon as we dropped anchor, I realized Shimoda was no more than a remote fishing village. Although I wanted to check out this area, my ultimate goal is to carry out a substantial trade in Nagasaki, especially since the agreement you obtained includes that port."

"An agreement achieved against daunting resistance, if I say so myself." Harris paused while the servant, a Japanese boy in his teens, forked wild boar steak onto each person's plate. "This country's cunning officials, ostensibly polite to the nth degree, used every means at their disposal to delay, obscure, and further impede the negotiations."

"Everyone talks of your great success," Jennings cooed, "and I'm ready to advance the American cause at Nagasaki next summer."

John studied Jennings' florid face. What was the man after?

"An admirable goal, Mr. Jennings," Harris said. "Tell me about your experience in these parts."

"Most recently, been working in Shanghai for the excellent firm of Taylors and Associates."

"I'm not familiar with Taylor and Associates." Harris leaned back in his chair.

"It's a new American company, formed six months ago. Rocketing up, passing a fizzle like Bick Trading Company." Jennings flipped his hand toward John. "I understand Mr. Cardiff here worked for Bick until he lost his job."

"You don't have the facts straight, my good man." John cautioned himself not to overreact. "I took a leave of absence from Bick's in New York in order to inspect the company's overseas facilities. Because I found evidence of opium smuggling, I ended my relationship with the company while in good standing."

Jennings chuckled. "All the companies with Far East branches cater to the Chinaman's craving for the drug. Have to be naïve not to know what every other trader knows."

"I was naïve when I started out, I admit. But no longer." John looked from Jennings to Harris. "While in Shanghai, I witnessed the horrors opium addiction inflicts on its victims. A sight I'll never forget."

"I quite agree with your assessment," Harris said, taking a sip of the cherry cordial the servant poured. "Two of my Chinese servants bought out all the medicinal opium in this town's apothecaries the first month we were here. Upset the local police. I finally got the two under control with the officials' helpful threat of prison time."

"If I can put in my penny's worth"—Whitson reverted to his captain's tone—"Mr. Cardiff knows what works. No American's ever heard of gettin' a special charter for trade under the Satsuma vermillion seal. But Mr. Cardiff got one—miracle like. That charter led to our runs 'tween Shanghai, Fuchow, and the LooChoos this last year. Good profit each time without one ounce o' opium. Not one ounce."

John's heart warmed to hear the captain express such confidence in him.

Jennings cleared his throat. "Don't want to leave the wrong impression. I wouldn't work for Taylors' if I thought it did anything banned."

Harris nodded in a perfunctory manner, then motioned for the servant to serve the next dish.

John stroked his beard. Apparently Jennings lied so much he was oblivious to his own prevarications. It would be hard for Harris or anyone with a lick of sense to miss the contradiction.

Harris turned to John. "And you are also interested in Nagasaki. Why is that?"

"The same bug took hold of me that latched onto many of our countrymen—fascination with this land's mystery and the lure of profitable trade. My company's made use of the Satsuma charter, with the help of my excellent Chinese comprador, to make two forays into Nagasaki so far. The harbor and bustling city couldn't offer a better location. But the officials are loath to let us trade beyond the Chinese and Russian bazaars."

"Then, it seems you've carried on a semblance of trade, at least."

"Yes, cotton calico and oolong tea in exchange for rolls of

silk. Yet the possibilities dwarf what we've done up till now."

Harris pursed his lips. "The Dutch in Nagasaki complain about the same constraints, rooted in hundreds of years of tradition. Our trade agreement provides only a beginning point. The consul I appoint for Nagasaki will have to tunnel through a mountain of barriers."

"So it seems you haven't made the appointment yet." John didn't envy whoever tackled the job.

"Not many men to choose from out here." Harris eyed John speculatively.

"Needs an experienced man." Jennings smile didn't hide a calculated look. "It'll take someone not afraid of pushing hard, remindin' the government of our country's power and, uh, good will, of course."

"Undeniably," Harris replied with a nod to Jennings. He began an account of the long negotiations he'd carried on before achieving the treaty. Possibly sensing the details were growing less interesting by the minute, he stopped in the midst of describing his journey to the capital and suggested they move and have their coffee and cigars outside, where they could enjoy the full moon.

Once settled at a round table, hastily trotted out from indoors, John gazed up at the myriads of stars, their twinkle unusually bright in the clear autumn air. A few steps away from where he sat, the moon's silvery light revealed scarlet maple leaves overhanging an impressive garden of molded bushes, rocks, and a rivulet. A breeze rustled a nearby grove of fir trees towering over deep purple shadows. Music and muffled laughter drifted up from the village at the foot of the hill. The setting struck John as perfect for a mythical tale.

"Tonight's the annual festival for the moon god," Harris

said as though responding to John's thought. "I suppose the natives would think it only natural for us to be out here, admiring the moon's splendor."

Whitson set down his coffee cup. "So that's what it is. Coming here, we dodged shoppers flockin' to every street-side stall. Workmen or fishermen, or whoever they were, filled the taverns—all this while troubadours strolled about strumming something like banjos. Couldn't miss the excitement, but seems admirin' the full moon could be done every month. Why the once-a-year turn out?"

"The officials don't want us barbarians, as they perversely call us, to investigate their carefully guarded land." Harris passed around a box of cigars before continuing. "However, Mr. Heusken talks freely with a few Japanese officials who speak Dutch. In return for learning a little about the rest of the world, they lift the veil a fraction on what takes place here."

One of the young Japanese servants lit a candle in the center of the table and bowed.

"Don't appreciate the term *barbarian*," George Jennings allowed while holding his cigar to the flame.

"A word used too loosely on both sides, I believe," John replied while lighting his cigar as well. "Few Western landscapers could do better than this temple's gardeners."

"At any rate," Harris said, "Mr. Heusken is our knowledgeable one about the festival." Harris turned toward his interpreter. "Tell us what you know, Henry."

Heusken straightened. "I guess you could say the moon festival has a somewhat romantic theme. I was told young ladies turn to the moon god for help in marrying a good man." He glanced up at the moon and shrugged. "Since they all face arranged marriages and have no say in choosing their mate, you can see how they'd seek aid. However, I'm not sure how much stock they put in the moon god's help. It seems people gather on balconies or in their gardens more for a good time, and less for venerating the god." Heusken paused to light his cigar at the candle.

"It hasn't been too long," Harris said, "since our own countrymen doubted their children could make satisfactory choices, especially those proud of their family line."

John wondered if Harris had tangled with his family over a match, then reminded himself that Catherine's father was close to being one of those old-fashioned fathers.

"I'd be happy enough to choose for my three daughters if they fell for rascals," the captain said, "although I imagine they'd object mightily."

"Arranged marriages are just the beginning of the female's hard life." Heusken's smile could be described as wicked or mischievous. "There's a book the whole populace swears by called *Higher Learning for Women*. The book claims the female is always inferior to a man except in bearing children. Imagine that." He grinned at his audience's intent looks. "The woman's supposed to consider her husband as if he were Heaven itself and not go anywhere without his express permission. She isn't to be the least bit angry or disobedient if her in-laws ill-treat her. To sum up, she has to make it her lifelong object to fulfill her husband's, as well as his parents', every command and desire."

Jennings chortled. "I can imagine it just fine. A pretty, almond-eyed wench, to fulfill society's obligations, bear you young 'uns, and satisfy your every craving as long as you live. No nagging or complainin' allowed. A man's fantasy, but actual reality here. Wait 'til my friends hear this."

Cringing at Jennings' crassness, John asked, "But what about love?"

"That's what the husbands have concubines for," Heusken said matter-of-factly. "Wives are admonished to avoid vices, especially the biggest one they call silliness. But a little silliness is overlooked in the pleasure quarters. There, the woman can titillate a man until he's begging for her attentions."

Harris frowned at his interpreter, who looked down.

John imagined Heusken knew of what he spoke.

Jennings smirked. "I've heard the natives don't approve of hairy faces. Think I'll shave my beard before long."

"We've discussed this subject long enough." Harris gave a big puff on his cigar.

John agreed. Yet he couldn't help thinking about how such a set up would affect Catherine and him. Due to the constraints her parents had exercised during their courtship, he wasn't sure just how deeply she cared for him. With an arranged marriage, he'd have no idea at all of her true feelings until too late. However, there was no question about one thing. Procuring a concubine would bring the roof down on his head.

In his next letter to Catherine, he'd mention the moon festival, but not the young ladies' situations. He'd like her to form good opinions about the land, maybe even be willing to visit if he settled in Japan for a time. He pondered whether to describe the Buddhist temple behind him with its thick thatched roof whose ends curved up to repel evil spirits. He hadn't told her how all their Christian objects had to be hidden at Amami Ōshima because of the persecution of the faith. But maybe Harris' negotiations had improved such a vital issue.

"How about the prohibition of Christianity here?" John asked. "Did the treaty address the problem?"

Harris sniffed. "To an extent. Every official considers our faith to be a vicious, evil religion that threatens the country's very existence. One time a governor inspecting my living quarters saw my picture of a child praying. I admitted my own practice of praying. But I didn't mention to whom in case the governor would fabricate an excuse to banish me from the country for proselytizing. It was against enormous odds that I managed to get a clause in the treaty giving foreigners personal freedom to practice their beliefs. But we are not to spread our faith among the natives."

"A good first step, considering such opposition." John sincerely meant it.

"You watch," Jennings muttered. "Our country's rabid missionaries will get themselves in hot water before they can say *bless you*."

Harris, Heusken, and Whitson all nodded.

The charge would be true of at least a few, John realized with a sigh.

Cigars finished, John joined the others in taking his leave. He and Captain Whitson urged Harris and Heusken to visit the ship for breakfast at the captain's table before the ship left, but the two declined, claiming prior commitments. John stepped onto the flagstone path as a servant, carrying a lantern attached to a long pole, prepared to lead them down from the temple's hill.

"Mr. Cardiff," Harris called out, causing John to stop and turn back to where Harris stood. "Sorry to delay you, but I failed to ask if you were also open to an appointment as consul in Nagasaki, as Mr. Jennings has already indicated about himself."

"I appreciate the question, sir, but . . ." John paused, uneasy at giving an unequivocal *no*. "I need time to consider such a large responsibility."

"The position as an honorary consul is part-time in nature."

"But a full-time job, I'd imagine, tunneling through those barriers you mentioned as well as dealing with our own countrymen—no doubt some upright ones, but also drunken sailors, gamblers, and belligerents."

"The appointment carries benefits you may not realize." Harris glanced around as though expecting an eavesdropper. "Priority in unloading cargo and clearing customs, an inside track in supplying government orders, much more freedom in travel, and the chance to carry out justice and do good for our own people." He pointed toward the tall flagpole, where the American flag had flown during the day. "The opportunity, Mr. Cardiff, to do one's duty as a true patriot. A true patriot in these troubled times."

"Mr. Cardiff might like the Hakodate posting instead." Jennings had turned back also. "Fewer ships dropping anchor up north. Less demands on a consul's time, seems to me, but a good market for wool, whale oil, items like that."

"The post's not available," Harris said. "I already have a suitable man in Hakodate, but your eagerness for the Nagasaki post is noted. Have no fear, Mr. Jennings. You are in the running." Harris looked pointedly at John.

It was hard to miss the intimation that Jennings would be consul if John refused. But there had to be other qualified men Harris could approach in the eight months remaining before the treaty took effect.

"You think about it, Mr. Cardiff," Harris said, "and let me know right away if you're interested."

"I'll do that, sir. Thank you for mentioning the opportunity." John turned back onto the path.

The three reached the village main street as guffaws came from a nearby home's garden. A few doors down, a *geisha*'s song trilled from a restaurant, its balcony filled with men and women chatting under large, red and orange paper lanterns. A group of drunken fishermen wove past, calling out incomprehensible words.

"I'm not one to ignore a good party," Jennings said. "You two gentlemen enjoy your night. I'll be on the longboat in the morning." He adjusted the scarf at his neck and headed toward a brightly lit saloon, where the local officials had given him a second-floor room.

John and Captain Whitson walked down to the quay, each lost in their own thoughts. Right before boarding the longboat, Whitson turned toward John. "Hard to be away from the wife and my girls on a night like this. Moon shinin' so bright and all." His voice carried a wistfulness John hadn't heard before.

"I was thinking a similar thing. I've a sweetheart in New York. She'd be pleased if she knew I'll be spending the night on my own cot."

"My wife, Bessie, too. And may I say, Mr. Cardiff, that sweetheart o' yours might just like marryin' a person with the title o' consul."

"Yes, I think she would if I could get her to come here. But I'm not sure that a title would be the best way to entice her to come . . . or to marry."

"Not a bad one neither," the captain said as he boarded the longboat.

After following Whitson on board, John stood at the stern,

listening to the rowers' low chant as they moved the boat away from shore. He glanced at the moon's splendor. What a difference there was in the idea of a moon god and his own faith. And in the ideas of marriage. He stood right on the edge of a land with an unintelligible language and truly alien beliefs.

Yet the country appealed to him as though it reached out and fastened onto his soul. When he'd landed that afternoon and strolled along the main street, the villagers had scrutinized his every move, while offering shy smiles and trying to quiet their barking dogs. The children had followed him like the pied piper. When he'd handed out copper buttons, they'd acted like he'd given them diamonds. After that, two little girls had run up to him with a bouquet. They'd giggled with hands covering their mouths as he'd returned their smiles and clasped the wildflowers to his chest. Anyone could see the commoners were a gentle people no matter how fierce the samurai and warlords proved to be.

Certainly, he wanted to make enough profit to return to his dear Catherine, but devoting all his efforts in this new land to making money seemed petty, especially in light of his promise to serve the Almighty better.

But how could he, a foreigner and a simple merchant, make any significant contribution? His own country's warships had forced Japan's leaders to expose their country's belly to people they feared—pale-faced, round-eyed barbarians like himself. How could he do something of value? Something noble? Would being the consul give him a bigger avenue to make an impact, or would the responsibility add constraints?

The fishermen's huts faded into the indigo shadows along the coast. As the boat moved into larger waves, he grasped the rail, while a thought tantalized him. Perhaps the evening had already given him two ways to begin. Small ways. Barely noticeable. Not dependent on profit or status. But, by Jove, enough raindrops could satisfy a thirst.

He would treat the Japanese women with the chivalry he'd been taught since childhood even if it made some of the men foam at the mouth.

And he would openly practice his faith. There were worse things than banishment.

CHAPTER 16

For three weeks following the night of the moon festival, Sumi's stomach lurched every time their gate swung open. Would the visitor be the *nakōdo*, bringing an offer from the Kurohashi family? When the person turned out to be a neighbor or her friend Taki or a deliveryman, she nearly collapsed from relief.

This day, the guest who had caused the range of reactions was Taki, who had just won their game of battledore.

"What's bothering you, Sumi? You never let me win. You act like you're half alive and half dead."

Sumi laughed and picked up the shuttlecock. "Enjoy your victory while you can. I suppose the bright sky dazzled my eyes."

Taki cocked her head. "I'm glad my betrothal is finalized, so bright skies don't blind me."

"You know I envy you—content with your elders' selection."

"Why not be content? Agonizing over it wouldn't change a thing." She handed Sumi her wooden paddle and leaned in with a confidential smile. "I hear even difficult men sometimes improve with age. Like *sake*."

Sumi tried to return the smile, but couldn't muster more than a twitch of her lips. "Some appear hopeless. My threatened betrothal is with a man who doesn't care for a woman's idea at all. It's as though we're dolls meant for his entertainment."

"You find that unusual? A big problem?"

Sumi nodded, not mentioning what truly sickened her. Her friend might even excuse the Kurohashis' attitude toward the Itō family's fate. She would certainly be horrified if she knew that Sumi and her father had touched a prohibited foreign object themselves.

"Your thinking is strange sometimes, dear friend. Why not choose to have a calm life? Agree with your elders' choices? Pushing against a stone mountain won't move it."

I—"

The gate swung open.

Sumi gasped, then bowed along with Taki, as her father walked toward them. He rarely returned home midmorning. Possibilities raced through her mind as well as a frantic denial of any unwished-for betrothal.

He nodded to Taki, then caught Sumi's eye. "I have important news," he said as he walked quickly past.

Taki gave an excuse for leaving and bid a hasty goodbye.

Her pulse accelerating, Sumi helped her father step out of his sandals at the vestibule, then stayed close behind him. After an interminable five minutes, the rest of the family took their places on cushions around the quilt-covered *kotatsu* table. Another five minutes was consumed by the pouring of tea and the formal greetings due her grandfather.

"I am ready to hear what you have to say," her grandfather announced at last.

Her father bowed. "Nagasaki is to be opened to foreigners

next summer." He paused at Sumi's indrawn breath. "They will be allowed to reside and carry on trade in the city. I have further news, but only our family can know this for now." He gave both Sumi and Kiyo sharp glances. "Governor Nakamura has ordered *me* to become interpreter for our city's first American diplomat, who will be known as a *consul*."

Sumi swallowed the joyful words about to erupt. Her father would be with a Westerner day in and day out. She wanted to leap and dance in circles, to shout the news to everyone in the city. But of course, she had to remain quiet and sedate. And tell no one.

Her mother drew out her fan. "Is it true?" She fanned her flushed face, the only clue to her recognition of the unmistakable honor Governor Nakamura had granted by such an appointment. Then she glanced at Sumi and handed the fan to her.

Kiyo, sitting next to Sumi, made a low sound, resembling a grunt.

Her grandfather's expression had reverted to its stolid mask. "If that is all the news you bring, then I also have an announcement." His eyes shone with determination. "I will accompany Kato-*dono* and his son's family on a pilgrimage, departing on my lucky day of the monkey next month."

Her father coughed, apparently to cover his surprise. "May I inquire the cause of the pilgrimage?"

"The coming of the barbarians. What else? Since I cannot resist the will of the Shōgun and our governor, I must resort to pleas for the gods' intervention."

"I apologize for my part in this difficulty." Her father bowed again.

Difficulty? Sumi fanned herself. Never, never could the

opening of the city resemble a hardship. If only the gods would remain aloof, or concern themselves with other people's pleas. Surely they were busy enough already with the thousands of requests on the papers fluttering at the shrines' portals.

Her grandfather tented his hands. "You could not refuse Governor Nakamura's command. Your fault was becoming fluent in the accursed languages. But may it never be said that my offspring shirks his duty."

"I try to fulfill my obligations despite my many faults." Her father bowed perfunctorily. "I find it amazing you have already made this travel plan. Did the *onmyoji* foresee my insignificant assignment in the stars?"

"No. I foresaw it myself when I learned of Nagasaki's opening seven days ago."

Her parents looked at each other, then stared at him.

"If you must know, Merchant Omura gleaned the information at the Ōhira Inn. The governor's servants have big ears and loose mouths."

Sumi covered her surprise that her uncompromisingly proper grandfather had also used their neighbor as a source of news.

"Anyone aware of the hours you spend on studying languages," he continued, looking at her father, "could predict your assignment once he knew the barbarians would be arriving. However, I do not believe the nosy merchant reached that obvious conclusion even though he tried his best to probe into our concerns. He reminded me of a rat digging for morsels, of which he did not get a whiff from me."

Her grandfather ran his eyes over the group. "This assignment could make our family a target. Vacillating samurai, even clans, may allow their understandable opposition to the barbarians to override their binding loyalty to the shogunate's decisions. The later this assignment to the barbarian diplomat becomes known, the better. Each mouth must be guarded."

Everyone bowed instantly. While being careful to straighten last, Sumi mulled over the allegation of danger. Her grandfather had repeatedly made dire predictions about war resulting from the barbarians' whaling ships drawing too close to their shores. No war had resulted. An agreement for trade with the United States of America, Russia, and a place called Britain, in addition to the existing trade with Holland, could hardly be called an invasion.

If her family didn't betroth her to someone like Keiji-*sama*, her dream of meeting foreigners would at last be realized. Right in Nagasaki. In seven or eight months. She had to fight back tears of joy.

Her mother poured more hot water into the teapot, then dipped her head. "May I ask the pilgrimage's destination?"

"Ise, *Amaterasu-Ōmikami*'s Grand Shrine."

"Such a long way to travel." Her father gazed into his empty cup as if it contained information. "We should not expect your return before two months."

"Longer. We plan to be in Kyoto for the New Year in order to petition the fox god and war god. Then we will proceed to Ise, where I will stay while the others travel to Edo by way of the Tōkaidō. Although still able to wield a sword, I have no desire to fight bandits alone, so I will rejoin the group for the return."

Her father grimaced. "Swollen rivers, storms, troop movements, other incidents could cause countless delays. Your return may coincide with the cherry blossoms."

"Most likely." He turned to face Kiyo, whose eyes widened before she lowered them. "The arrangements for your betrothal are nearing completion. A samurai from my own clan. The agreement should be finalized before my departure."

Kiyo scooted around on her cushion and bowed her forehead to the mat.

Her grandfather nodded, then pursed his lips. "The man pursues artistic endeavors with sandalwood, but has an honorable ancestry. He did not object to your modest dowry."

Sumi caught a flash of anger in her cousin's eyes. Kiyo's next bow was stiffer. She wouldn't be sheltered under a big tree if her husband had to supplement his rice allotment.

Her grandfather turned toward Sumi, and her heart skipped a beat.

"Negotiations for your betrothal have begun also. But these negotiations are more complicated."

Sumi smothered the thousand-and-one questions striking her mind and fought against the dread roused by the word *complicated.*

"My pilgrimage will slow the arrangements, but only a little. Although I do not doubt their eventual success, I will not reveal them yet, lest a careless word throw a rock into the wheels."

"Thank you, Honorable Grandfather." She also bowed her forehead to the mat, then kept her eyes lowered and her body still despite her plummeting hope. Complicated negotiations could well be with the Kurohashis, made difficult by both her untoward boldness and her father's position as a Dutch Scholar. If a union with their grandson was indeed being proposed, she wouldn't want to hinder it with just a rock, but with a boulder, like the enormous one she had once watched thunder down the hillside, barely missing a cottage and landing in the middle of a rice paddy.

CHAPTER 17

June 1859 (Year of the Sheep)

Sumi twirled her oiled-paper-and-bamboo umbrella in the thick fog. To her left, she pictured enormous, white-painted houses complete with glass windows, small shutters, and central chimneys, sitting behind long, open yards, like in the grainy picture she'd seen in one of her father's books. Wooden shoes clopped on the cobblestones, too, until she remembered wooden shoes belonged in Holland, not in the United States of America.

The fog began lifting in time to keep her from running into a plank that jutted off a workman's shoulder, but the sun's effort to break through the clouds wasn't welcome. Her city's ordinary gray shops with their banners, balcony overhangs, and tile roofs were poking through the mist. Her countrymen, too, were now populating the street—aggressive peddlers, several housewives, a pilgrim, more muscular workmen, *not* long-nosed, round-eyed foreigners. The spell had been broken.

She lowered her umbrella with a sigh and stepped into Omura's bronzeware shop.

He offered a drawn-out bow lower than his usual one.

"What does the young lady desire today?"

Sumi smiled at the greater deference he showed her, now the eighteen-year-old daughter of a samurai, despite not being married.

"Please give me a minute to see what is available." She glanced over the full shelves. A handsome washbasin caught her eye, but she hadn't come to buy any items. Without appearing too eager, she wanted to hear everything she could about the foreigners, whatever recent gossip the merchant had collected.

"I suppose I can tell you what news I've heard." He tucked his dust cloth into his sash and clasped his hands behind his back. "An American ship is expected to leave Hong Kong within two weeks, headed for our harbor."

She caught her breath. "Truly? You hear so many unusual things . . . and have such nice items on display today."

She set down the packet holding her grandfather's tobacco and picked up a shiny bronze mirror, pretending an interest in it. One look at her bright pink cheeks made her put the mirror down as if it had come to life and pinched her.

The merchant watched, his eyes intense.

"Concerning the ship"—she casually fingered a small statue of a bug-eyed cat—"do you know if it will come here directly? Arrive early next month as expected?" Try as much as she could, she couldn't disguise the eagerness in her voice.

"Nagasaki is its first port of call. The ocean-going ships can weather storms. And a typhoon this early?" The merchant cut off his snort with a quick bow. "Most unlikely. The ship will arrive on time."

Let him poke fun. He'd told her what she craved to know. A delicious shiver raised her neck's hair.

"Would you have time for tea?" Omura took a sideways step toward the shop's raised platform and paused.

"No, thank you. After I look around a little more, I'll need to deliver my Eldest's package."

"I fear I have been remiss. How is your honorable grandfather? Not still indisposed, I hope."

"He has nearly recovered. I'll tell him you inquired."

Her grandfather had returned from his pilgrimage when the irises bloomed, long after the short-lived cherry blossoms. He'd rested for a week, but still appeared subdued. Sumi sympathized with the hardness of his trip. But from the moment the gatekeeper had rushed into their vestibule announcing her grandfather's return, dread had competed with the good feeling of his safe arrival. Every day brought the foreigners closer, but if she were betrothed to Keiji-*sama*, the poet Issa's *dewdrop world of suffering* would be a reality, not the illusion the poem implied.

Omura bowed again. "Please allow me a minute before you leave. I do have an item that would please an attractive lady." He walked over to his storage cabinet and withdrew a wrapped object. "I noticed your interest in the mirror. This is a new type. Its glass reflects much more accurately." He unwrapped the mirror and held it up in front of her.

Sumi flinched when she saw her cheeks, all the pinker in the shockingly clear reflection. "It is a wonder—almost too revealing, in my case."

"Not at all. A nice, clear image."

She gave a half-smile as he lowered the mirror. "Where did you acquire it?"

"A Chinese trader purchased it . . . from Englishmen in Siam. However, I don't like to talk about my sources. Not everyone approves of foreign merchandise. This mirror may be the only one in our city, perhaps in the entire country. But since your family and you are such good neighbors, I offer it for 22 *momme*, my actual cost."

"I believe my father mentioned seeing one like it himself. In our city."

"Ah well. He has privileges that I don't. So apparently there are two."

"Might that mean a lower price?"

"As I said, I offer it at my actual cost."

The precious mirror was expensive, too expensive, more than the price of one of Hiroshige's woodblock prints. But she'd never owned something made outside her country, and the quality was much better than the bronze mirror's. She could use part of her small fund accumulated from her elders' New Year gifts.

"You are certain it's legal to own one of these foreign items?"

"Since the Shōgun is permitting foreign people into our city, it stands to reason that foreign objects are permitted so long as they are not related to the Evil Religion. Still, it would be wise not to say where the mirror originated if you buy it."

She pushed away the bad memory of Taki's neighbor and stroked the smooth glass. "I am afraid I can't resist. Could you keep it for me until I bring the money from home?"

"Please take it with you. I'd be happy to receive payment anytime . . . in the next few days."

Sumi pulled out the *furoshiki* scarf she carried in her sash. Glancing in the mirror as she took it from the merchant's hands, she started at the reflection of a person standing in the doorway. His flat lacquer hat, worn only by samurai, cast a shadow on his face. The glare of the outdoor light further masked his features. His stance, however, looked threatening, as though he were about to draw his sword.

"Oh, I think someone . . ." When she turned, the entranceway was empty. "I thought someone had come to see you, but no one is there."

Omura glanced at the shop's entrance too and frowned, then gave a seemingly forced chuckle. "Perhaps you are holding a magical mirror. It may be worth more than I'm charging."

She shook her head and smiled, covering the prick of fear. A mirror was one of the three sacred treasures in a Shinto shrine. The Shōgun might not mind, but the sun goddess herself could be repulsed by foreign mirrors invading her country, the special land of the gods.

But then the foreigners would bring additional mirrors when they came, and also forbidden books of the Evil Religion, and who knew what other queer objects. This lone mirror was inconsequential compared to all of that. So why should she worry about a reflection of what was surely a passerby, not a supernatural form?

"Let me wrap this more securely for you." Omura shot another glance toward the empty entryway. "The glass in it can easily crack." He reached into the cabinet and pulled out more of the wrapping material.

"*Oya*! Look here." He spun toward her. His fist held up three sheets of paper separate from the wrappings. "Pages of foreign print. The inspectors must not have seen these."

Sumi's heart beat faster. "They probably thought the papers were of no consequence," she suggested, knowing that was extremely unlikely. "I've learned a few foreign words. Perhaps I can identify their nature." She kept her hand from shaking as she held it out to take the papers.

Holy Bible met her eyes. She leaned over the pages to hide her shock. Someone had torn the sheets out of the forbidden book. Her father's warning rang in her ears. She felt faint at the dizzying opportunity, laced with unspeakable danger.

She tilted her head up casually and met the merchant's eyes. "It appears to say something about cleaning with a cloth. Maybe the surface retains fingerprints." She wiggled her fingers to take his eyes off her face. "Does the information seem troublesome?" She wrapped the papers halfway around the mirror and stopped, waiting for his answer while forcing down her guilty feeling. Honesty was important, but this was a lie that protected both of them.

He hesitated, then shrugged. "Not at all. I suppose the instructions belong with the item. Please keep them if they interest you."

She nodded with what she hoped was an assured, calm look and slipped the thoroughly wrapped mirror and the packet of tobacco into her scarf.

Outside the shop, she looked in both directions, but saw no threatening samurai. A trickle of sweat rolled down her back. The papers inside her scarf offered a far more tangible peril than a phantom face. The sun had completely banished the earlier mist, but she pulled her umbrella down closer to her head, treasuring the anonymity it offered.

If her cousin discovered the pages and guessed they hadn't been cleared by customs—or worse, guessed their identity—she could report Sumi to the police. Even if Sumi said she thought the papers were instructions for the mirror, she could still be imprisoned while the officials debated her fate. She shuddered at the horrible thought.

But Kiyo had taken shelter in her aunt's home. She wouldn't want to endanger Sumi's mother. Rather than telling the police, a more probable consequence would be for her cousin to tattle to their elders. Then Sumi would be guarded until betrothed to the least suitable man her grandfather could locate in the whole country. If not Keiji-*sama*, another rabid traditionalist just as bad.

Holding the scarf close to her chest, she gripped the umbrella tighter. She would be careful, very careful, so no harm would come. The papers weren't just a foreign object like the mirror. If she could one day read them, they would be like a tunnel into the foreigners' minds. The papers could be a curse. Or they could be a blessing.

Merchant Omura congratulated himself on his first sale of the new-style mirrors. Perhaps he should have lowered the price for his neighbor, but if one considered his overhead and the danger, doubling the mirror's true cost was reasonable. Normally, he earned a three-hundred percent profit. He would use the same technique for the remaining fifteen hidden deep in the storage cabinet—selling them to trusted customers, carefully.

Ah-ee, he gasped at the next thought. What about the foreign papers that escaped the inspectors' scrutiny? Should he tell the warrior about Taguchi Sumi's interest in them? How he'd allowed her to take them? That wouldn't sit well even though they were only directions for cleaning. But walls had ears, and *shōji* panels had eyes. Governors' servants weren't the only ones who gossiped. If Ōta-*sama* somehow learned of the failure to tell him about the girl's questionable conduct, or even what the warrior might deem her treachery, his outrage could be deadly.

He'd have to admit to having sold one glass mirror, but being able to say it had come from a Chinaman would make it less odious. He stood up, realizing he'd better make sure there weren't any more sheets mixed in with the packaging materials. And if there were, he wouldn't be passing them on to the Taguchis' pretty daughter.

The two round Buddhas on the shop's god shelf looked down on him as he headed for the cabinet. These gods of industry and wealth had given him success so far. He would burn an extra stick of incense each day to keep their good favor.

CHAPTER 18

The next morning, Sumi curled up on a cushion and leaned against the column by the open small shōji window in her bedroom. Her yellow cat padded across the room and rubbed against her arm until she took it into her lap and scratched behind its ears.

All at once the cat sprang out of her lap and onto its feet as a sparrow, carrying a twig, flew onto the overhang extending from under Sumi's room.

"You can't reach that bird. You'd have to risk your neck, and if you made it over there, I couldn't rescue you. I wouldn't even try."

The cat threw Sumi a backward glance as if to say it cared nothing for her opinion. However, it must have realized the bird was out of reach because it stretched out on the floor, keeping its eyes fixed on the opening.

Sumi rose on her knees to see out the low window. The nest looked halfway finished. She watched the energetic little bird until it flew away. What freedom it had. Nobody told it how many twigs to gather or where to build its nest . . . or which bird to choose as a mate.

Yet not only cats, but also falcons relished a sparrow feast. And falcons could reach a sparrow anywhere. Even snakes could threaten the hatchlings, like the fiend years ago in the pear tree.

Was freedom really such a good thing?

The sound of a broom being knocked against a downstairs post cut into her thoughts. She could explore her precious prize right then no matter what calamity the future held. She retrieved one of the foreign sheets of paper from the book of *haiku* where she'd hidden them. The slight odor of her grandfather's tobacco reminded her of the risk.

Her fingers shook as she held the page in the light. A few words were familiar: *friends, love, one*. The phrase, *God is love*, caught her eye. What was a G-*o*-*d*? What object could be defined as *love*?

"You always bury your nose in a book."

Sumi's head jerked. How had Kiyo crept up on her? And why? Did she sense a forbidden secret like a homing pigeon sensed its base?

Folding the paper casually, Sumi willed her face to appear unperturbed. "Just looking over some *haiku*." She gestured at the book's cover. "It calms my mind." She hoped her eyes didn't betray her panic.

Her cousin scowled. "Are you searching for more poems to share with our guests, like the one about clothing?"

Careful. Not too meek, nor too irritable. "I . . . I can read you several good ones I've found. You can use them yourself at the next festival instead of your usual plea."

"If I were interested, I would read the book for myself. But I'll let you be the one to embarrass the family with impertinent poems. And besides, my coming betrothal means I won't be making any more pleas." She grabbed a scarf from her cabinet and left the room in a huff.

Sumi lay flat on the floor, watching the nest and waiting for her heartbeats to return to normal. The sparrow, heedless of danger, brought another twig. The cat's ears moved forward, and it sat up on its haunches, its muscles taut. Like Kiyo, Sumi thought, the cat waited to pounce if its prey made one false move. The cat and Kiyo detested each other, but they had more in common than either might realize.

Sumi rose and began pacing. Kiyo had almost snared her. She might not be so lucky next time. What was she thinking, taking those pages from the merchant? Then keeping them in the house? She had to get rid of them immediately.

But how? Where? She must not disrespect the Evil Religion's book if it was connected to any real spirits, even foreign ones. After all, her father had said the *kirishitans* had fought and even died for the *Holy Bible*, so great was its words' importance.

A natural setting would be most appropriate, but she couldn't risk being spotted hiding the pages in their garden. Making an effort to control her trembling hands, she rummaged in her cupboard. A flat, narrow cedar box containing her best tortoise-shell comb caught her eye. She emptied the small box, tucked the papers into it, and slipped it under her sash.

According to the sundial in the garden below, it was close to the time to meet Taki at the nearby tearoom. Since Kin rarely accompanied her while she stayed in the area, she could walk farther to the nearest park after leaving her friend and dispose of the pages there. That should be good enough for words from the *Holy Bible*, whether the book's ideas were sacred or evil.

After descending the stairs, she glimpsed her father

kneeling at his low desk in the main room. Apparently dressed for an important meeting, he wore his formal pleated *hakama* trousers and second-best tunic. Although he looked the part of a staunch samurai, he wasn't exceptionally handsome, having a rather long, narrow face and bony body structure. Nevertheless, no one outshone her hard-working, intelligent father.

He turned halfway toward her. "Is it already time for you to meet with Taki-*san*?"

She approached him and bowed. "I am leaving a little early." She glanced at the open book. A foreign one. Dare she ask him about the word *god*? The word had also been in the *Holy Bible*'s first sentence she had seen a year ago, the night her father had warned of the book's great danger. He might remember that sentence.

"Yes, this is a foreign book I am reviewing for the vice-governor," he said as if answering an unspoken question. "One you would find boring despite your insatiable curiosity. It teaches about banking."

She wrinkled her nose. "Curiosity is a great fault of mine, but I can withstand the temptation to study banking." She gave a slow smile. "My curiosity is only about a small thing today." She caught her breath. Would he see through her tactic?

"What insignificant thing is that?" He straightened his notes and faced her more fully.

She glanced around to be sure they were alone. "Uh, just an English word or two."

He pointed to the cushion by his desk. His eyes narrowed with suspicion.

She knelt on the cushion and bowed, scolding herself for her foolishness. Her father knew her too well.

"What English words?"

She might manage to skirt the quicksand if she couched the question well enough. "I remember you taught me that *saw* means *mimashita*, and *was* means *arimashita.* The letters' reversed order makes the meanings entirely different." She swallowed. "I know *dog* means *inu*, so I wondered if *g-o-d* would have an entirely different meaning too."

The packet scalded her hand when she felt under her sash to assure its position. She should have waited to ask this question until after she'd gotten rid of the pages.

"Are you remembering a word from the forbidden book?" He scrutinized her face.

No plausible denial came to mind, so she finally nodded.

"Strange how that book's memory persisted." He searched her face again. "I suppose dangerous memories outlive safer ones. That is a fact of life. I'll answer your question this time, but in the future, you must not only remember but also *obey* my order to never again speak about anything related to the Evil Religion's book."

She bowed her assent, feeling her face heat.

"G-o-d means *kami-sama.* Instead of referring to the millions of spirits that actually exist, the English word is for just one god. The Westerners worship it as though it were the *only* god."

"Then English speakers are truly ignorant."

"Which is one reason people often call them barbarians. One of *many* reasons." He grasped her left shoulder. "Do not allow your curiosity, Sumi, to lead you into trouble. Even though we no longer trample on the crucifix to please the Shōgun, the foreign god is prohibited." He pinched her shoulder a little harder. "I discarded that forbidden book the day after you saw it."

"I understand."

He released his grip, but maintained his grim expression.

She bowed and left for the tearoom, shaken, yet pleased. She'd gained a little more insight. But she also had more puzzles to consider: Why did her countrymen so greatly abhor a god characterized as *love*? Did the god have a forbidden longing for human women, or was his love similar to a good parent's affection for a small child? Maybe the foreign god had other emotions too, dangerous ones, like jealousy or anger. If so, she was wise to dispose of the pages respectfully.

Still, equating a god with any kind of love was different from everything she'd heard before. Some gods were known to be kind and merciful under certain conditions. But loving? That idea was impossible to grasp.

After finding the tearoom's first floor empty of patrons, Sumi started up the stairs to the second floor. She stopped when a gravelly voice called out. The shop owner's ancient mother tottered toward her.

"Your friend left. She sent her apology. Our other customers left too."

Sumi sniffed, but didn't smell smoke. "Was there a problem? A wild creature?" A rabid dog or a large enough rat would certainly empty the shop of people, herself included.

"A two-legged, wild creature, a Chōshū samurai I never saw before." The old woman gasped. "Forgive me please. My mind tangled. I forgot you're not one of us."

"Never mind. You are upset. As you were saying about the stranger . . ."

"He came inside, swords still at his side. Scanned the room like he owned it. Not even our samurai customers muttered objections. Maybe even they feared his swords." She scrunched her brow, adding more wrinkles to her forehead's mosaic of lines. "No one wanted more tea. Our customers left one by one. Soon only him stay."

"How strange. Did the man say anything? Do anything else?"

"He sat back there." She pointed to the room's rear platform. "When I brought tea, he eyed the pot. Then puffed up an' said it was good our countrymen made the pot." The old woman's filmy eyes blinked several more times. "I said I thought so too."

"Of course the teapot was made by our countrymen. Why would he say that?" Sumi felt a nervous twinge.

The woman fanned her face with her hand. "Something else strange happens these days. At Merchant Omura's shop." She darted her eyes toward the door, around the room, and back at Sumi. "My youngest daughter is a maid there. A samurai—the same one who came here, I think—visits the shop once or twice a month. Used to be once or twice a year. And each time, he buys nothing. Doesn't want tea. Waves her away. Only comes when no customers are there. Merchant Omura is in a bad mood afterwards."

Sumi shook her head. "Not good for our merchant or our neighborhood. Disrupting *wa*, harmony. I suppose your daughter didn't hear any of their conversation? Why the stranger might visit the shop so often." She doubted the mother would admit her daughter eavesdropped, but she had to ask.

"She minded her own tasks upstairs."

"Merchant Omura was once a samurai. The warrior might have trained with the merchant and be trying to get him to close the shop, take up his swords again."

"My daughter says the merchant sells foreign goods

sometimes."

"That may be so."

Suddenly remembering the figure in the mirror, Sumi tensed. But if that had been the reflection of the upset samurai, what did it matter? Even if he were against Westerners and their goods, he couldn't have detected the foreign style of the mirror in her hands. And he certainly couldn't know about the foreign pages she'd kept. Surely, Omura wouldn't dare mention them, especially since he'd allowed her to take them.

"Seems a conspiracy's brewing 'gainst the merchant and others like him." The woman's voice had dropped to a loud whisper. "The barbarians bring danger."

Sumi frowned. "Foreigners should not be blamed for an overzealous samurai. And what plot can the stranger carry out if he tries to stir up trouble? Since the shogunate has opened our city to the foreigners, the officials will do their duty. They'll keep everyone safe."

"Forgive this old grandmother's prattling." She made a deep bow, then pointed her trembling, blue-veined hand toward a low table. "Now you wish your bean cake and tea?"

"The clouds are gathering for another shower. I'll return next week instead."

"May the gods protect us." The woman bowed low.

Sumi gave a nod to acknowledge the woman's old age, while thinking how fearful ordinary townspeople were. Although she might never measure up to the brave heroines in her country's history, she did have a little of a samurai's courage. At least—she grimaced—she could think herself brave when compared to the tottering old grandmother.

But a *conspiracy*? Preposterous. One irritable samurai did not make a conspiracy.

CHAPTER 19

At the park, Sumi walked briskly along the pathway that meandered among red flowering hibiscus shrubs and smooth copper-tone boulders. But she slowed her pace when the ancient stone path entered the cool, deep shade of evergreen trees towering over masses of lush ferns. The greenery surrounding her gleamed, refreshed by the rainy season.

How she loved this place. She breathed in the smells of the cypress and pine trees and the newly turned soil, a fragrance free from the odors of tobacco, food, and sweat. Here she was free. Free from high expectations, free from tedious lessons, free from Kiyo's interference.

Free like the little sparrow. And in danger if not careful.

She clutched the box. If only she could keep the pages longer. There might be some more unusual ideas. But she dared not. Not even one more day. She shivered, remembering Kiyo's unexpected appearance.

Voices carried from farther along the path, around the next bend. A shy giggle from a female. A soft, rumbling male voice.

A secret rendezvous?

She'd heard that a few people, peasants or even spoiled

children of merchants, sometimes rejected arranged marriages, and that the so-called lovers were intimate even before marriage. What kind of man and woman did such a thing? How could they insult their families? Their ancestors? The gods? She could never reject her elders' arrangement outright. To do so would be monstrous.

But if *permitted* to choose, like the Westerners' rumored custom . . .? An entirely different matter.

She glanced at a little trail to her left, most likely used by gardeners as a shortcut. It would allow her to stay out of sight and view the couple without disturbing them. She hesitated, embarrassed at the thought of spying. But what harm could there be in a quick peek? The couple was temptingly close. She glanced around to be sure no one was watching.

The brown carpet of needles muffled her footsteps. The voices became more distinct until she could glimpse the forms of the young man and woman through the feathery branches of bamboo. They were sitting on a blanket back from the main path.

Careful to avoid a thorn tree, she squatted down and leaned back against a maple, ready to appear absorbed with the birds flitting in the overhead branches if the two turned toward her. But after watching the couple for a few minutes, she concluded there was little chance of their looking in her direction. The two lovers brazenly gazed at each other's faces.

The female tittered at something the male said. Then he leaned toward her.

His lips touched hers! Unheard-of behavior! Sumi's gasp escaped before she could swallow it.

The couple glanced her way, and she crooked her head back. Had they caught her gawking through the leaves? Heat rushed to her face. She withdrew her fan from her sash.

The girl murmured some sort of complaint.

Sumi raised her fan and peeked over it. The man helped the girl rise with one hand. They moved their blanket a little farther down the secluded trail.

She was about to stand and retreat to the main path when the sound of two male voices reached her.

The men stopped on the path just outside her view. "I believe there are two wayward youngsters secreting themselves behind those bushes." The man's speech identified him as high-status samurai—a warlord's retainer or relative.

"Peasants and artisans would be hard at work. Must be the offspring of merchants. They are an immodest nuisance. We can't have them stumbling around the teahouse," the other said, his voice low.

Sumi clapped her hand over her mouth to prevent another unwanted gasp. The second speaker sounded just like the Kurohashi grandson, Keiji-*sama*.

The men came into view. Sumi stared through the leaves, thunderstruck. She'd been right. The second man was the grandson. But the bigger shock was the first man, whose tunic's crest identified him as a member of her own Chōshū clan. A basket hood covered his head. Why? Why would a high-status samurai wear a hood, like a pilgrim or masterless warrior striving to be incognito?

She swung her gaze into the treetop again in case either one spotted her.

A shriek from the female made Sumi jerk. Birds squawked and took flight from the closest branches. After making sure the hooded warrior and Keiji had disappeared from sight, she stepped onto the main path, curious to see what had happened.

The smell of urine assaulted her nose. The couple looked at her and then back at their blanket the young man held in his hands. A dark patch showed on its edge.

Muttering curses, the man finished rolling the fouled blanket up, while the girl stood in the middle of the path, sniffling.

Sumi turned her head away, embarrassed. Even though Keiji-*sama* was repulsive, he couldn't be that crass, so the unknown clan member must have been the vulgar one. Men released their water routinely in public, but not deliberately next to someone.

Taking no further notice of Sumi, the couple hurried off in the opposite direction from the offending men.

She stood still, her thoughts racing. Most likely, the ill-mannered warrior was the same Chōshū samurai who had disturbed the tearoom patrons and Merchant Omura as well. Why had he decided on a disguise? And what had brought him to her neighborhood in the first place? Most puzzling of all was the sight of Keiji-*sama*, a staid Confucian scholar, associating with him.

She should heed her mother's admonition to *avoid hazardous bridges*, a warning applied to whatever her mother feared, from blind beggars to the matrons' tentacles of the pleasure houses. If the two men noticed her, not only would she have to chat with the detestable grandson, but also face the stranger, who appeared more untrustworthy than even the wobbliest bridge.

However, the men's reason for meeting might become obvious at the teahouse, where the path ended. Perhaps they wished to strengthen a friendship and enjoy the calmness of the tea ceremony or discuss Keiji-*sama*'s Confucian studies without attracting onlookers. The hooded warrior would certainly benefit from a lesson on expected behavior.

But could their meeting be something nefarious? Her skin prickled. Since she might end up betrothed to Keiji-*sama*, it seemed wise to find out.

She continued down the path in the direction the men had taken. When she reached the teahouse, two pairs of *geta* clogs outside the entrance gave proof the men had already entered the building. The lack of an accompanying pair of sandals indicated the resident Buddhist monk had not yet joined them.

She tiptoed around the side of the small building to where only the paper sliding *shōji* covered the wall's opening. Not wanting to cast a shadow, she kept behind a wide wooden post.

"We have all sworn loyalty to the Shōgun, haven't we?" Keiji's high pitched voice indicated his discomfort.

"Yet the Divine Emperor has Heaven's mandate, does he not?" The hooded warrior's tone rang with condescension. "Any bumpkin knows the mandate lies at the core of Confucius' teaching."

Sumi tried to make sense of the warrior's words, which seemed to pit imperial authority against the shogunate.

"When the Divine Emperor does not approve," the hooded warrior continued, "loyalty toward the Shōgun must come second. Opening the door to the devilish barbarians—"

Footsteps crunched at the front of the teahouse. Sumi leapt away from the building and angled in the direction of the trees.

"Stop, *Ojō-sama*!" a voice called.

She covered her face with her fan, turned, and bowed toward the elderly monk. Then she walked quickly away.

"Wait, please!" the monk called again, his voice more urgent.

Not sure whether anyone was following her, she didn't

stop. Once back on the main path, she padded down it as fast as possible. The urine's acrid scent alerted her to the hidden shortcut. She dashed onto the tiny trail and ducked behind a boulder.

No footsteps sounded.

Her heart beat erratically. Had the hooded man tried to get Keiji-*sama* to come out against the shogunate? If so, the grandson had resisted speaking treason . . . at least, in what she'd heard. But the exchange must have been a philosophical discussion, a theoretical one. Who could imagine the Shōgun would ever act without the Divine Emperor's approval in real life?

How foolish to argue over imaginary situations when there were enough real-life puzzles.

One thing was certain, however. The hooded man despised foreigners and was rude. He was the last person she wanted to meet face to face. Anywhere. But especially not in the park. And Keiji-*sama* was a close second. They were badgers from the same hole. She would stay hidden until the men left. She hunched down lower behind the boulder and tucked in the edges of her kimono.

A few minutes later, the strange warrior strode by on the path. She held her breath until his footsteps faded. Now she had to wait for Keiji-*sama* to pass.

Time crawled by with no sign of him. Where was he? Could he have taken a different route out of the park?

She continued to crouch despite the cramping that attacked her calves. Finally, no longer able to endure the pain, she managed to push herself up. The pain lessened as she perched on the boulder and kneaded the sore areas.

Regaining the use of her legs, she cautiously followed the

path back toward the teahouse. She passed a housewife and her child, engrossed in studying a line of ants, and a gardener busily trimming a bush. Satisfying herself that Keiji had left by another way, she headed for the park's pond and its border of irises, where she would dispose of the worrisome pages.

Although it should make no difference, she checked for anyone who might observe her. A little boy and his elder were admiring turtles on the other side of the pond. At the far end, two women chatted on the small arched bridge. No one was close by, perhaps because most of the irises had stopped blooming.

Near the water's edge, she leaned over to smell one of the few purple flowers still raising their velvety heads. Its gorgeous color and sweet scent brought tears to her eyes. If only such beauty weren't temporary, teasing admirers with its short life.

Maybe the foreign god had an answer for this brevity. She pulled out the small box and slid it open. Holding the papers, she ran her fingers over the mostly incomprehensible words. But scanning a random page seeking a particular insight was a ridiculous idea. Had these few pages bewitched her?

After tucking the papers back into the box, she found a small, thin stone and added it to keep the box solidly on the ground when it rained, hidden among the flowers. After the box crumbled in the dampness and the papers disintegrated, the stone could act as a remembrance years later—just in case the foreign god had any power in her country and cared.

"What are you doing, *O*-sumi-*san*?" Keiji gave a half-bow and reached toward the box.

Sumi jerked it out of his reach and tossed it.

"Oh, you startled me! Look what I did." She pointed to the ripples where the little box had sunk in the water, two arm-lengths away.

"You meant to throw it into the pond. I saw you place a rock inside."

"I did plan to dispose of the old box eventually." *He doesn't know anything. Stay calm.* "I don't blame you for startling me. I was inattentive. Now please excuse me. It grows late." She bowed.

He returned a shallow bow, his eyes narrowing into slits. "I am surprised at you, the daughter of a samurai. Don't you feel shame at littering this pond? What—"

"Please pardon my interruption. I believe I felt a few drops, didn't you?" She drew out a tissue and patted her forehead. "I do not want to delay you with a shower coming." She bowed again and turned away, perspiring in spite of the cloudy coolness.

After a few more steps, she turned and made the obligatory third bow.

Keiji still stood by the pond, frowning. He didn't return her bow.

She walked on and resisted looking back. If he rescued her box and the papers were still legible, her life as she knew it would be over. But surely he wouldn't want to wade into the pond and dig into the mud, not only getting wet and dirty, but exposing himself to ridicule if others noticed him.

Exiting the park, she turned toward home, berating herself. She'd been a fool. She should have disposed of the papers while both men were inside the teahouse. But what was done was done. She walked past two shops displaying wooden clogs and paused under the awning of the third one to catch her breath. Attractive images had been painted on the inside of the clogs' soles. Her gaze settled on a pair with an iris design.

She closed her eyes against the memory of the pond. The

encounter had tarnished the beauty of the irises—maybe forever.

Someone stopped behind her, and she moved on.

A person's pulsating shadow, blurred by the people and animals crowding the street, kept pace with her. She walked faster, and the shadow sped up. She swerved to the right around a tattered beggar and then to the left around two housewives examining a straw broom. The person fell in behind her again. Keiji-*sama*? The basket-hooded warrior?

The next second, she clearly saw the hood's shadow, and then the rude samurai appeared next to her. He spit, splotching her sock and sandal.

She jerked her foot aside and swallowed a shriek.

The samurai swung around on his heel and headed in the direction he'd come from.

She watched him saunter down the road, acting like nothing had happened, until she lost sight of him behind a gang of laborers. Sucking in agitated breaths, she fisted her hands.

Foreigners cannot be half as barbaric.

A shiver rippled through her. The uncouth man had identified her as the eavesdropper. The villain must have heard the monk call and caught a glimpse of her kimono. How reckless she'd been. Crossing hazardous bridges didn't come close to describing her foolishness.

Standing at her bedroom's high open window that evening, Sumi watched the shadows in the garden shift in the moonlight. A nightingale's trill came from somewhere in the neighborhood. This time of night should enchant her, but instead it taunted her.

If only she could concentrate on the pleasant things in life and forget the day's events and her looming betrothal. The strange samurai's insult shouldn't disturb her. No one would dare conspire against the Shōgun's decree to open their city. He couldn't do any real harm to a family like hers, could he?

But what about Keiji-*sama*?

If he'd even noticed the pages in her hand, he probably suspected they were from her diary. And for him, women's opinions were worthless. He couldn't suspect the pages' real nature. It was his reprimand that galled her. He'd acted as though he already owned her. The encounter had been awful, and the worst part was she mostly brought it on herself.

She sank down on a nearby cushion. In addition to all that had happened, she was in her *mae-yaku,* the "pre-calamity" eighteenth year, for the sages warned that the age of nineteen threatened females. Were calamities already underway?

She could be safe in a household like the Kurohashis'. Her acceptance of such a life would especially please her grandfather and delight her mother. She wanted to please her family, to make them proud. But letting go of her dreams seemed impossible, like slicing off a leg or both arms. Why couldn't she sacrifice herself as a true samurai?

The moon cast its beautiful beams, impotent against the dark cloud that stalked her.

CHAPTER 20

After folding her umbrella, Sumi stood in the shadows of the bronzeware shop's vestibule clutching the coins she'd brought to pay for the extravagant mirror. She could hardly believe what she was overhearing. The merchant—their *good* neighbor—had lied to her about the mirror.

"I can supply you with eight of these," Omura said from the other side of the partly closed partition, apparently addressing a fellow merchant. "They sell well. You should have seen our neighbor's delight. Her face turned positively crimson."

Sumi clenched her hands tighter.

"How much for the eight?"

"I'll sacrifice for such a long-time friend. "Fifteen *momme* each."

*Fifteen momme? After I agreed to twenty-two? So Omura-*san *lied and cheated me.*

"Too much." The visiting merchant turned to go and met Sumi as she stepped into the shop. "Looks like you have a customer."

"All right. All right. You can have them for fourteen each." Omura finished wrapping paper around the purchase, which had to be the eight mirrors.

The two men completed the transaction. Then the buyer bowed to Sumi and triumphantly carried his bundle to the vestibule.

"Ah, *Ojō-sama,* welcome," Omura said smoothly, his smile ingratiating. "Despite the rainy weather, I knew you would grant me the kindness of paying on time."

"Yes, I value honesty. But from what I heard just now, it appears you had more mirrors than you said."

"Surely, my good neighbor has not eavesdropped on a confidential transaction."

"I didn't want to interrupt. I hope my politeness is not taken as eavesdropping."

"Yes, you describe an important distinction." He paused and gazed at her. "One would not want a reputation for habitually eavesdropping on private conversations."

A chill shivered up Sumi's spine. Had the rude warrior visited Omura and told him about her hearing part of his conversation? That didn't make any more sense than his spitting on her sandal. No one would care that much about eavesdropping. Servants did it all the time. Unless . . . unless the discussion she'd overheard did border on treason. Even advocate treason.

Biting back a retort about the need to shun dubious characters, she held out fourteen of the *momme* she carried. "I wonder if the price can be lower now that you discovered more mirrors in your possession."

"My, my. You are a good bargainer. I rarely meet a member of a samurai family interested in practical matters of money . . . so unabashedly." He bowed.

"I'm interested more in good faith than in money."

"But you see, your mirror was the only one of its particular type."

"Maybe I'd like a second glass mirror. May I see one of those?" She pointed around the merchant to the stack of mirrors still sitting on the shelf behind him.

Omura glanced over his shoulder at the shelf and blinked. "Only an expert can see *your* mirror's superior quality. But to keep our good relationship, I'll take seventeen *momme*, a considerable discount, even though I expected the agreed-upon payment."

Sumi fished out three more coins and set them with the others on the low stand next to her. Were all merchants so greedy?

He scraped up the coins with a huff. "May this humble merchant give you a word of caution?"

"Certainly. I wish to hear all words of wisdom." She gave a half bow while thinking the advice of a liar and a cheat would have no more value than the bronze fox with nine tails he'd tried to sell her.

"But first, please take a seat and let me pour you some tea to improve this damp day." He gestured to the nearest cushion on the platform's *tatami* mat.

She knelt without replying, reluctant to spend a longer time at the shop.

He poured the tea and waited for her to take a sip.

After accepting the expected compliment on its flavor, he stroked his chin and sighed. "I recognize your interest in the world outside our blessed country. I share a like interest, albeit for different reasons. However, these are perilous times." He narrowed his eyes. "*Perilous*. I cannot say it strongly enough. Dangerous even to keep mundane papers of instructions for the care of a mirror."

She struggled to appear nonchalant while her body tensed. "They seemed insignificant. But I agree. One cannot be too careful."

"After you left the other day, I found one more such page. That was when I woke up to my duty."

Sumi strangled a gasp. Was her world crumbling before her eyes?

"I destroyed it immediately," he said.

Sumi managed a nod as her breathing started again. "I . . . I disposed of the papers also. Since I know only a little English, the pages you kindly gave me were not useful after all." Surely he recognized his equal responsibility for not having reported the pages to the customs officials.

"Wise indeed. Now there is a little more advice I'd like to offer. I am only a merchant these days, but I have lived long enough to have many experiences."

"Please. What is it you wish to say?"

"Even when a young lady's heart tells her to explore new customs and ideas"—his eye twitched—"she would do well to listen to her elders and marry into a fine, traditional family. Doing so will not only please her ancestral spirits but also result in a much safer life. A long and peaceful life."

How dare the lowly merchant try to advise her about marriage? She was tempted to leave right then, but stopped herself. The formerly good-natured merchant had changed since the rude samurai's visits had reportedly increased in frequency. The question was why.

She pasted on a smile. "We all desire a peaceful life. I have been concerned about safety for this neighborhood since I observed an unruly samurai yesterday. Perhaps you heard about the stranger." She couldn't mention what the maid had said about the visits.

Omura half shrugged. "I heard, although servants tend to exaggerate." He strung her coins onto a string and slipped it into a pouch.

"But I see you are still selling foreign goods in these *perilous* times."

"You should not worry about me, an insignificant merchant, or about what I sell. But if a lady, like you, comes between the foreigners and a strong-minded samurai, such as the one you observed, she could face great difficulty. It's as if she came between a dog and a monkey. The monkey escapes, but the interloper gets bitten."

A tightness formed in her chest. The merchant shouldn't expect her to cower because someone behaved like a dog. "Couldn't the interloper wield a stick? Make the dog retreat?"

"I will answer with a question. Why get in the middle? Why care so greatly about the foreigners when you have no goods to sell?"

For her, the real question was just the opposite. Why wasn't the whole country eager to explore every facet of the foreigners' thinking, learn all their discoveries about the stars and the oceans and medicine and the spirit world? However, since her passion baffled everyone except her father, she could hardly expect a merchant obsessed with money to understand.

"It's hard to explain . . ." She glanced around and noticed the washbasin she'd seen the previous time. "But that basin might help if you truly want to know."

"Of course. Of course." He carried the basin over and set it on the stand before her. "A handsome piece. Moderately priced."

She picked it up and turned it so the dragonflies etched

around its sides appeared to take flight. "I admire the design. But notice how the dragonflies fly in circles, not darting to flowers and fountains and even to distant hills. And the basin itself speaks of frustration, like in Issa's *haiku*."

Omura frowned. "Your familiarity with *haiku* surpasses mine."

"He wrote an unusual poem."

From the first basin
To the final washbasin
Reflecting riddles

"Everything a muddle." She swallowed hard and set down the basin. "What a sad way to come to the end of a day, or to the end of this life. Yet I find riddles everywhere. Riddles about words. About people. About the sun and moon. About the afterlife. Riddles. Riddles. Riddles. Answers might be discovered if we could explore beyond what we know now, what we assume is true." *I might as well shock him.* "I even want to find out how evil the foreign religion actually is."

The merchant's face paled. "Remember what happened to your friend's neighbor. Our country's officials constantly guard against the seeds of rebellion."

"The foreigners and the secret *Kirishitan*s haven't brought about any harm since their downfall centuries ago, have they?" She didn't wait for an answer. "And now the Shōgun has permitted a treaty for trade with countries full of *Kirishitan*s. Is the religion an evil sect because our countrymen have always said so, or is it really diabolical?"

Omura glanced around. "If you value your life, *never* repeat those words. Chief Inspector Sato is not the only one who would find such ideas treasonous. There are others, too, that no brandished stick would make retreat. In fact, striking at one dog would bring a pack of snarling beasts." He walked to the entrance and bowed. "I thank you for your business." His voice was sharp, cutting.

Not trusting herself to reply, Sumi nodded, retrieved her umbrella, and left the shop.

The spitting rain spread a gray haze over the neighborhood as she turned toward home. Her previous bravado shriveled in the gloom. She never should have revealed her private thoughts to the deceitful merchant.

She stepped around a puddle, feeling the start of one of her rare headaches. Eager for a hot, cleansing bath, she picked up her pace. At the sector gate, she tilted her umbrella and acknowledged a guard.

Then she stopped, unable to move another step. Paralyzed.

Chief Inspector Sato, standing next to his horse, had turned from talking to the other guard and was staring at her, rain dripping from his flat hat and down his straw raincoat. His mouth formed a stern line.

She forced herself to bow.

He returned a nod resembling a slight bow before mounting his horse. He shot another piercing look at her, then flicked his crop and rode off.

She shuddered at the enormity of his glare. He'd been examining her. Had he been searching for a sign of guilt? Of fear? Could he sense those emotions like a dog sniffed out a weasel? If so, he couldn't have missed her sudden dread at seeing him.

She managed a few steps before stopping with the horrible realization that if Sato had been examining her, it had to have been because of the illegal pages. If Keiji-*sama* had actually retrieved the box, he could have given the papers to an official for investigation, and the chief inspector would have received the result. Maybe Omura warned her because Chief Inspector Sato or another official had asked about the pages. That might explain the merchant's sudden concern for her intimate affairs.

She closed her eyes, struggling to push the arrest of Taki's neighbor from her mind. The notion of three rough policemen forcing *her* into the prison cage made her want to cry out like Itō's wife. She imagined standing in front of a high official, confronted by the chief inspector holding up the incriminating papers.

You, Taguchi Sumi, claimed these pages were instructions for cleaning a mirror. But look, an interpreter of the first rank reports that these bear the words, Holy Bible, *and not one word about a mirror.* Then he was pointing at her, his face like a temple gargoyle. *You lied! LIED to keep the forbidden pages. Why?*

Dizzy, she stumbled to the side of the road and leaned against her own home's front wall, unable to continue to the entrance gate.

How could she answer the charge? *I . . . I wanted to understand the people coming in just two weeks. Just two weeks. Two weeks*. Her heart beat wildly.

With the chief inspector accusing her, how could a judge not find her guilty? *This woman questioned my arrest of a* Kirishitan. *She told the merchant Omura she could decide if the foreign religion was evil, disdaining the judgment by our august rulers. And now, we find she concealed pages from the Evil Religion's forbidden book itself.*

Guilty . . . Guilty . . . Guilty! The ship waiting to take her and her distressed family to the northern wilderness filled her vision. Her poor family, ruined by her stupidity! If only she could take back her decision to ask Omura for the papers. If she could go back in time, she would raise her hands in revulsion when he made the discovery and flee out of the shop.

A wolf-like dog, soaked by the drizzle, slunk past her. She watched it turn its head from side to side, searching for refuge. It marked the sector's gate in an attempt to claim its own territory before a guard booted the yelping stray away. Would she and her family be hunting for refuge too, kicked at like dogs, despised?

A friend of her mother's came briskly toward her.

Sumi straightened. She had to get control of herself. She shouldn't look guilty before actually being charged.

"Sumi-*san,* nice to see you." The lady peered at her face, then gave a shallow bow. "But you must get out of this weather. You have a warm, dry house waiting for you. I would not be out here myself, heading for the herbalist, if two maids and our cook were not all ill."

Sumi returned the bow, imagining what a bedraggled appearance she gave while standing in the rain like a fool. "Thank . . . thank you for your good advice. I felt a little dizzy, but I am all right now. Just a few more steps to my gate."

"Then I will not detain you." The lady bowed and hurried away.

Despite the loose cobblestones conspiring to trip her and the water sloshing under her sandals, she forced her wobbly legs to take the remaining steps home. She grasped a side post while waiting for the gatekeeper to answer her call.

A man with an umbrella hiding his face exited as she stepped forward. He lifted his umbrella and bowed.

Matchmaker Kato! Sumi ordered her body to continue functioning. She managed to return the bow.

"Sumi Ojō-*sama.* I look forward to finalizing a fine match for you tomorrow. It was challenging to find someone from a line comparable to that of the Hino family—such a regrettable outcome—but I am pleased with this new prospect."

"May I ask, who—" Her voice wobbled.

"Ah. I am not at liberty to say. You will be given that information tomorrow, but I know you will be pleased with the man's fine scholarly accomplishment. It should restore the cheerful countenance this bad weather has stolen."

Sumi returned the *nakōdo*'s final bow, certain she had an even worse countenance than the one a minute earlier.

Keiji-*sama*! Who else could it be? What other unattached, young man was so well-known as a scholar? She rubbed her forehead, trying to ease the pain.

The rain had become harder. The drops that blew under her umbrella mixed with her tears—tears no worthy samurai's daughter had permission to shed. She collapsed on the veranda, not daring to meet her elders.

"It's a shame women can't perform in the theater dramas." Kiyo looked down at her while she opened her own umbrella. "You are always convincingly pathetic. I take it you are weeping about your betrothal?"

"Yes," Sumi mumbled. If Kiyo knew the whole reason, she would dance with glee until she grasped the possibility the family name would be sullied, everyone banished, and the house confiscated.

"Your betrothal will not be to a fiend. Not even to a samurai who works with sandalwood." Kiyo raised her chin. "I find it impossible to sympathize." She adjusted her umbrella and promenaded toward the front gate.

You wouldn't be sympathetic if my betrothal were to a demon guard from the frozen caverns of the Naraka hell. She wiped her cheeks, aware that irritation had dried up her tears.

She rose and fixed her mind on the steaming bath waiting for her. She had to do better. The illicit pages almost certainly were awash in the water seeping into the box at the bottom of the pond. The chief inspector could have been recalling how her grandfather had compared her to a foolish monkey. Maybe he was checking for a tail. She rolled her eyes at her own mockery.

However, her betrothal wasn't imaginary. It was bearing down on her like a juggernaut. There wasn't any time left to cast a boulder into its wheels. Unless something like a miracle occurred, she was out of options—if there had ever been any.

CHAPTER 21

Sumi pushed herself off the futon and shoved back the shutters. She half expected nature to match her distress, but the sun's mocking rays brightened the neighbors' gray tile roofs. Far down the street, the voice of the soybean vendor rang out, *Nattō, nattōō.*

"What's the matter with you now?" Kiyo grumbled, still half-asleep.

"I'm sorry if I woke you. It's difficult to face today."

Kiyo pushed aside her wooden pillow and rose up on one elbow. "You are impossible. Whoever your grandfather has chosen for you, it is with the gods' blessings."

"The gods first matched me with a man who is dead now. If the gods truly spoke, they didn't know the future well. How could Makoto-*sama* have been the right one?"

Kiyo sat up all the way. "Must you question everything? The matchmaking Idzumo gods are not responsible for people's deaths . . . or even for their fickleness. You have absolutely no reason to complain. Besides, if your betrothed is the Kurohashi grandson, you will marry a scholar. Other people respect him, no matter how *you* malign him."

"Then I wish those other people would marry him. I do! Why should matches, especially *if* the gods determine them, have to depend entirely on family name and a dowry?" Sumi fought against a lump in her throat. Couldn't her cousin show the tiniest bit of understanding?

"Then in your lofty opinion, what should marriage depend on?"

"Suitability. Maybe even friendliness or . . . love, and that's not just my opinion. Father says Westerners often choose marriage partners because they are *in love*."

"Love?" Kiyo huffed. "Love is just a man's desire for a woman's body. I am sick of hearing your outrageous ideas. You will learn to accept your situation. You will have to."

Sumi's protest died on her lips. What good would arguing do?

She dressed and straightened her side of the room in the uncomfortable silence between them, then followed Kiyo down the stairs, expecting an equally awkward breakfast.

To her relief, Kiyo asked their elders to excuse her from eating. However, she made a show of burning a stick of incense in front of the *Butsudan* before taking her leave to view a flower arrangement exhibition.

Sumi's mother refilled the teapot and turned to Sumi. "Kiyo-*san*'s attention to the gods and the traditional arts is admirable, is it not?"

"Yes." Sumi forced herself to sound agreeable. "Especially since the gods' benevolence is greatly desired today." She glanced at her father, whose face showed no trace of sympathy. She decided to delay her own worship. The gods might take offense if they sensed her cynicism. And they would be infuriated if they guessed her interest in a foreign god who was mysteriously identified with *love*.

She pushed away the thought of the foreign god and Sato. She would not allow her imagination to overpower her good sense on this day of all days.

The matchmaker arrived, and Sumi returned upstairs to await the outcome of his conference with her grandfather, parents, and her mother's brother and his wife. Thankfully, the Kurohashi family hadn't made their appearance. Not yet, anyway.

After Kin helped her put on the special kimono and thick facial powder, the minutes dragged by. Sumi glanced down at the sundial in the garden. The contract should have been quickly signed since the betrothal had been hammered out during the previous months. Was there a chance her betrothal wasn't to Keiji-*sama*? Her heart said yes, but her mind said there was no chance whatsoever.

To pass the time, she dampened the ink stone and prepared paper and brush to write her thoughts. Arguing with her elders was out of the question, so it was no use marshalling her objections to Keiji. But how about a short poem? She could write a *haiku* to *commemorate* the occasion if Keiji-*sama* was indeed the one being proposed. And the suitable subject of her poem resided right outside her room.

Dipping her brush into the ink, she wrote in broad strokes on the long sheet of rice paper. The words flowed from her brush:

> Menacing falcon
> Overtakes the small sparrow
> Claws sealing its fate

Reading over her poem, she grimaced at its stark message. But if she minced words, her elders wouldn't understand the extent of her misery. Then she studied the overall effect of the three vertical lines, imagining the paper under her grandfather's artistic eye. He would fault the stiffness of the *kanji* and her failure to make full use of the grayer shades of ink, but she probably couldn't do any better if she rewrote the poem a hundred times. She blew on the paper to make the ink dry faster, wishing she could infuse the poem with an enchantment.

"Miss, my masters desire to meet with you." Kin waited for Sumi to roll up her paper and precede her down the stairs.

The cat, which had given up its interest in the fluttering sparrow, started to follow. Sumi blocked it with her foot, motioned for the maid to pass by, and slid the panel to her room shut. She started to bow toward the door as though apologizing to the cat, but caught herself.

Her grandfather met her at the main room's door with a frown. "The *nakōdo* left without finalizing your betrothal. Some further difficulty has arisen. Although the Kurohashi elders and our family are agreed on the betrothal's terms, the three Kurohashi men have asked to meet with our family this afternoon. You are to be present."

A moan escaped before Sumi could stop it. So her betrothed would be Keiji-*sama*.

Her grandfather's frown deepened. "Do you know what this difficulty is? It seems to be a problem troubling the grandson."

Sumi tried to gather her wits. She shouldn't think about the forbidden pages. The difficulty could very well involve her abruptness at the pond or her *stiff spine*, to use Kiyo's words. "No. I am sorry. I do not know." She kept her eyes cast downward. "The scholar's thinking is very different from my common ideas." She bowed low, feeling the stiff kimono crinkle.

"Common?" Sharp irritation laced the word. "Your ideas could hardly be called *common.* But different? Yes, unfortunately."

He stood stock still in front of her for what seemed like five lifetimes.

She itched to bring out her poem. *Show him. Now.* Her fingers tensed, but her hand wouldn't move. Then he turned toward his room, her best chance disappearing with him.

After beckoning for her to join him and her mother at the low teakwood table, her father lit his pipe and puffed out a ring of smoke. He studied her as she settled on her cushion. "You look elegant in your ceremonial kimono although your face's natural color is better than the powder that conceals it."

Sumi wasn't sure she should thank her father for his observation, so she merely bowed.

"At least her attire and make-up are proper." Her mother rose. "I must delay the plans we had for a celebratory lunch. Even though my brother and his wife say there is no need for them to return, I assume we will be entertaining the Kurohashi men this evening if all goes well." Her stiff posture gave a warning to Sumi as her mother caught her eye. "Our whole family readily agreed on the betrothal's stipulations."

"Thank you for your effort on my behalf." Sumi cast a gloomy look at her.

When they were alone, Sumi pulled her *haiku* from her kimono sleeve to show her father even though her betrothal was in her grandfather's hands, not his.

"You are greatly exaggerating the situation," he said

between puffs on his pipe. "Neither Keiji-*san* nor you resemble a falcon or sparrow in the least. Be more sensible."

She felt the trickle of a tear and bowed her head.

"The daughter of a samurai," he continued in a softer voice, "must not yield to weak, childish emotion. If Keiji-*san* is indeed a falcon, then his betrothed must become a falcon too."

She bowed her assent.

Become a falcon. The words made sense in a way she knew he didn't intend. *But how?*

Sumi waited for the afternoon's resumption of talks between the two families in an area adjoining her home's main room. Would the preliminary cordialities never end? Facing the Kurohashi family would be torture, but so was kneeling apart, waiting and waiting. What could the *difficulty* be? If she knew, she might be a better falcon.

The closed partitions did little to block the sounds. Even more tempting, the crack between the sliding panels offered the possibility of a narrow view of the proceedings. Taking a big breath, she inched across the *tatami* mats right up to the thin barrier. She peered through the crack, thankful for the daylight pouring into the other room from the open shōji and the dim light cloaking hers.

Across the room, her grandfather and father puffed on their pipes. The eldest Kurohashi, seated in front of the alcove, was speaking with the *nakōdo* between his own puffs. Keiji and his father, their backs to her, were squatting in front of the door panels, apparently waiting for the others to assume their more formal positions.

Keiji coughed, then leaned toward his father. “When I think of the girl, despite her faults, I can’t help thinking about the story of the ancient tea master, Rikyu, and his prized flower.”

“What’s that?” His father’s voice rasped. “Are you comparing her to the tea master’s chrysanthemum?”

“Yes, in a way. She strikes me as the exquisite specimen Rikyu wanted to display for the Shōgun.”

Sumi blinked. *Maybe he’s a little better than I thought.*

“Is this related to one of your recent lessons from the teachings of Master Zhuang? Natural spontaneity?”

“No, nothing so erudite. I am merely saying I admire her appearance like the Shōgun admired the tea master’s blossom. The lovely oval shape of her face, her willowy figure. Of course, I will have to put her in her rightful place. She has a defiant streak. I would not want a thorny weed replacing my flower.”

It just did.

His father chuckled. “She will take, I expect, some thorough pruning. Since she has no siblings, her parents may have doted on her.”

“I have seen how opinionated she is. And while pruning, I *will* cut out the wayward fascination she exhibits toward the barbarians.”

Sumi’s chest constricted. What type of pruning did he intend? Scolding? Ostracism? Disagreeable tasks? And how did he know about her interest in the foreigners?

The grandson drew crinkled papers partway out of his tunic.

He had the papers! Stomach acid nearly gagged her.

“This will get everyone’s attention.” Keiji tapped the pages. “She will be crawling to her elders, to our family, and to *me*, begging for forgiveness." He smiled at his father. "The pruning will have begun."

He can't know what they say. He can't! He wouldn't still plan to marry me if he did. Feeling faint, she moved back quickly from the door. Her mind whirled, searching for the best response.

Only her father would know what the papers really were, and only if he looked at them. She could claim she'd thought they were insignificant instructions, like she'd told the merchant. But then she would have to beg her family, the Kurohashi elders, and Keiji-*sama* for forgiveness for not having reported the unauthorized papers to the authorities. And what if the Kurohashi family turned them in to the customs officials on her behalf? The terrible truth would come out.

Maybe she could say they had come from her father's work. But she didn't dare without consulting him. And if the papers were ever checked, he would be blamed for her crime.

If only she could talk with her father, they might make a plan. But it was too late.

Her mother bustled into the room. "It's time," she whispered.

CHAPTER 22

Sumi stood, smootHED her stiff, yellow kimono, and took a step. When she didn't fall, she took another, then followed her mother into the main room. *I'm an object to be appraised, like a merchant does a box of tea leaves. But worse, an opponent to be humiliated.*

Keeping her eyes lowered, she bowed to the visitors and took her place on a gold cushion in the corner of the room.

Her mother was watching her, concern written in the deep lines in her face.

Her grandfather rose to his feet, and Sumi stiffened. The confrontation was seconds away. She thought about how the Lady Nii had jumped into the sea with the child emperor to protect his honor. Other women had been heroic in the past too, fighting to defend castles, giving their lives to save their clan. She was the daughter of a samurai. She had to be a falcon.

Her grandfather's face was a mask as usual. "My family is ready to respond to the perceived difficulty. We wait for an explanation from Keiji-*sama*."

Everyone looked at the grandson.

The air around Sumi threatened to suffocate her.

He stood up and stuck out his chest as if taking on a lion. Turning toward Sumi, he gave a bow so shallow it could scarcely be called a bow. "An acquaintance of mine advised me to rescue your little box from the bottom of the park's pond. He surmised you had used it for items of value to you." He drew the box from his tunic and set it on the teakwood table. Splotches of dark brown stained the wood. "This is yours, is it not?"

The eldest Kurohashi cupped his hand behind his ear to hear her answer. Keiji's father and the matchmaker exchanged whispers. Her parents had both leaned forward.

Sumi offered what she hoped was a sweet smile while her heart hammered as if it would break through her skin. "How thoughtful of you to rescue it." *Be a falcon.* "Please also express my gratitude to your acquaintance. Was he . . . that unusual man you met at the park's teahouse?"

Keiji opened his mouth, then paused.

Did he appreciate that she hadn't mentioned the basket hood covering the man's face? That the rude stranger's words appeared to urge disloyalty to the Shōgun? Sumi steadied herself, daring to hope Keiji would return the favor.

His face flushed. "You mistook me for someone else. I met no one at the teahouse."

"I regret my foolish error." She bowed her head to the mat, wondering how he excused his lie.

The cat's faint mew from upstairs was the only sound in the room. When she raised her head, the eldest Kurohashi and her grandfather were both gazing at Keiji with puzzled frowns.

"I swear! I met no one, just my acquaintance when I exited the park." He raised his chin. "I have also brought the contents of the box." Looking at Sumi, he pulled out the stone and the crumpled papers. "I suppose the stone served only as a weight. But perhaps you could explain the value of these *foreign* papers. Their contents? Their source?"

Sumi froze. How could she act as a falcon? If she brazenly defended her initial interest in the foreign words, the Kurohashi family might reject the betrothal, yet the danger would be immense. The Kurohashis were the type of people who would hand the papers over to the authorities—out of spite.

If only she could disappear through a hole in the floor or fly out the open *shōji*.

Keiji tapped his foot. "O-sumi-*san*, perhaps you are considering a *haiku* to share with us, but I would like to hear your explanation first about *illegally* possessing the barbarians' material."

My father has foreign papers, cleared by the authorities. How does he know mine were illegal? Merchant Omura?

"Please excuse me. You asked about their contents," she managed to utter. "I cannot tell you. Their message was in English."

Like the sudden gust that precedes a storm, Sumi's grandfather rose and grasped the papers out of the grandson's hand. "I will dispose of these properly."

Keiji gasped along with everyone else. "Excuse me. I want—"

The eldest Kurohashi, having risen on his knees, shot out his hand. "I ask for the papers' return."

Her grandfather bowed to the Eldest. "I am certain an excellent man like you agrees the work of the abominable barbarians is unworthy of consideration." Leaving the Eldest with his mouth open, he took three strides over to the brazier and slapped the three papers onto the coals.

Sumi drew in a breath. In a daze, she watched a flame flare and curl the pages into ashes. For a second, she questioned if the *Holy Bible*'s god would overlook such disrespect, but realized her country's officials—even her father—had destroyed many such pages, and they hadn't been struck dead.

She groaned to herself. It would have been helpful if she'd thought of that before she'd gone to such lengths to dispose of her pages. But no matter what else occurred, the foreign god couldn't be angry with her. And the evidence could no longer be shown to the chief inspector. Her family would not be banished to the coalmines.

Her grandfather turned his back to the brazier. "I assume the pages were discards from my son's translation work." He turned toward Sumi's father, who gave a noncommittal bow. "Obviously, the barbarians' words held no value for my granddaughter, who could not read them." He pinned Keiji with his gaze. "Since you are not a member of the interpreters' guild, I assume the barbarians' words held no value for you as well. Am I not correct?"

"They held no value for *me,* but—"

"Then let us proceed unless there is another difficulty." Her grandfather lowered himself onto his cushion.

Distress replaced Sumi's shock. Her grandfather had smoothed the way for the betrothal.

Keiji knelt back on his heels and arched his eyebrows at his elders.

"There is a related problem," the eldest Kurohashi said, his tone sharp. "I also am disturbed by the fascination with the barbarians that your granddaughter is *rumored* to entertain, and as her behavior at the park may confirm." He bowed to her grandfather. "Do we have a guarantee the young lady will follow in your noble footsteps? That she will conform to *our* household's standards of loyalty and obedience? That she will not shame us by associating with the barbarians when they pollute our city?"

"There is no difficulty in what you ask," Sumi's grandfather said.

My life is ending, Sumi thought, forcing herself to remain composed.

"Excuse me." Keiji rose and bowed to his grandfather and hers. "Would you permit us to hear the assent from O-sumi-*san* herself?"

As soon as her grandfather nodded, the eldest Kurohashi also gave his consent. Keiji settled back down on his cushion, then folded his arms, obviously expecting her meek, apologetic answer.

Amazingly, a door had opened—one last chance. She gathered her courage. "I wish to comply with all that you request. But would you ask me to forsake my father?"

Her mother moaned.

Keiji snickered, then half-bowed an apology. "I laughed only because a Dutch Scholar"—he gave a half-bow toward Sumi's father—"rarely has to dirty his hands by dealing directly with a foreigner. Certainly not with the new *Amerikans*."

They don't know about the appointment! Sumi dared a look at her father, whose eyes were glued on her. *But I'm bound to secrecy. And if I reveal it now, my father will appear deceitful.*

She straightened her shoulders, then bowed her acknowledgment, a rush of blood making her ears ring. "I will strive to please my future husband . . ." Her voice sounded weak, so she forced herself to speak louder. "I will conform to his esteemed household's standards." Although the black cloud she had fought against for months enveloped her, she blinked back threatening tears. She might not measure up to a falcon, but she wouldn't be a weak sparrow either.

Keiji's lips curled. "We did not hear the full guarantee." He darted his eyes at his elders, who nodded. "About the barbarians?"

She drew in a sharp breath, as a thought came—a way to be a falcon after all. "May this simple female also ask a question or two of her future betrothed? I wish to emulate his honored mother in submitting to his esteemed wisdom, and I am puzzled about this last issue."

"Are these questions necessary?" The eldest Kurohashi's tone came close to a sneer. "What can be confusing about not associating with barbarians?"

Sumi's father gave a bow. "I believe she would not ask, otherwise."

"I do not mind the questions. I am curious to hear her female thinking." Keiji glanced at his father and grandfather, who grimaced.

Sumi bowed to Keiji. "Although I mistook the person speaking with the hooded samurai at the teahouse, I overheard the stranger make a puzzling statement, one I cannot solve with my limited knowledge."

Every face frowned at her, but the eldest Kurohashi nodded for her to continue.

"The samurai indicated the Divine Emperor's disapproval of the foreigners should affect a person's loyalty to the Shōgun." She heard one of the elders draw air through his teeth in a hiss. "If the Divine Emperor truly disapproves, should our families refuse to fall in line with an order by the Shōgun to welcome the Westerners into our city?"

"You dare ask a trick question?" If the daggers in Keiji-*sama*'s eyes were real, Sumi would find out what happened to people in the afterlife.

"I also would like to know your answer to the question," Sumi's father inserted, "since a stranger spoke suspicious words in our daughter's hearing."

"Only because she eavesdropped." Keiji half rose in his outrage.

Gasps came from the Kurohashi elders.

Keiji's face turned crimson, as red as a snow monkey's. "I mean, surely such a discussion would not knowingly take place in front of a female."

Her father raised an eyebrow. "May we be privileged to hear your wise answer?"

Sumi's pulse increased, anticipating Keiji-*sama*'s response and her final chance to escape the talons.

"Subjects of the Divine Emperor," Keiji said, fully standing, "must honor his divine will above that of the Shōgun, his appointee. Confucius made that clear."

The eldest Kurohashi pursed his lips.

Keiji's father frowned.

Her father and grandfather's faces remained masks.

"This wise answer leads to my second question." Sumi spoke in her smallest, most humble voice. "If one's husband chooses to disobey the Shōgun, who is his overlord and has *not* been removed from power by the Divine Emperor, should his wife obey the *overlord*, or obey her husband's order?"

"This trick question is clearly unconscionable," the eldest Kurohashi muttered. "It smells of rebellion and a fancy for the barbarian. My son need not answer."

Everyone in the room glowered at Sumi except her father.

Sumi bowed her forehead to the mat, then faced toward Keiji. "Since my foolish question is unworthy of an answer, I must finish my pledge with what limited understanding I have." She raised her head higher. Samurai committed suicide for their masters, loyally cutting into their intestines. To yield to this man was a far smaller requirement. "I will not disobey by associating with foreigners."

Keiji slowly nodded and sat down on the cushion as if he were the supreme ruler.

Her father cleared his throat. "I wish to reveal a recent development, which will explain much of my daughter's unfortunate inquisitiveness and actions."

Her mother's eyes closed.

Sumi gripped the edges of her cushion. Surely he wouldn't reveal the secret of his appointment now. The family had to present the news at a later time, as though they themselves had just been informed.

Hard lines creased her father's face. "The Taguchi family line has a long history of *loyalty* to the shogunate. Based on the decision of the Shōgun, who has not been deposed, Governor Nakamura has *ordered* me to become the new American diplomat's interpreter, beginning with the Americans' arrival in two weeks."

Sumi could hardly suppress the impulse to bow at her father's feet. She had never imagined him a fierce falcon.

"What is the meaning of this?" The eldest Kurohashi shot out both arms and nearly choked on his spit. "Why are we just now learning of such . . . such a repugnant change in your position?"

The matchmaker's jaw dropped.

"This is unbelievable!" Keiji's father clamped his teeth

together as though restraining a torrent of words. "Hiding this development until this last minute is reprehensible."

Her grandfather cleared his throat and rose. All the room's occupants swiveled their focus to him. His eyes flicked in Sumi's direction, narrowing in disapproval.

Her stomach twisted. Hadn't she bowed to his will in the end? Made the ultimate sacrifice? Her father was the one who had made the scandalous announcement.

He faced the Kurohashi men. "I deeply apologize for this late revelation." He bowed low. "During my four-month pilgrimage, I earnestly petitioned the gods to stop the barbarians. But they have not yet seen fit to intervene. Therefore, my son has no choice but to obey the will of the Shōgun and Governor Nakamura. B*ushido* demands his adherence." He bowed again before kneeling back on his heels.

The eldest Kurohashi stood, arms crossed, eyes sparking. He faced her father, who also rose, hands clasped in front of him like a priest.

"In your close work with barbarians, Kenshin-*dono,* you risk contamination." The old man's voice shook with anger. "Before finalizing any plans for a future union, we will require evidence the foreigners have not tainted all of this family irrevocably."

Keiji-*sama*'s glare scorched Sumi before she could duck behind her fan.

Her father bowed. "These are turbulent times. We understand your thinking and accept your unavoidable decision to withdraw from the negotiations."

Withdraw! Her father had said *withdraw*! Elation bubbled up from deep within, expanding so fast, she felt she would burst. She was free! Free of Keiji-*sama*! The nightmare finished.

Sumi fanned herself. Now was not the time to faint.

The concluding formalities were brief. With correct politeness, her grandfather invited the guests to stay for the special evening meal, scheduled to replace the original one.

The eldest Kurohashi tersely stated their regrets. He motioned to the matchmaker to carry out the betrothal gifts they had brought, and the men marched out.

"We will discuss this later," Sumi's grandfather muttered. His sharp look could have penetrated a stone wall.

Sumi bowed and headed up the stairs, wanting to dance and leap for joy despite the looming strong rebuke.

Kiyo looked up from arranging her hair when Sumi entered the room. "Are you not betrothed?" She gave a sly smile and wet her lips—a hunter closing in on her prey. "I saw our guests leave in what could be described as high indignation. Were they privileged to hear some of your unusual ideas?"

"The Eldest has promised to discuss the outcome this evening. I'm sure you will have your curiosity satisfied soon enough." *And be given a quiver full of barbed arrows.*

"Dinner will be interesting." Kiyo put a final comb in her hair. Then she shooed the cat away from her dresser.

The cat stalked over to Sumi, who picked it up and rubbed under its chin. Here at least was one creature in the house not disgusted with her. "Let's see how your prey is doing," she whispered while walking over to where she could see the sparrow's nest.

The sun was dipping behind the trees. The sparrow, still in its nest, turned its head so that its left eye focused on her. Apparently not frightened by the cat in her arms or the threat of a falcon, the little bird fluffed its feathers and pecked under its wing.

Peace that Sumi could almost touch wrapped itself around her—the first sense of well-being in weeks, even months. The meal downstairs promised to be uncomfortable, miserable, abysmal, but that would be nothing compared to facing arrest and exile or a lifetime with Keiji-*sama*. The wished-for miracle had occurred.

The original meal of red rice, soup with nine lucky vegetables, and a whole little red snapper fish for each diner had been given to the gatekeeper to carry to a shrine, or more likely to his family. The ordinary dishes of fish soup, noodles, and vegetables were eaten in near silence, with only her parents speaking occasionally to each other about inconsequential things. At the end of the meal, her still smoldering grandfather rejoined them.

Sumi steeled herself to accept whatever came.

"Exactly as I predicted." Her grandfather towered over her. "The barbarians have already brought evil. As for you, Sumi-*san*, we chose the Day of the Bird for your betrothal so the union would bring rich silks, silks as abundant as a peacock's feathers. Instead, your unbecoming behavior plucked out the bird's feathers." He shook his long, thin finger. "I do not want to know what you did in the park, what those devilish papers were. But your untoward action caused concern. Then your obnoxious questions were inexcusable." He paused for her response.

"I am sorry," Sumi murmured, lowering her head.

"In the times of clan warfare, consorting with the opposing side risked the castle's downfall. If the enemy succeeded in crossing the moat, led by the wayward clansman, the erring one's later willingness to throw himself into the water would not save the clan . . . even though some in the clan might appreciate the sacrifice. Call it admirable." He paused again.

"Please forgive me." Sumi bowed low. "My curiosity about the foreigners and my overly-bold questions caused much trouble."

Her grandfather exhaled. "Forget about your curiosity or boldness. The main problem was your inability to recognize the enemy. You still have not. Who are the enemy? *Not* the Kurohashi family. *Barbarians* are the *enemy*!" Her grandfather spun on his heel and headed toward the garden.

Kiyo gave Sumi a why-must-you-always-cause-trouble look and went toward the kitchen, as she had begun doing each evening, to ensure the rice god was honored by having the cooking fire properly extinguished. Sumi's mother picked up her needlework with a sweep of her hand, grasped an extra lantern, and left for her room. Her father motioned for Sumi to stay seated.

"Do you understand why we had not revealed my appointment privately to the Kurohashi elders?" He used the wet cloth on his stand to wipe his face.

"No, I'm sorry." She swallowed the thickness in her throat. "At first, I wanted to do everything I could to fight the grandson. But when I realized his family didn't know you would be the American's interpreter, I wanted to protect our honor." She gulped. "Was that throwing myself into the moat?"

His eyes softened. "I recognized the reason for your silence. Not even a falcon destroys its own kind. Loyalty and duty—a samurai's highest virtues. Your grandfather recognized it too. He rarely calls any action admirable, even indirectly.

"As for myself, I cannot blame you for wanting to learn about the foreigners. You seem to have been born with that curiosity. I suppose, too, I inspired you to fight when I said to be a falcon." He gave a thin smile. "However, I cannot entirely excuse your rashness. Harboring foreign pages, which surely did not come from my discarded materials, was a discredit to the family name and to you."

She bowed. "I should not have been so rash." She struggled not to show any relief at his reprimand, far gentler than she expected.

Kiyo reentered the room, bowed to Sumi's father, and headed for the stairs.

Her father waited until the creak of Kiyo's footsteps could be heard on the top steps and then her shoo of Sumi's cat. "We had an excellent reason for not revealing my appointment to the Kurohashi family and matchmaker, even with the opening of our city only weeks away." He paused, then leaned forward. "We wanted to enable that family to save face."

She cocked her head, puzzled.

He nodded. "Yes, for them to save face. If they had found out about my official assignment a week or so *after* finalizing the betrothal, their traditionally-minded relatives and acquaintances would not have expected them to *break* the contract. After the Kurohashis moaned sufficiently about the calamity of my appointment, everyone would have simply expected the bride—you— to become an invisible seam in the household's fabric. If Keiji-*sama* wanted to marry you as much as the *nakōdo* intimated, he could have had his bride, and his family their supposed honor."

"I apologize," she said as required, while longing to ask if her father's admission to the Kurohashis had been unavoidable after her rashness. Or had he *chosen* to come to her aid?

He half-smiled, half-grimaced. "The falcon was real. The

sparrow flew bravely. I willingly opened the way for its escape."

Sumi bowed. Warmth flooded her.

In her room, Sumi took the betrothal sash off her dresser and shoved it into the farthest corner of her storage cupboard. She wouldn't need it, at least not for the Kurohashi family. They already considered her too opinionated, and after the Americans arrived, they'd find her family deeply *contaminated*. She plopped down on a cushion, nearly giddy with relief.

Kiyo set aside her embroidery and gazed at her. "I don't understand you at all. You carelessly botched your betrothal to someone far exceeding what you deserved."

"I agree. I did not deserve Keiji-*sama*."

Her cousin squinted at her. "How can you so blithely turn your back on a good future? Are you truly so blind to reality?"

"I am very happy because of the future."

"We'll see how happy you are when the disgusting barbarians arrive." Kiyo picked her embroidery back up and jammed a needle into the cloth. "You have two more weeks to indulge your dreams, two weeks of ignorant bliss. Then your eyes will be opened to the truth."

"Having my eyes opened is exactly what I want."

But unwelcome thoughts whispered in her mind. What if Kiyo and the Kurohashis and her grandfather and the hooded samurai, and perhaps the Divine Emperor, and many other people were right, and the foreigners really were uncouth barbarians? What if Merchant Omura was right, and associating with foreigners would imperil her life?

She wanted to shout, *No*! She would not fall prey to such thoughts. She would not allow all her hope for the future to be destroyed. She would judge the Americans for herself.

CHAPTER 23

July 3, 1859, Nagasaki

John leaned on the ship's rail and scanned the infamous cliffs of Pappenburg Island as the ship steamed closer to Nagasaki Harbor. Remnants of the early morning mist clung to a craggy precipice as though ghosts remained where hundreds of Japanese Christians in the seventeenth century had been hurled down to die on the sharp rocks below. The Japanese ruler in 1638, expelling the last foreigners, had thundered: "So long as the sun warms the earth, let no Christian set foot here again!"

The sun hadn't stopped warming the earth, yet here John was, and not just for a few days of trading. This time he would plant his feet in Nagasaki. For the next two or three years at least, he'd get to know the inhabitants, solidify the trading company, and fulfill his commitments as consul.

Consul!

When Townsend Harris wrote John a month earlier that Jennings would be named to the post if John refused the honor, he had accepted the appointment. The Consul General could have been bluffing, but there was no way to be sure. John rubbed his forehead. Had he made a mistake? In the Japanese zodiac, it was the Year of the Sheep. An ambiguous omen. Would the Year of the Sheep attract wolves or provide an abundance of green pastures?

"Look there!" George Jennings' blue eyes glittered with anger as he strode toward John, waving an arm. "That fool cannon's trackin' us."

"I see it all right, but no sign they're about to fire it." John moved a few steps away, wondering why the person most resembling a wolf kept trailing him. Did John resemble a vulnerable sheep?

Not only had Jennings boarded the *Retriever* for transport from Shimoda to Shanghai—an escort of Japanese officials had made sure he didn't miss that departure—but he'd also dogged John and Edward in Shanghai, snapping up one of their trade deals for himself. And now the wolf had managed to be on the same naval ship bringing John into Nagasaki.

"Commodore Perry had enough sense to use a squadron to pry open the country," Jennings grumbled. He pulled a cigar from under his rain slicker and snipped the tip. "Need a squadron here too, not this measly twenty-four-gun frigate."

John pulled out a cigar of his own. "Trade treaty's being honored. No need for a squadron now."

"You expect the natives to keep their word? They'd as soon lie as drink a cup of their stinkin' green tea."

"I recall we both congratulated Consul General Harris on negotiating the fine treaty of Peace, Friendship, and Commerce. We expected good results then, seems to me."

"Treaty of friendship's a strange way of putting it, considerin' they call us good-for-nothing barbarians. Mealy-mouthed diplomacy won't get anywhere with a country run by warriors."

"Tell me something." John waited while Jennings lit his cigar. "Why Japan? Why aren't you helping Taylor and Company expand its business elsewhere? Fuchow? Macao? Or Bangkok?" *Anywhere but Nagasaki.*

"Best chance for profit's right here. Same reason as you." Jennings puffed a circle of cigar smoke close to John's face.

John waved the smoke away. "By all accounts, the situation here won't be like the wheeling and dealing in Shanghai." Grabbing Mr. Jennings' cigar and pitching it into the bay was tempting, but he settled on launching a not-so-subtle warning.

"And your point?" Jennings glared.

"This government, I'm told, keeps a hawk-eye out for any prohibited activities—shady business deals and especially smuggling. Some traders may find that a problem, don't you think?"

"What're you implying? My dealings are goin' to be above board!" Jennings' face turned dark red.

"Just telling you what all traders here need to remember. Watching out for my compatriots. Doing my duty." John offered a frosty smile.

Muttering about officials too meddlesome for their own good, Jennings stomped down the companionway.

John turned back to observe the bay.

The ship had entered what resembled a very long, but narrow lake. Only the salty smell and dark water indicated they were still in an arm of the ocean. Fishing boats, their black and white sails folded down, dotted the bay. The unfolding scenery, which still fascinated him despite the two previous trips, dissolved the image of Jennings' shock of red hair and mocking expression.

Terraced rice fields now rose steeply one after another from the water's edge. Wisps of smoke curled up from unseen cottages in the more distant high hills. With a familiar ache, John wished Catherine and he could experience this once-in-a-lifetime event together. She wouldn't want to roam those hills like he did, but she would enjoy painting the remarkable scenes.

When the forenoon watch's eighth bell sounded, John took a last glance at the bay and climbed to the quarterdeck cabin where the frigate's captain would host him and the ship's other five civilian passengers.

The walnut-paneled room, though elegant, was cramped, the air oppressive. John exchanged greetings at the captain's table, then resigned himself to another meal of pasty chicken stew for the fifth time in the last nine days. He missed the cook's dishes on the *Retriever,* but felt no regret his ship was well on its way to California. Martin Li, with Edward's initial help, would establish a branch of Cardiff & Associates at San Francisco.

Captain McDougal, after signaling to the waiters to carry on, surveyed his guests. "Consul Cardiff here has been plying these waters for a time now. I'd wager he'd agree this country we're about to visit resembles a porcupine. Blamed land sticks out its barbs before you get close enough to investigate. We keep hearing about clans and warlords. Anyone have an estimate on how many clans there are? Hundreds?"

"That's what I heard," John offered when no one else answered. "More than 250, each clan living in a domain headed by its own warlord with samurai providing the barbs.

"So this country's crawling with warlords, is it?" The captain grasped a spoon from a waiter and piled stew onto his plate as though he'd never eaten anything as tasty. "And the bloody samurai? How do they operate?"

"I've read," Richard Pendleton interjected, "that samurai place loyalty to their master above life itself and cling to tradition. In fact, they are said to disdain the use of guns."

John nodded. He'd come to like and admire the well-versed, older man and his wife, Margaret. Richard had signed on as the frigate's assistant chaplain in order to have free passage to Nagasaki, where the couple planned to retire.

"Looks like the samurai have plenty of fire power now," Jennings grumbled, his mouth full of chicken.

"Fortunately for us and this country's peace"—John forced his eyes away from Jennings' overactive jaws—"most clans are said to be loyal to the Shōgun, the country's dictator."

"And we all hope that is so," Richard Pendleton said, laying his napkin by his plate. "The samurai's loyalty is a fascinating subject." He glanced around the table. "The after-dinner stories have been first rate. If nobody else has one this time, I heard a tale that demonstrates just how intense the samurai's devotion can be. It's about forty-seven warriors, considered great heroes here. Supposed to be true."

"Do you want to tell it right before we disembark, Richard?" Margaret Pendleton drew her shawl closer around her. "It unnerved me when I first heard it."

Captain McDougal chuckled. "Don't worry, madam. These people feed on adventure or they wouldn't be on this ship." He turned toward Pendleton. "Let's hear it, sir. Go ahead."

John kept quiet. Tales were interesting, sometimes insightful, but also could be misleading, mixing a little truth with a lot of fiction.

"All right," Pendleton said. "If not from me, you would hear it sooner or later anyway. As I said, it's famous." He adjusted his wire-rimmed spectacles. "The story goes that at the turn of the last century, a rural warlord visited the Shōgun's castle, where strict rules regulated the visitor's behavior. However, the castle's Master of Protocol, named Kira, gave the naïve Warlord Asano the wrong information on purpose, causing him to lose face. A huge insult in this country."

"A good thing to remember," John said.

"Yes, indeed. So now, the warlord, mortified by his bungling, attempted to assassinate Kira, but only wounded him. For disturbing the great Shōgun's peace—mind you—the Supreme Council condemned Asano to death by suicide." Pendleton glanced at the two ladies at the table. "The man obediently disemboweled himself with his own hands."

Both ladies lifted handkerchiefs to their noses.

"A barbaric custom, but I've heard of worse," the captain said. "Carry on."

"To continue, then, the Shōgun enhanced the penalty by confiscating Asano's castle and booting out Asano's family and forty-seven samurai, who turned out to be particularly devoted vassals. The disinherited warriors, known as *rōnin,* formed a secret pact to avenge their master's death. To lessen suspicion, the warriors scattered, and the chief disguised himself as a drunken good-for-nothing, lolling in street gutters and houses of ill repute.

"Now we come to Kira's comeuppance." Pendleton lit his pipe and puffed out smoke while looking at his audience. "The forty-seven *rōnin* stormed Kira's castle one dark night, forcing their enemy to hide in a secret spot. When a *rōnin* thrust a spear through the disguised compartment's thin wall, Kira suffered a wound, but exerted unbelievable self-control. He made no sound and wiped the blood off the weapon while it was being withdrawn. However, his self-control didn't extend to his cough. So in the end, he was promptly beheaded."

Jacob Mann, John's new secretary for the consulate, screwed up his face. "What happened to the forty-seven so-called heroes?"

"The government condemned them to ritual suicide too."

Sighs rose from the ladies.

"I swear," Jacob said, "the idea disguised warriors could be lying in wait for you is enough to make your blood curdle."

Jacob's wife Beth patted her chest. "Have you heard whether there are any *rōnin* nowadays with this same kind of obsession?" She reached for Jacob's hand.

"Of course there are," Jennings said. "The children grow up hearing a story like that and want to be famous demon warriors too."

John sat still, digesting the unwelcome implications. Obvious dangers, such as cannon, might not be as perilous as a harmless-looking drunkard. What was he getting himself into?

What he was not entering, he reminded himself, was an ancient tale. "Hold on, friends. A story from the last century shouldn't overly concern us." His words broke the heavy silence. "The treaties in this new era guarantee our protection. If we're prudent in what we do, we should be safe enough. Townsend Harris lived among the people for over two years. No one attacked him."

After a pause, all but Jennings and Mrs. Mann murmured their relief.

When the after-dinner coffee and cigars were finished, John returned on deck just as the powerful engines in the ship's bowels changed from their hammering pulse to a humming vibration. Sailors at the winches finished lowering the ship's anchors. The ship shuddered and stopped its forward thrust.

Beyond the high sea wall ahead, lay the city of Nagasaki and his residence. A shiver of anticipation slid up his spine. Who wouldn't give their eye teeth to be in his place?

A Japanese sampan pulled out from the shore. Peering through his spyglass, John detected three samurai in the forward part, their decorative tunics with extended shoulder pads announcing their officialdom. Another boat followed, apparently carrying the officials' six attendants. John moved back up to the quarterdeck in order to impress these first officials with his stature as consul.

The men, who were from the customs house, took a tour of the ship, then partook of refreshments, filling their tunic's voluminous sleeves with wrapped-up leftovers. As this initial party left, they stated all would be ready the next day for John's welcome by the governor.

Glancing at his fob watch, John decided he had just enough time to visit Nagasaki's Chinese sector and update his standing agreement with the silk supplier. He'd already requested a boat be readied if circumstances allowed for his shore leave.

"I see you're already makin' hay, Consul." Jennings' leering face greeted John at the gangplank. "Having a cutter at your disposal must be one of those advantages the consul general described. Mind if one of your subjects catches a ride?"

John minded, all right, but could hardly forbid it when the boat had plenty of room. "No, come ahead. However, I have business to carry out alone."

"I got no intention of trailing you. Have my own plan." Jennings cradled a package.

"You remember that all goods must go through customs, right?"

"I'm no dunce." Jennings turned and preceded John onto

the boat.

Once on shore, the two men headed in different directions. Careful not to lose his bearings, John followed the route to the silk shop he'd located previously with Martin. Chinese merchants had to live in a walled area guarded by resident Chinese guards. However, Merchant Huang had a small shop outside the community, possibly because his features enabled him to pass as a Japanese man. His wife was really Japanese.

After placing an order for forty rolls of shimmering blue silk to be picked up when the *Retriever* returned in three months, John accepted Huang's invitation to join his wife for tea. He followed the merchant into the miniscule, one-room home at the back of the shop. Sitting on a cushion by the room's central fire pit, he sipped the steaming drink and basked in the companionship even though he understood less than a third of the merchant's Pidgin English.

"Here! The offender's in here," came from the shop's entrance.

John stopped in mid-sentence and half-rose, recognizing Jennings' voice. What was the wolf up to now?

An authoritative-sounding Japanese voice called out a moment later.

The silk merchant sprang up, and John followed him back into the shop, a cloud of worry descending on him.

Jennings stood in the shop's vestibule next to a samurai wearing a somber, gray outfit with shoulder pads resembling short wings. Two other samurai next to him wore much plainer clothes. All three had the double swords of a full-fledged samurai slung at their waist.

John's Chinese host fell to his knees and banged his forehead on the *tatami* floor.

"You better bow quick," Jennings said. "They raise a bump on your noggin' if you don't."

Searching his mind for a way to communicate, John stared at the official with the shoulder wings, who returned a cool stare.

"I am Dutch Interpreter of Second Rank," the man of lower status announced. "I speak poor English, but I try interpret you."

"Thank you." John heaved a breath, relief pouring through him. "I am John Cardiff, the new United States of America consul for your city."

The interpreter reared back and translated for his chief, who frowned. Then the interpreter bowed low to John.

John returned a similar bow to the interpreter.

The interpreter flushed. "Please not bow to me. Only Chief Inspector Sato."

"All right. What is the problem?"

"This American"—the interpreter glanced at Jennings—"tried sell five bottles his medicine without customs' seal. The loyal shop owner's neighbor reported crime to block foreman, who reported to customs inspector, who reported to Chief Inspector Sato—Chief Inspector *all* Nagasaki. But American here say he not know bottles not pass through customs because they your bottles."

"Mine?" John scowled at Jennings, who gave a half shrug.

The chief inspector took one of the bottles from the bag Jennings had carried from the ship and held it out.

John took it, and after sniffing the liquid inside, handed it back to the inspector. "Those bottles of medicine, called laudanum, did not come from me." He held the samurai's steady glare, but inwardly cringed at the thought of being expelled from the country on the eve of his official welcome.

If the inspector declared both of them smugglers, the American State Department would have to intervene. By the time the messages traveled back and forth and the truth was discovered, months would elapse. Another man would have become consul, and Cardiff & Associates' reputation would be in rags. His company would definitely not be on the ground floor in Japan. It would be under the ground. This time the wolf bared sharp, pointed teeth.

A crowd began to gather, pointing at John and Jennings, chatting with each other, and laughing.

Then the inspector pivoted and rapped out three syllables. The people dispersed in less than a minute.

The spectators had been a small nuisance in John's mind—a housecat's hiss compared to a lion's roar.

"Have you got your pistol on you?" Jennings asked in a loud whisper.

"That isn't something to discuss," John muttered, restraining from calling Jennings an idiot. He noticed that the interpreter looked puzzled, probably not knowing the word *pistol.*

"I have mine." Jennings glanced at the samurai out the corner of his eye.

"Don't draw it. If you do, it will be four against one. The four includes me."

Apparently catching on, the interpreter blanched and spoke to the chief inspector in excited Japanese.

The inspector barked a command at the other samurai with him. The companion samurai headed toward a group of men waiting down the street with bamboo contraptions resembling cages. The men lifted the cages and moved about twenty yards closer.

His heart pounding, John breathed a quick prayer for help,

then clasped his hands in front of his waist. "I have forbidden this American to use his gun. I will not use mine. However, I represent the United States of America. If you arrest me, you will break a treaty stipulation—a rule your superiors agreed to follow. My government will free me, using force if necessary, and require your government to pay a large amount of money."

After hearing the translation, the official narrowed his eyes and growled a response to the interpreter. John feared the worst.

"You are ordered to prove you are the American consul," the interpreter said.

John let out a breath. At least, here was one sign the inspector might become reasonable. "Please come with me to the ship. I will give the proof."

The official, eyes hard as steel, agreed with alacrity.

John turned to say a word to the merchant Huang, but the trembling man had retreated into his back room. A good move, John realized. If a lion failed to catch a larger prey, it might go after a smaller one.

"Didn't want to lose my head," Jennings simpered as the four headed to the cutter. "Figured our lofty consul could take care of the mix up."

"And because I am a consul, the officials won't arrest me once I prove my status, but they may bar my entry, courtesy of you." John forced an even tone. Displaying raw emotion in a land of stoicism would not impress the chief inspector. "However, Mr. Jennings, you face the possibility of a Japanese prison. If you'd listened to my warning and used decent, common sense, there wouldn't be a charge of smuggling, would there?" John knew better than to expect more than a snort as an answer.

Jennings snorted.

CHAPTER 24

On board the ship, John introduced Chief Inspector Sato to Captain McDougal and asked for the captain's assistance. After leading the group to his cabin, John unlocked his small safe and pulled out the document signed by Harris appointing him consul.

Captain McDougal nodded. "Aye, John Cardiff is the bona fide consul for Nagasaki. You'll not meet a finer man."

Sato ran his hand over the seal during the translation, then handed the document back to John with a scowl and a jerk of his head.

"Now, I would like to address the five bottles falsely attributed to me." John paused, eyeing the Bible lying on his desk. If he risked expulsion, he might as well make it for a better reason than a false accusation. He walked over and picked up the book.

The interpreter gasped, apparently recognizing it.

The chief inspector asked the interpreter a question, then put his hand on his sword.

Captain McDougal moved his hand to the ceremonial sword he still wore following the visit of the customs officials.

"I have fifty marines on board," he warned, not raising his voice.

Sato removed his hand from his weapon after the translation, but spoke his objection in sharp staccatos to the interpreter, who returned a deep bow.

"Chief Inspector Sato objects to that book." Beads of sweat spotted the interpreter's forehead.

"This ship belongs to the United States of America," John said, his jaw firm. "Furthermore, the treaty signed by your government's superiors guarantees *my* freedom to practice *my* beliefs even if I were not on this ship."

After the translation, Sato's mutterings were translated as, "American warship and treaty cannot make evil action into good action."

"In the United States of America, we hold this book in great honor. We put our hand on it when we swear to tell the truth—a good action. And so, I swear to tell the truth, the whole truth, and nothing but the truth, so help me God."

The interpreter stuttered while translating, as though searching for words.

Chief Inspector Sato scowled and folded his arms.

"I swear that those bottles containing tincture of opium do not belong to me." John replaced the Bible. "You may thoroughly inspect this room for any more bottles. And since Mr. Jennings"—John made an expansive wave at Jennings, who was leaning against the room's porthole—"claims the bottles are not his either, he should also permit an inspection."

"No head-choppin' native is going in my room," Jennings said. "Guess the policeman here will just have to balance my word against yours and what he terms your *evil* action."

The captain sent a message through the first lieutenant, who had also joined them, ordering the steward to come on the double. Then he turned toward Jennings. "This is a military ship, Mr. Jennings. You signed the paper acknowledging that fact when you boarded at Shanghai. I have the authority to inspect every inch of this vessel anytime I wish."

"I'm not one of your underlings." Jennings raised his chin. "I am a civilian."

The steward rushed up with a salute.

The captain ordered the man to unlock Jennings' cabin door.

"This is an outrage," Jennings fumed. "Secretary of State Cass will hear of this unAmerican invasion of privacy."

Ignoring Jennings' glower at the door, John strode into Jennings' room with the others. The cabin held the same standard furnishings of a bed, shelves, washstand, and narrow wardrobe, with the addition of a large chest Jennings had brought from Shanghai, sitting at the foot of his bed.

"My good man, you can either unlock your chest, or a sailor can hack it open for you," the captain said.

Jennings produced a key from around his neck and opened the chest. It had canisters of tea and wadded up packing paper, but was empty, otherwise.

"I resent this barbarous treatment," Jennings sneered and slammed the chest's lid down.

John had seen this Chinese style of chest before, ones that sometimes hid spring-triggered compartments. But finding and opening the compartment, if there was one, would be tricky. Martin Li would know how, but Martin wasn't there.

The steward stepped forward. "Asking permission to speak."

"Given," the captain said.

"I was passing by when a sailor tried to deliver coffee to Mr. Jennings this morning. Since our passenger ordered the coffee but wasn't responding, I took the liberty of using my key to enter the room. Mr. Jennings threw his bedsheet over the chest, but I noticed five brown bottles next to it."

After the translation, the Japanese official strode to the chest, raised the lid, and drew his sword.

"Wait just a minute!" Jennings headed toward the inspector but stopped when the man raised his sword.

For a second, John thought Jennings might lose his head before anyone could act. But instead, the official sliced a swath from the false bottom of the chest.

Covered glass trays filled with round balls of opium lay exposed. Small brown bottles could be seen in another layer underneath the trays.

Jennings' face blanched. "Why, I never! By my mother's gray hairs, that's the strangest thing I ever seen. Must have been there when I bought the chest."

"So you'd have us believe," the captain said, shaking his head, "the former owners of the chest gifted you with the opium without your knowledge, and those five bottles of laudanum appeared at the snap of your fingers."

The official spoke in harsh tones to the interpreter. "Chief Inspector Sato say drug illegal. Red-headed American go to prison."

"Over my dead body," Jennings said, a noticeable tremor in his voice.

"What do you suggest, Consul?" McDougal asked. "I don't have to release anyone from my ship, but I'm more than willing to rid it of riffraff."

"The provisions of our treaty officially take effect

tomorrow, not today." John fought the desire for revenge. "But if they were in effect, I'd ask Jacob Mann to record the testimony of the eyewitnesses, the evidence of the chest's contents, the defendant's plea, and my verdict."

"And what would that verdict be?" The captain folded his arms. "It's good for us to be in agreement."

Jennings had stopped swearing and muttering, and now glowered at John.

"If the defendant pled guilty, was willing to dispose of the opium, and foreswore future smuggling, I'd forbid him to disembark in Japan, order him to work as a ship's hand on the return trip, but allow him a fresh start elsewhere."

"The treaty's not in effect," Jennings spit out. "You're not my judge. And opium's not illegal under U.S. laws."

"Of course, if you relinquished jurisdiction over this passenger," John continued addressing the captain as though Jennings hadn't spoken, "the official here could hold Mr. Jennings under the Japanese laws until the treaty takes effect. I fear Mr. Jennings would find himself in an unpleasant cage in the Nagasaki prison, perhaps flogged, until finally released into my custody days from now."

Sato had listened to the translations in silence, the strength of his anger matched by an apparent rigid self-control.

Captain McDougal whistled between his teeth. "I'll do everyone a favor. Opium that's not for the surgeon's use is prohibited on this ship." He turned to the First Lieutenant. "Get two of the crew to dump this contraband into a barrel of water in front of everyone standing here. Then the solution is to be dumped into the bay. Mr. Jennings will return to China as part of the crew, assigned to stoke coal. He is confined to quarters for the three days in port. There's a suitable room available on the orlop deck. If he gives any trouble, clap him in irons."

John breathed a little easier, knowing Jennings wouldn't be prowling Nagasaki, looking for shady deals and the *wenches* that enticed him.

Sato continued his stony silence as the opium was dumped into the barrel.

Jennings warned again about his complaint to the secretary of state, but when told he would be moving to his new location at the end of fifteen minutes—voluntarily or forcibly—he began throwing belongings into the cleaned out chest.

Sato pivoted and ordered, through the interpreter, to be returned to shore. John accompanied the two men to the leeward ladder after the inspector waved away a gangplank. Right before taking the ladder, the inspector spoke gruffly to the interpreter.

The interpreter turned to John. "Chief Inspector Sato order me introduce self because Governor Nakamura say I interpreter for American consul. So I serve you. My name Taguchi Kenshin.

"You've been assigned to me as interpreter? On a daily basis?"

"Yes, assigned. Every day I work for you."

"That's grand. I wasn't sure there would be anyone here nearly as fluent in English as you. And now I learn you'll interpret for me. I can't think of any finer news that that."

John observed the slender, middle-aged man more closely. Worried eyes looked out from a clean-shaven face, and in the manner of all samurai, he had the shaved pate and a top-knot of black hair. He was scrupulously immaculate, in fact, more so than the usual Westerner.

"Chief Inspector Sato say he want no more very bad

foreigners come Japan. He say all foreigners in danger, but danger bigger if very bad foreigners come. Also danger bigger if put hand on foreign religion book in front people. He work protect foreigners because he has order to protect. He do his duty."

"Please tell him I appreciate his effort to protect foreigners. Also, tell him I will not be a secret Christian because I am loyal to God. I think he understands loyalty."

Sato nodded stiffly after the short translation.

John felt sure Mr. Taguchi had not translated his last two sentences.

"Maybe I disappoint you. My English not yet good. I speak gooder Dutch."

"No, you are doing very well, but I want you to try to translate everything I ask you to say."

"I work to improve." Mr. Taguchi's eyes conveyed his understanding.

John took a breath and nodded. He wouldn't resort to secrecy about his faith, but at the same time, he'd consider how his actions might affect Mr. Taguchi before he pushed his interpreter too hard. It didn't bode well, either, to have an important official as an enemy. For starters in building a better relationship, John bowed to Sato with a slight smile.

Sato hesitated, then returned a bow without a smile. A bow a little shallower than John's, but a decided bow.

An early shower had cleared the air the next morning, and the sun attempted to shine through the clouds. John sat at his desk and reread the verses from Isaiah 40 that a ray of sunlight brightened on the page. *Why sayest thou . . . My way is hid from the LORD, and my judgment is passed over from my God? Hast thou not known? Hast thou not heard, that the everlasting God, the LORD, the Creator of the ends of the earth, fainteth not, neither is weary.*

John recognized the gentle rebuke. Even if the chief inspector had thwarted his entry into Nagasaki, the Creator of the ends of the earth would have been involved in the situation. John bowed his head, agreeing that whether the day ahead promised green pastures or wolves, he needed to lean on this passage's bedrock truth.

At the second bell of the forenoon watch, John, the Manns, and twelve of the ship's officers in blue dress uniforms climbed aboard the longboat to be rowed to shore. John took hold of the rail and stood, facing the prow, careful not to snag his blue jacket's dozen brass buttons. His heart thumped with anticipation.

The Navy band, posted on the frigate deck, played "Hail, Columbia" as the boat moved forward, its three trumpeters sounding clear notes remarkably on key. At the end of the anthem, a boom sounded. For a second John thought the Japanese soldiers had fired off a cannonball after all. Then he realized it was the frigate's own action. Of course. The captain had begun a thirteen-gun salute in honor of John and the United States of America.

He—John Cardiff—was the U.S. consul arriving at his post. And it was the Fourth of July. Fireworks couldn't compare to a salute of cannon. His heart seemed to keep pace with each boom.

After the boat was secured at the quay, John stepped onto the land and approached the small group of officials standing

motioned for John and his fellow Americans to follow. Mr. Taguchi stayed next to John. A Japanese militia moved up to the rear.

John stood still for a minute, taking in the view. Puffs of smoke from wood or charcoal fires and a fresh breeze off the surrounding hills, picking up a garden's fragrance, modified the salty smell of the bay. Before him lay the teeming city of Nagasaki. Lining their route were hundreds, perhaps thousands, of its citizens. An unbelievable sight.

The cobblestone street ahead had been swept clean of trash and animal manure if any had marred it. Box-like, two-story, gray wooden buildings, packed together, were too numerous to count. Homes? Shops? Some were definitely shops. Fluttering upright banners announced the shops' contents in giant Chinese-type characters against dark blue backgrounds. Two arched bridges cut across their visible route. He had dreamed of crossing Japanese bridges like those. Now in a few minutes, he would cross them into a new world.

If he lived to be a hundred, he would never forget this day.

CHAPTER 25

The distant booms of the cannon had stopped. Shivers darted up Sumi's spine, knowing the blasts saluted the arrival of the Americans. They were stepping foot onto the shores of her city at that very minute.

She took a deep breath and straightened her best, cherry-colored kimono. The rain-washed air was fresh, invigorating, like the new era the distant cannon had signaled. Snippets of conversation between her mother, Kiyo, and their family friend, Mika, reached her where she waited on their friend's balcony. Accounts of a drunken brawl. The price of the best brocade. Another government edict. On and on they talked.

Sumi almost laughed. Why would anyone care about such mundane topics? Discussing the opium smuggler's false accusation of the new consul would be a more interesting topic, but her father had ordered them not to repeat his account. Even that incident paled in significance compared to the fact today's procession would pass by within the hour. It would be as if foreigners in the photo in one of her father's foreign books had come to life before her eyes.

Beneath her, throngs of spectators bowed and made way for

one another on the sides of the stone road. Most of the people still held their oiled-paper umbrellas despite the clearing skies. The constant bobbing of the orange, brown, and yellow disks mirrored the grasshoppers jumping in her stomach. She pressed her cheek against the balcony's lattice, straining to see the length of the thoroughfare.

The drone of chatter, mingling with vendors' cries and the *gata gata* of wooden clogs and carts, fell to an expectant hush. Bystanders knelt at the edges of the street.

Sumi spun toward the guest room behind her and bowed toward the three inside. "Excuse me. I can see the procession. The forerunners are almost here."

A large group of her country's officials and militiamen escorted the fifteen Americans. Two male foreigners and a lady were followed directly by twelve United States military officers in gold-braided, blue coats and long pants.

"Look. There's Father. On this side of the street." Sumi pointed him out as the others joined her. "How distinguished he appears, parading with the dignitaries."

Their hostess nodded. "He puts the foreigners to shame. The lady's attire looks like a mushroom, doesn't it?" Mika extended her arms sideways and fluttered them, mimicking how the brown skirt ballooned out from the woman's pinched waist. "And she walks next to the man, as if she had the right to do so."

Sumi shook her head at the American woman's outrageous audacity.

The man next to her father strode as though he led an army of mounted warriors instead of the twelve men marching behind him. His air of authority surely marked him as the consul. His height was impressive too. He would tower over most men even without his black headgear.

Her father looked up at the balcony. The American followed his gaze, then turned and spoke to her father, who nodded with a quick bow. They both looked at the balcony again.

The whole procession slowed, then stopped.

Her father gestured urgently for them to come down to the street.

"Quickly. Quickly," her mother commanded.

Trying to grasp what was happening, Sumi turned to obey. Questions stung her mind as she trouped through the rooms with the others and down the stairs. What was wrong? Was the consul objecting to the procession? Would he not cooperate with her country's high officials, proving he was uncivilized? Truly a barbarian?

Muttering that this was most unnatural and apologizing to Mika, Sumi's mother led the way out of the house.

They met Sumi's father in the front garden.

With repeated apologies, he asked Mika to bring tea for the consul and his two companions. Then he turned to Sumi's mother. "You three must meet the new diplomat. He claims he wants to show proper respect to my family. Something about demonstrating a custom called *chivalry*."

"And he demands tea?" her mother asked.

"The tea was my idea," her father replied, more curt than usual. Then he preceded them out the front gate.

Sumi sighed with relief. If the consul talked about showing respect, he wasn't trying to insult anyone.

"Shameful," Sumi's mother told her. "Your father had to ask for the tea so the officials wouldn't blame our family for the interruption."

Admiring her father's quick thinking, Sumi joined her mother and Kiyo in bowing low to the mystifying consul.

The consul swept off his headgear and—unbelievably—returned their deep bows.

Stunned, Sumi took a step back. Why had he bowed? Not only were they women, but the consul was her father's superior, not the other way around.

Sumi dared to look for a moment into the consul's gray eyes—kind eyes that seemed to study her. She was face-to-face with a foreigner!

She felt herself blush and looked away, her mind reeling. Giving such honor to her family was truly disturbing behavior, because everything should be done in proper order, as Confucius said. But how could anyone not consider his random act appealing?

Mika made quick bows as she extended cups of steaming tea to the three honorees.

The consul raised his eyebrows in surprise as he accepted his cup, but then responded with a small bow to Mika.

The couple with the consul also bowed to Mika, belatedly and tentatively.

Sumi kept herself from laughing at their poor imitation of their leader. She dared a glance at the consul's face again.

He smiled at her, then put on his headgear and reentered the procession of officials winding their way to Higashi Park for the welcoming ceremony.

Wishing she could fly up the stairs, she followed her slow-moving mother and still slower Kiyo, a veritable tortoise, back to Mika's balcony.

Peering through the lattice once more, all Sumi could glimpse of the consul was the back of his head as he and the man and woman accompanying him approached the next intersection. But the poor view didn't truly matter because she'd seen the American up close.

His features were definitely strange, yet intriguing. His gray eyes had not been the least bit ghoulish despite their other-worldly color. Although his nose was long, it wasn't as elongated as portrayed in the caricatures of foreigners sold on the street. Brown hair surrounded his face, and his upper lip supported an additional swath. An unusual amount of facial hair, but not at all beastlike or frightening. She fanned herself to cool her warm cheeks.

Her lack of composure earned a frown from her mother. Sumi slipped her fan under her *obi* sash and murmured, "It's a little warm." But her mother's eyes remained troubled.

Her cousin turned from the lattice. "As I expected, the foreigners are wholly barbaric. As if the consul's bows weren't uncouth enough, did you see how he and the other man, as well as the officers trailing him, wore long pantaloons to hide their legs' deformities, and used leather bags to cover their feet? Feet like horses' hooves."

Sumi's throat tightened. "Nobody knows that for sure." Kiyo's criticism was as predictable as their neighbor cat's midnight yowl.

"Will you raise a barbarian's leg coverings next time to check?" Kiyo grumbled.

"No. I'll find out when I read their books."

"In this lifetime or the next?"

Sumi sniffed and turned back to the spectacle, unwilling to lose more precious moments. Too quickly, like a dissipating mirage, the last of the procession passed by. A shaft of sunshine silvered the wet cobblestones in the procession's wake.

The others standing with Sumi turned to reenter Mika's guest room. Sumi raised a finger, begging a moment for a final glance. One look told her something had happened. The procession had slowed to a crawl. She scanned the bystanders and squinted at the arched stone bridge in the distance. Surely the consul hadn't stopped to bow to more spectators. The officials would be scandalized.

Her mother stepped next to her. "You must—" She gasped, then pointed to a basket-hooded figure snaking through the crowd.

Bursting onto the road, the man planted himself in front of the consul.

A bolt of astonishment struck Sumi, then fear for her father. The intruder had to be a *rōnin.* Usually hotheaded. Totally unpredictable. None other would dare confront the officials in broad daylight.

The belligerent samurai bellowed something that distance muffled. Whatever the message, her father's translation must have shocked the Americans, for the lady behind the consul stumbled backward, nearly tripping over her billowing gown.

"Do something!" Sumi ordered under her breath. She turned to her mother. "Why is every guard just standing there? Useless?"

Her mother, ashen faced, shook her head.

As though roused from sleep, shouts ripped from the governor's militia in the procession's rear. One of the American officers snatched out what seemed to be a gun.

The hooded man leapt back into the crowd and threaded his way in Sumi's direction.

She flinched at the possibility this fanatical scoundrel could be the same samurai who had been at the teahouse and spit on her sandal. That man had been uncouth, possibly treacherous, but she'd never thought he could be a ranting *rōnin*.

Swords flashing, militiamen surged after the culprit. Moments later, they paused in their onward rush, a few turning left and others to the right, apparently losing sight of their quarry.

The *rōnin* headed toward the dark alley opposite where Sumi and her mother stood.

A chill slithered up Sumi's spine. Whether or not this was the same arrogant samurai, the police had to capture him. A fanatic couldn't be left free to prowl the streets.

"Over here! He's over here!" burst from her lips.

Sumi clamped her mouth shut. Had those words come from her? Unbidden?

The hooded man whipped around and raised his head toward the balcony.

She froze until he vanished into the alley's gloom. Seconds later, a militiaman rushed into the alley after him.

Her mother yanked her back from the lattice and into the guest room. "What madness possessed you? To take such a risk? To ignore all your training?" Her voice shook.

"I am sorry." Her neck heating, Sumi offered a protracted bow. At the flick of her mother's fan, she settled on a satin cushion next to Kiyo, who glared at her, before turning her attention to Mika.

Sumi pinched her lips. Was her action that terrible? Hadn't her shout helped the militia in their search? A scowl from her mother warned not to voice her thoughts. She braced herself to wait. When the *rōnin*'s capture became known, everyone's censure would become a distant memory.

"Sumi-*san*, pay attention." Her mother rapped her fan on

the low lacquered stand in front of her. "You can learn something from Mika-*san*'s careful work. Look how Kiyo-*san* takes this art seriously."

Her cousin sent Sumi a self-satisfied smirk and continued to examine the needlework their hostess had done for a cushion cover.

After Kiyo finished, Mika smiled proudly and passed the needlework to Sumi.

She forced herself to run her finger slowly over the stitches, then looked at Mika's expectant face. "It's beautiful. My hope is to embroider so well."

She lowered her eyes, knowing that only Mika believed her.

Her pulse rising, Sumi knelt at the end of the low teakwood table in front of their home's alcove, waiting for her father to finish his evening meal. She tried not to stare at him or her grandfather, both seated across the room from her. At last, her father swished a little green tea into his rice bowl. He frugally swallowed the remainder of the fine grains, then used a damp cloth to wipe his forehead, his cheeks, his mouth, his chin, and finally, finally the back of his neck.

Rising abruptly from his place, her grandfather stalked out of the room. Before Sumi could stand and complete her bow, the panel door slid closed behind him. She knelt back down, not surprised, yet sorry he refused to participate in the special evening. Couldn't he loathe foreigners yet still be curious?

"Listen to me," Kiyo hissed as she took a place next to Sumi. "You knew our family faced danger because of the barbarians. But by the gods, you've made the peril a hundred times worse. Shouting like a street vendor, loud enough for that *rōnin* to hear."

Sumi sucked in a breath. "He couldn't identify me from those few words coming from he-knew-not-where. At least, he couldn't know *exactly* where." She ignored Kiyo's disparaging grunt. "People shouldn't be like cowering turtles, always keeping their heads inside their shells."

"And too-brave turtles get their tiny-brained heads lopped off."

"Governor Nakamura himself welcomed the foreigners. We saw his militia. How much peril can there actually be? "

Kiyo drew herself taller. Her dark eyes grew darker still. "Have you heard any report of the *rōnin*'s capture?"

"No, but—"

"And what makes you think the governor *wanted* to welcome the barbarians? You are forever babbling about learning, learning, learning. In reality, you understand nothing."

"I don't. I mean, I . . ." Why wouldn't the right words come?

"For once, see your foolish obsessions for what they are. A grasping at clouds." Kiyo shook her head in disgust, then bowed low as Sumi's parents knelt to join them at the table.

Sumi also bowed as her mind churned. Was it possible the horrible *rōnin* still roamed the streets? But even if he had eluded the militiaman, the ward guards would have inspected each person passing through the gates, and the police would have scoured the city until he was caught. Surely he'd been caught.

Her jaw tightened. She would not fall prey to her cousin's gloomy outlook. Even the most reactionary people had to eventually warm up to the foreigners. Closing the country again would be like pulling a thick shroud over the land.

Her father leaned back against the wall and crossed his arms. "I suppose you want to hear from the beginning." He gave a knowing look in Sumi's direction. "Unfortunately, the day did not start well. The vice-governor was prepared to shake hands with the consul at the quay, but the consul bowed. Imagine our officials' consternation."

Sumi winced.

Her father nodded at her. "I could have been demoted on the spot for having advised the handshake, but the vice-governor overlooked it. Not only that, the officials also excused the procession's delay while Consul Cardiff met each of you." Her father chuckled. "I'm afraid he gained a reputation as an inordinate lover of tea. A servant was stationed by the three honorees to refill their cups throughout the afternoon."

Sumi grinned behind her quickly raised fan, but her mother and Kiyo frowned.

"I hope the officials continue in such a generous mood." Her mother's voice was tense. "The consul seemed too sure of himself. He should be more humble."

"The odd behavior is not as bad as you might think," her father said, addressing her mother. "Although Consul John Cardiff's documents say he is only thirty, he displays a calm disposition. As a matter of fact, his behavior was flawless during the welcoming ceremony and later at the sumo exhibition."

Thirty, yet he's the consul!

Sumi half listened to her father's description of the afternoon's entertainment while mulling over the fact the American ruler had sent such a young diplomat to represent him. The consul had to be an extraordinary samurai, his fighting skills far exceeding those of the United States' other warriors.

"Foreign manners, after all, are the least of my worries," her father concluded.

He had her full attention again. "What worries, Father?"

"Ah, problems would be a better word." He filled his silver pipe and held it for a second at the brazier's edge to light the tobacco. "Only matters of land allocation." He puffed on his pipe, mixing the scent of tobacco with the lingering smell of the evening's steamed fish.

Kiyo raised a dubious eyebrow. "May I ask if what I heard is true? My friend said the *rōnin* shouted to honor the Divine Emperor. Expel the barbarians. And slaughter all refusing to leave. She said the lady and man next to the consul quivered like trapped mice." Kiyo cast a sly look at Sumi. "Then Sumi—"

"Some rudeness occurred, obviously," her father cut in. "Our officials are taking care of it as we speak. You need not concern yourself."

Sumi let out a relieved breath. Her cousin's fake question had yielded exceptionally good news—the rōnin was being handled, and her father had apparently heard about her shout and excused it.

"We should respect these Americans," he continued, looking straight at Kiyo. Then he turned his eyes toward Sumi. "Yet they are stranger than you can imagine—wearing their dirty shoes indoors, cluttering their rooms at the temple with huge, bulky furniture, displaying their emotions on their faces for *everyone* to see, and even putting cow milk in their tea. I saw a sailor draw milk from a cow today, a ludicrous sight."

Sumi tried to imagine how milk was drawn from a cow. Apparently, the foreigners weren't afraid the milk would cause protrusions to sprout from their heads, like she'd heard a farmer claim. Drinking such milk and the other foibles were peculiar—no one could deny that—but even people from distant parts of her country had unusual tastes and mannerisms.

"I never want to drink animal milk." Sumi shook her head and grimaced. "But these customs do not mean the foreigners are barbarians, do they? Especially someone with a calm disposition?"

"They are not barbarians, yet all of us must be careful. I will tell you one more detail about the incident with the red-haired smuggler, but what I report cannot be shared with anyone."

Kiyo leaned forward. Sumi steadied herself, glad now that her grandfather wasn't in the room to find fault. Her mother increased her fanning.

"Consul Cardiff swore to tell the truth while he *openly* held the Evil Religion's book in his hands . . . as though it held the power to force him to be honest. His action incensed Chief Inspector Sato, who nearly drew his sword."

Her mother gasped. "This man is dangerous! A lawbreaker!"

Sumi stiffened. The consul shouldn't be called a dangerous criminal for simply holding the book. After all, she and her father had both held it. Yet the consul was clearly a believer in the foreigner's god, and that *was* against the law of the land.

"No, the consul is not a lawbreaker," her father said. "In the treaty, the shogunate gave permission to the foreigners to practice their beliefs. The consul did not insist that I translate all of his religious words, the ones that would have further offended the chief inspector. I think he wanted to spare me trouble."

A warm relief slid through Sumi. Here was additional

evidence of the consul's kindness. And if his thoughtfulness was related to his belief in the foreign god, then his religion couldn't be entirely evil.

"May I—"

A wave of her father's hand stopped Sumi from asking for more details.

"Enough for now." Her father snuffed out his pipe. "There will be sufficient time later to assuage your endless curiosity."

She comforted herself with the fact her father was right. This day was simply the first of hundreds to follow.

After retiring to her room, she peered out the open panel at the moon shining on the garden, thankful to have a few minutes alone since Kiyo still hadn't come up from below. The sparrow's head wasn't visible. A dark shadow indicated it snuggled in the bottom of its nest. She glanced at her cat in the corner, which opened one eye, but chose to resume its sleep. A breeze whispered about her face and rustled the pear tree's leaves, making them shimmer in the moonlight.

She closed her eyes, remembering an afternoon in the early spring. She had been standing under the pear tree when a series of breezes brought showers of blossoms swirling around her, the white petals scenting the air, dusting her head, delighting her with their other-worldly beauty.

When her city had opened itself to the Americans a few hours earlier, the same wonderful sensations had swept through her. Kiyo had predicted her disillusionment, but aside from the *rōnin,* the day had been perfect. Far exceeding all she expected.

She pictured the consul's gray eyes, his smile, his bow. Apparently unfamiliar with her country's most basic manners, he was making a valiant effort to enter a place that was a mystery to him. His life energy had to be strong. Of course, you couldn't judge the *ki* of a person from one or two actions. Just as no one could judge the quality of a pear tree from its blossoms or one solitary pear. But if the first pear was good, you always wanted more.

The year she'd waited for all her life had begun—the year of the tall, bold barbarian.

A civilized barbarian.

A barbarian she yearned to know.

A NOTE FROM ELIZABETH ANN

Thank you for taking time to read *The Year of the Barbarian*. If you enjoyed the story, please consider leaving a review on Amazon or Goodreads even if it's only a line or two.

Do you want to learn about the dangers that threaten Sumi and John and whether romance blossoms in their lives? Don't miss the release of Book Two of the *Dragonfly Trilogy*! A preview of *Dragonfly Wings* is at the back of this book.

You can discover more about the culture underlying the story world and receive writing updates and giveaways by going to my website and subscribing to my newsletter at www.elizabethannboyles.com/my-books

I hope we can stay in touch. You are greatly appreciated.

THE FICTITIOUS CHARACTERS

In the general order of the name's appearance

Taguchi Yoshikatsu* – An elderly retainer of the Chōshū clan
Taguchi Kenshin* – Yoshikatsu's son and a linguist, having a rank as a Dutch Scholar
Haru – Taguchi Kenshin's wife
Sumi – Kenshin and Haru's daughter
Kiyo – Haru's orphaned niece, Sumi's cousin
Merchant Omura – A bronze-ware merchant
Suzuki-*sensei* – Sumi's tutor
Kato-*dono* – A family friend and matchmaker
Hino Makoto* – A distant samurai betrothed to Sumi
John Cardiff – A New York trader
Catherine Gray – John Cardiff's fiancée
Ōta Nobumitsu* – A reactionary clansman
Taki – Sumi's close friend
The Itō Family – Taki's accused neighbors
Sato Rinzo* – The Chief Inspector in Nagasaki
Edward Cardiff – John's older brother
Fan – A Chinese cook
Henry Li – Comprador for Rubert & Company
Martin Li – John Cardiff's comprador
Jim Whitson – Captain of the *SS Retriever*
Inspector Kawata – A samurai in charge of Amami Ōshima
Kurohashi Keiji* – A Confucian scholar desiring to marry Sumi
Townsend Harris – The actual American Consul General for Japan, but referenced fictitiously

Henry Heusken – The actual secretary-interpreter for Harris, but referenced fictitiously
George Jennings – An American Far East trader
Kin – One of the Taguchi family's servants
Captain McDougal – Captain of a U.S. naval frigate
The Manns – The secretary assigned to the American consulate in Nagasaki and his wife
The Pendletons – An American couple on the ship
Merchant Huang – A Chinese silk merchant

* The surname is given first in the Japanese names.

JAPANESE TERMS

These definitions are specific for *The Year of the Barbarian*, not comprehensive in scope.

Beigoma – Top spinning competition
Bushido – Moral code of the samurai.
Chan, Dono, Sama, San – Titles affixed to names, like Miss, Mr., Mrs. in English, but reflecting status.
Chawan – A large bowl for drinking tea.
Edo – The city which was the seat of power for the secular government from 1603-1868. Renamed Tokyo.
Gata gata – A mishmash of noise.
Haiku – A poem whose first line consists of five syllables, the second of seven, and the third of five. Its meaning relies on cultural understanding.
Hakama – Wide skirt/trousers worn by samurai.
Ki – A person's life force in this story.
Kirishitan – Christian.
Kotatsu – The kotatsu's wooden frame is placed over a recess in the floor. The frame is covered by a heavy blanket, and a charcoal heater is placed under a bottom grate.
Koto – A 13-stringed zither about six feet long.
Mōshiwake gozaimasen – A humble apology.
Naginata – A smooth, long spear ending in a curved steel blade, used for defense especially by women in very old samurai families.
Nakōdo – Matchmaker.
Nori – Seaweed.
Ojō-sama – Polite word to refer to a young lady.

Rōnin – A masterless samurai.

Sake – A rice liquor.

Samurai – A warrior in the service of a clan's warlord. Samurai is the singular and plural form.

Sensei – Teacher or an expert in a certain fields.

Shōgun – The title of the supreme secular dictator.

Shogunate – The national government, led by the Shōgun and supported by the Council of Elders.

Shōji – A sliding panel used as a door, window, or room divider, made of translucent paper covering a lattice.

Sumimasen – A humble apology; excuse me.

Tale of the Heike – A historical tale recounting the struggles between two clan in the 12th century.

Tatami – Framed mats of rice straw that make up a traditional room's flooring. One mat is approximately six feet by three feet.

Tengu – A goblin.

Torii – The lintel entrance of a Shinto shrine.

Tsukuyomi – The moon god in Shinto belief and legend.

Uta-garuta – A game based on 100 famous waka poems. The players try to be the quickest in matching the card having the last two lines of a poem with the card having the poem's full text.

Waka – A Japanese poem. The tanka is a subcategory form having phrases of 5-7-5-7-7 syllables.

stiffly at the foot of the embankment. The Manns caught up with him, and the American officers fell into a formation of four abreast behind him.

Mr. Taguchi bowed to John, and motioned to the most elaborately dressed of the three Japanese officials. He explained that the official, who wore colorful silk pantaloons, an open tunic over white crepe, blue and white shoulder extensions, and two swords slung in his wide sash, was the number one, vice governor of Nagasaki.

John bowed just as the vice governor extended his hand. Then the vice governor bowed as John extended his hand.

John swallowed back a chuckle in the nick of time. The officials were frowning as if the crown jewels, or their equivalent in Japan, had just been stolen off the king's head. He stood still, waiting for someone to make the next move. Surely this breach in protocol wasn't anything like the mistake causing the loss of face in the tale of the forty-seven *rōnin.*

Then everyone looked at Mr. Taguchi, who kowtowed with his forehead to the damp ground as if accepting all the blame for the *faux pas*.

The officials turned around without further introductions and led the way toward the top of the embankment separating the harbor and the city. Apparently, the interpreter's bow had solved the problem. The thought came to John that if the rural warlord in Mr. Pendleton's old tale had been blessed with such a good man as Taguchi Kenshin, no one would have needed to cut into their intestines. From what he'd seen of his interpreter the previous day and in the last few minutes, the hand of providence had brought John an invaluable ally.

At the top of the embankment, men holding streamers aloft stood ready for a procession. The officials moved into line and

DISCUSSION QUESTIONS

Spoiler alert: Questions 7 – 12 should be discussed after reading all the story.

1. Do you think Sumi's strict, samurai-type training helped her build strength of character? What parts of her training struck you as good or harmful?

2. What do you think contributed to Sumi's yearning to meet foreigners?

3. Have you experienced a longing for a new opportunity as strong as Sumi's desire?

4. Do you think of Sumi as a gifted young woman? If so, how?

5. What characteristics of Catherine struck you as particularly undesirable or admirable?

6. Does John appear misled in choosing to court Catherine? If so, what factors could have contributed to that?

7. How would you judge Merchant Omura's reaction to Ōta Nobumitsu's demands?

8. Have you ever been forced into a very tight spot where you were not pleased with the options?

9. Do you think John's original motivation in establishing the trading company was based on impulse, wise analysis, or assurance of God's leading?

10. John had questions concerning the reality of God's providential care. Did any events in the story impress you as truly providential? Have you seen clear signs of providential occurrences in your own life?

11. How did John show he wasn't just a "foxhole" Christian after the storm?

12. In addition to the rescue of the kitten, did Sumi's grandfather demonstrate any affection for Sumi elsewhere in the story?

13. Was Sumi's willingness (or unwillingness) to sacrifice her happiness justified? Are Christians also called upon to make sacrifices? Is there a difference in the characteristics of the samurai sacrifice and the Christian sacrifice?

14. This book is meant as a foundation for the two remaining books in the series. Were the plot and character development in this book sufficient to make a good story in itself?

15. Were you surprised by any of the customs? Did you gain any new insight into historical Japan or Shanghai? What was your favorite part of the story?

ACKNOWLEDGMENTS

During the many years I worked on the *Dragonfly Trilogy*, numerous people kindly offered suggestions and encouragement. Here, I'll mention just those who contributed improvements specifically for *The Year of the Barbarian* although I deeply appreciate all of the help.

Many thanks to Maki Brown, Yuki Watanuki, Mamoru Ishida, and Michiko Shin for their guidance in balancing a present-day sensibility of what is genuinely Japanese with the Edo period's ways of speaking and acting.

Thank you also to members of critique groups who read this book's manuscript and offered advice: Janice Olson, Lyndie Blevins, Kay Learned, Jodi Grimes, Suzanne Disheroon, Randy Oxentenko, Amanda Caudill, Lee Carver, and my daughter Sherry Boyles. I won't name all the beta readers, but you are treasured for being a friend willing to donate your time.

I'm very grateful to two wonderful authors. Although we had never met, Elizabeth Camden graciously read and endorsed *The Year of the Barbarian*. Lena Nelson Dooley kindly featured an interview with me about the book on her blog.

Kellie Coates Gilbert, Patricia Carroll, and Jackie Castle led me through the maze of publishing. Julie Flickner rescued my website, enabling more people to find the book.

And last of all, a big thank you to my family, who put up with my book chatter and time-consuming writing day after day.

ABOUT THE AUTHOR

Elizabeth Ann's love for Japan developed when she lived in Japan for several years while in her twenties. The Japanese people went out of their way to acquaint her with the food, language, flower arrangement, tea ceremony, and other unique and wonderful customs. Now that she teaches at a Christian university with a global outreach, she is privileged to spend time with international students from Japan and many other fascinating countries as well.

She and her husband live in a suburb of Dallas, where they enjoy family times with their two grown children and grandchildren as often as possible.

Visit her at Facebook.com/elizabethannboyles
Twitter.com/AnnBoylesTX

Read on for an excerpt from
Dragonfly Wings*, Book Two of the *Dragonfly Trilogy

CHAPTER 1

July 1859 (Year of the Sheep), Nagasaki, Japan

Taguchi Sumi took a closer look at the charcoal bucket for the brazier in her home's main room. A wadded paper lay half buried as though intentionally concealed. She plucked it out and uncurled the tight ball, careful to keep the black dust from dirtying the *tatami* floor's spotless straw mats.

Her breath caught. Words written in the squiggly English alphabet as well as in Japanese met her eyes. Tingling with excitement, she tore through the Japanese translation.

English lessons. Taught by Americans. One class for young men. Another for young ladies. Unbelievable! Nothing on earth could be more wonderful. Nothing.

Two afternoons each week. Even once a week would have thrilled her.

Third house from the Oura River Bridge in the new international sector. She could walk there in an hour.

Three weeks had passed since the Westerners' arrival,

cracking open her country's two-hundred-fifty years of isolation, and she hadn't glimpsed a single one of them after that first day. But with these classes, she would meet Americans twice a week, maybe even the amazing United States consul himself. She had to comport herself with the dignity required for a samurai's daughter. But inside her, fireworks exploded.

"That paper does *not* concern you."

She started and then bowed. "Ah, good morning, Grandfather. The strange paper attracted my curiosity." She crumpled the precious notice, fitting it within her fist, bracing for his next words.

"It announces barbarian trickery. Throw it into the fire."

Her hands obeyed, but her heart didn't let go. The paper disappeared in a fiery puff.

She sighed and darted a look at her grandfather. Despite the thinning white hair, his firm jaw hadn't softened a bit. His dark eyes glittered with determination. She'd occasionally wheedled a concession from him in her childhood, but not recently.

"What now?" He picked up a metal stick and poked the brazier's charcoal chunks.

Her chest tightened. "I regret the trouble I've caused the family."

"Trouble especially for me, in arranging your marriage." He gave the coals a final hard poke.

"I will strive to improve. Instead of being a burden, I wish to contribute to our family, if possible."

"And how is that?" He motioned to the teapot, then lowered himself onto a cushion with a groan.

"Might not Father find translation work day after day . . . tedious? Perhaps I could aid him if I spent only little time studying languages."

She glanced at the Eldest again, knowing he saw through her pretense. She could never truly consider her father's work tedious. As Dutch Scholar of the Second Rank, her father had access to the writings of the world, like having a banquet at one's fingertips. And he didn't just read about the Westerners. While interpreting for the American consul, he met them every day.

Her grandfather grunted and pointed to the cushion across from him.

She set his *chawan* bowl of golden tea on his nearby stand and took her place, kneeling back on her heels and smoothing her kimono. At his stern look, she straightened her spine.

He slurped the steaming tea, then dabbed the moisture from his cheeks. "The barbarians are perilous in ways you refuse to acknowledge. Their *ideas* can destroy the naïve. Moreover, I have asked Kato-*dono* to continue as matchmaker and search out another worthy family who upholds our country's traditions. Such a family would never approve of your studying barbarians' languages no matter the reason."

Sumi forced down the acid that rushed into her throat.

"When Kato-*dono* hesitated because of the botched negotiations with Kurohashi Keiji-*san*, I convinced him that your odd interest in the foreigners had been an ignorant phase. You should thank the gods he is still willing to represent us, especially since the age of eighteen far exceeds the time for betrothals."

She bowed, afraid to speak. The matchmaker would no doubt seek another man as repugnant as Keiji-*sama,* who had belittled her, ranted against foreigners, and worst of all, applauded—actually relished—the banishment of a pitiable man to the coalmines for cherishing one ancient Christian charm. She shivered at how close she had come to a lifetime with the closed-minded traditionalist.

"Do you remember the old tale of Urashima Tarō?" Her grandfather's voice sounded less gruff.

"Yes." She kept her eyes lowered and tried to speak normally. "It appealed to me as a child."

"When the young Tarō left the sea princess's palace, a calamity lay in store. Describe it." He squinted at her as she looked up.

"Returning home after his adventure in the underwater palace, Tarō found years had passed and his family had died. Yet—"

"Dallying in an alien place destroyed the boy's natural life." He leaned forward. "In addition, the ocean covering the palace enabled sharks to prowl. Invisible. Dangerous. Waiting for people foolish or stupid enough to go where they did not belong."

Sumi blinked. Sharks weren't in any version she'd heard. But since he freely manipulated the tale, maybe she dared use the tale too.

"May I ask if the story might be looked at in an additional way?"

"Eh? What way?"

"Since Tarō deserved the extraordinary reward for having treated the turtle kindly, it seems he could have chosen to stay at the enchanting palace."

"Stay?" he spluttered.

She plunged ahead. "But since he chose to leave, he should

have followed the princess' instructions not to open the mysterious box. If he had been wise, he could have avoided the box's curse and faced a better future." She held her breath.

"The tragedy was not the curse of aging. It was the boy's neglect of service to his family." Her grandfather plunked down his tea bowl. "Without *loyalty* you are nothing!" He rose and pointed his finger at her. "No matter how you construe the story, I forbid you to attend that class." He headed for the door.

Sumi stood and bowed, then stared at the paper's ashes. Loyal? She *was* loyal to her family. Couldn't she be loyal yet explore a little? Dip her toe into new waters without being swept away? Or attacked by sharks? Her grandfather had toured the largest domains, climbed Fuji-*san*, visited the Shōgun's magnificent Edo castle. He hadn't been in a magical palace, of course, but close to it.

Glancing toward the doorway, she caught her grandfather looking back. Likely as not, he had no idea how much pain he had just inflicted. And he couldn't know how much she yearned to please him, yet how impossible she found it.

He continued toward his room, and she turned in the opposite direction, holding back a forbidden tear.

At their home's entrance, the summer heat already seeped through the paper panels. She slid back the *shōji*, seeking a breeze, but found none. Pulling out her fan, she sat on the veranda's step, imagining years of empty days ahead.

A dragonfly flew past her, its wings a flash of silver.

She straightened and watched it dart from one bush to another, heading toward the front gate. Was it a sign? A reminder to persist in her dream? Samurai admired the courageous insect, which always flew forward, never backward, and overcame lesser insects. Bashō, revising another poet's *haiku*, had written:

Simple pepper pods
Add gossamer wings to them
Behold: Dragonflies

Pepper pods and dragonflies. One essence to the poem's authors, but not to her. A pepper pod drooped in a garden until picked. However, the dragonfly could visit new, distant places on a whim and then return unscathed. She couldn't endure remaining like a pepper pod. There had to be more to living than flower arrangement, tea ceremony, embroidery, and plucking the *koto*'s strings, each lesson progressing as slowly as the poet Issa's snail crawling up Fuji-*san*, stone by stone by stone.

Oceans no longer separated her from the foreigners. They were here, in her city. She closed her eyes, picturing the tall, confident consul during the welcoming procession. He couldn't be an uncivilized barbarian. Her father wouldn't have said he had a calm, thoughtful disposition if he were. She'd sensed his fine life's energy, his *ki,* herself.

Regardless of danger, whether real or make-believe, she had to find an opening into the world beyond, into the world the consul inhabited.

The following morning, cooler air blew in from the ocean, inviting an outing. Seeing her father gazing at the book shelf over his low desk, Sumi bowed. "Father, please excuse my interruption." She drew in a shaky breath. Had her grandfather foreseen her request and already blocked it?

He turned toward her. "Yes? What is it?"

"Might I accompany you on one of your visits to the international sector? I'd like to observe a few of the strange sites you've mentioned." She drew out her fan and tried for an unruffled countenance while slowly fanning her face.

"I suppose you'll need to see the area sooner or later." A smile flickered at the corner of his mouth. "If you have no lesson today, you may come with me. Perhaps we can satisfy a little of that boundless curiosity of yours."

Her spirits rose as she bowed her thanks. Somehow, against all odds, he had gained her grandfather's permission to become a Dutch Scholar and linguist. Of course, that was before anyone knew the Shōgun would open the country to the Americans, and then to other countries as well. But her father's victory showed the impossible could become possible.

An hour later, she wiped damp palms on her cherry-colored kimono and nearly tiptoed out the house. She needn't have worried, however. Her grandfather was in the back garden, where he didn't like to be disturbed.

They each rode in a *kago*, the hammocks swaying from the broad poles carried by jogging, bare-legged porters. At the Oura River Bridge, they left the *kago.*

Her father waved her forward. "Walk next to me. Foreigners, both men and women, walk side by side. In fact, when entering buildings, the men insist that the women enter first."

Sumi immediately complied despite unease at not following three steps behind. Did foreign women get used to such royal treatment?

After they passed through the guard gate, the road filled with swaggering sailors, workmen, horseback riders, men and women in bizarre outfits, and aggressive peddlers hawking fans, umbrellas, ink stones, and other paraphernalia. Two seagulls swooped overhead, their squawks mixing with the caterwauling of fishmongers selling eels and squid. The strong smell of seawater announced the bay's proximity.

Sumi tried to drink in all the sights at once, her body tingling with excitement. Her country's door had opened wide, and hers had creaked open a tiny bit in spite of her grandfather.

The dark river next to her teemed with sampans and large barges. Six men unloading barrels of whale oil shouted to each other in a language she'd never heard her father practice—not sounds of English or Dutch. She turned toward him.

"Russians," he said, anticipating her question. He pointed to several Chinese with long pigtails earnestly bartering for *daikon,* foot-long white radishes, from a green grocer. "Foreigners' cooks. The world has come to us. To our own city."

They walked by the third house from the bridge. Its occupants had turned the Japanese house into a semi-foreign one. White wooden planks and glass windows took the place of the original sliding panels. Sumi forced her eyes away from the building. Behind its strange exterior lay the English treasure trove. She sealed her mouth against the pleadings longing to burst forth. *Forbidden!*

Up ahead, a group of foreigners chatted, two men and two women. The ladies wore the amazing mushroom-style skirts that nearly swept the ground. A hat covered with feathers perched on one lady's head. The other lady wore a smaller, less startling hat with one feather poking up. The foreigners talked and laughed in a familiar fashion. Then the lady with multiple feathers signaled to another couple across the road and marched over to them. The foreign women enjoyed astonishing freedom, the extent almost dizzying.

As they drew closer, she noticed a cane poking out from under the elderly man's arm. The cane's top curved into the shape of a . . . a parrot's head. Could that possibly be his clan's insignia? The characteristics of such a bird would hardly make an enemy tremble. She snickered at the thought of a parrot swooping down on a helmeted warrior.

The man gave the lady's words his full attention. Gray streaked his once dark hair and beard. Why foreign men wanted hairy faces was beyond her.

At that moment, the man recognized her father. He held out his hand—the *handshake* she'd heard about. The white-haired lady turned toward them and smiled. Then the second man, whose back had been toward Sumi, turned around.

She took a step backwards before she stopped herself. The tall American consul himself faced her. Only thirty years old, according to the documents her father had seen, yet he was a powerful country's envoy. Although he didn't shave his pate or wear his hair in a topknot, he had to be an extraordinary samurai.

The consul and her father shook hands too. No one bowed. When the elderly lady spoke, white teeth showed. They weren't coated with black enamel. Wasn't she married at such an advanced age? Didn't all married women dye their teeth and pluck their eyebrows?

English words swirled all around.

Her father said something that caused the three foreigners to look at her. She raised her fan, but dared a peek at the consul's face. He didn't at all have the sinister look attributed to barbarians by so many of her countrymen. His gray eyes appeared just as kind as the first time she'd seen him. In spite of his brown beard and the swath of hair over his lips, his jaw exuded strength, as expected of a samurai. She'd heard rumors he was a good swimmer, accounting for his muscular, lean look.

She fanned her warm face. She would give everything she owned to be able to understand the conversation.

For more information and to purchase Book Two, go to
www.elizabethannboyles.com/my-books

Made in the USA
Columbia, SC
18 April 2021